MEDIOCRE BUT ARROGANT

Photo courtesy Varun Madan

ABHIJIT BHADURI works as the chief learning officer of Wipro and lives in Bangalore, India.

He has led HR teams in several organizations including Microsoft, PepsiCo, Colgate and Tata Steel. He is on the Advisory Board of Wharton's prestigious program for chief learning officers that is run by the University of Pennsylvania, USA. He is frequently quoted in the business press and has written columns for *The Economic Times*, *Hindu Business Line*, among others.

Abhijit has an MBA from Xavier Labour Relations Institute, Jamshedpur.

Mediocre But Arrogant is his debut novel. The story continues in his second novel *Married But Available*.

Abhijit is a cartoonist and prolific blogger at http://abhijitbhaduri.com. He can be reached at abhijitbhaduri@live.com and you can follow him on twitter @abhijitbhaduri.

MEDIOCRE BUT ARROGANT

ABHIJIT BHADURI

HarperCollins *Publishers* India

First published in 2005 by Indialog

This edition published in India by
HarperCollins *Publishers* in 2012

Building 10, Tower A, 4th Floor, DLF Cyber City, Phase II,
Gurugram Haryana – 122002, India
www.harpercollins.co.in

4 6 8 10 9 7 5 3

P-ISBN: 978-93-5029-121-4
E-ISBN: 978-93-5029-516-8

Typeset in Bailey Sans ITC TT 11/14
InoSoft Systems Noida

Printed and bound at
Microprints India, New Delhi

Friday 15th April 1983

Jamshedpur

The MIJ Song

CHORUS: The two years I spent at MIJ
Studying for my MBA
Precious hours spent ~~at Dadu's~~ with pals
~~Studying~~ Drinking the night away

Those ~~te~~ Term Papers we had to write
Every prof had a strange quirk
It took Rascal Rusty to figure out
For each prof what would work
Some liked "quotes", some liked graphs
Some liked humour in papers – just for laughs

CHORUS: The 2 years I spent at MIJ
Studying ....

Dadu's Dhaba was our usual haunt
Whether for chai or cigarettes we'd want
Where Arunesh Sang Dylan's Songs
~~With the shiny guitar he'd flaunt~~
~~With his shiny Yamaha guitar he'd flaunt~~
To be continued

– POET LAUREATE ABBEY

This song is dedicated to the QT class without which ...

Must ask Arunesh to add chords to this.

yes

SHOULD BE IN OUR COAT OF ARMS

don't show off

ALPS?

NAAH!

don't be mean

paws

What are these

OH!

For

Buli, Feni and Jojo

Behind the Scenes

Ever since *Mediocre But Arrogant* got published, the question I have been asked most often is, 'How much of this is autobiographical?' There are some similarities I share with Abbey. I lived in the Railway Colony at SP Marg, studied Economics at SRCC. I did my MBA at XLRI, Jamshedpur while Abbey went to do an MBA at the Management Institute of Jamshedpur (MIJ). So we are 'same same but different' as they say in some parts of the world. Or maybe 'different different but same same'. *Mediocre But Arrogant* is really a story of growing up in India. Anyone who has lived in a college hostel will recognize the characters in this book: Gopher who sucks up to every prof and generally annoys the hell out of his classmates; Arunesh the guitarist who plays songs of Dylan; the crazy room-mate Pappu who sleeps more than anyone I know; the enigmatic Rascal Rusty who has the most ingenious solutions to life's problems. These characters live in every college.

To survive the terrible food in the Students' Mess there is Dadu's Dhaba where you are more likely to find the students than you would in Prof Chatto's class. Chatto teaches the incomprehensible Quantitative Techniques that has been the nemesis of many generations of students. This is also the place where Abbey discovered Ayesha and Keya. He has a sneaky feeling that back home in Delhi, his friend from college, Priya loves him. That is so not on. Then again, isn't this what your college days were like? So this book is all about that.

I want to say thanks to many people who helped me as I chased my dream of writing my first novel. Nandini for being the first one to critique my ideas! My children for patiently letting me pretend that I knew what it meant to be a father. To my parents who taught me the basics of writing. To my in-laws who bought the first copy of this book. Thanks Madhukar and Geeta for helping me make sense of the chaos over numerous cups of chai. To the professors and friends from XLRI, Jamshedpur for all the good times.

Thanks to Basant Pandey of Indialog for bringing out the first edition of the novel and giving me a break as an author. To Keerti Ramachandra who edited the first version of the book.

HarperCollins, for bringing out the latest edition of my debut novel—*Mediocre But Arrogant*. The second novel, *Married But Available*, continues from where this novel ends. Thank you, Karthika for editing both the novels that have changed what MBA stands for!

Abhijit Bhaduri

Chapter 1

I do not know why I landed in corporate India. Nobody in my family had ever ventured there and they were doing fine. That it was a combination of serendipity and stupidity is what I think it was all about. Why I chose to do Human Resource Development is another mystery. In fact, I did not even start off in Human Resources.

When I joined MIJ, Management Institute of Jamshedpur, Bihar, in the summer of 1982, the course I had enrolled in was called Industrial Relations and Social Welfare. At that time, there were only 'welfare officers', and that term really sucked. So some smart cookie, like Rascal Rusty, decided to tweak the formula, change the packaging, and make a new commercial with a babe in a skimpier bikini, as the marketing guys did with all their soaps and toothpaste brands every year. They called it a 'relaunch'. That's how the new and improved version of the Personnel Management and Industrial Relations (PM&IR) course (positively Neanderthal) came to be called Human Resources. And those who graduated from the institute were re-christened 'HR professionals', instead of the previous personnel managers.

After struggling through two years at MIJ and eventually completing the course in PM&IR, I was let loose on the corporate sector. In the course of time, I was anointed the head honcho of HR at a reputed firm, all because of the stamp that MIJ had put on me; or as they say in management jargon, because I bore the MIJ 'brand'.

'In the good old days cattle owners used to brand their cattle by using a red hot metal marked with their own name or initials or symbols—in marketing terms, these were "logos". Slowly, some such marks or brandings began to get associated with superior quality of cattle. So customers looked for those "brands" when they were buying livestock. That's how the term brand has come to represent a particular standard, a quality, a method by which your products and services can be differentiated from those of your competitors. Life is all about brands.

'For the next class, please come back with a thousand-word write-up on "The Brand I Want to Be". Describe the brand you currently are and the one you want to be in two years. The focus of your write-up should be on the marketing strategy you will use to become that brand.

'Do not waste time copying your answers from some marketing journal in the library. I have read them all and will be able to instantly identify the plagiarized portions in your paper. If that happens, your assignment will not be graded. I want you to be creative and...'

Thus spake Professor Suri, Head of Marketing at MIJ. His knowledge and sarcasm were both legendary. And he was right. It was indeed all about brands. How else to describe the transformation of scores of university graduates into much sought after brands in the corporate bazaar?

Given the number of applicants every year, it seemed as if the branding machine at MIJ worked overtime, though the earliest batches of MIJ students must have found it difficult to give themselves a distinct identity.

Tell me, what would you logically want to call the students of MIJ? MIJ-ians—but that sounds like we are trying to copy IIT-ians. Be creative, da!

How about MIJ-icians?

Ha ha ha! That would be a stretch. This is not a term-paper, da... Give us real options.

What do you want students of MIJ to be called—MIJ-ets? Or, worse still, 'mijiocre'?

This would all have become a big time branding issue if it had not been resolved by Brainy Bala—one of our brilliant super-Seniors. He came up with the term 'MIJ-ite', which immediately earned the seal of approval at the Students General Body meeting. Even Prof Suri approved of it. That became our brand. In futures we would collectively be known as MIJ-ites.

Despite its unglamorous name, MIJ had an impressive campus, a fancy library and a state-of-the-art auditorium where we held our annual one-act-play festival. In the administrative block were the dean's office, the classrooms, and above them, a large chapel. Next to it, believe it or not, was the Girls' Hostel, making it the butt of innumerable jokes. 'Hostel' was a generous word; the girls' dwelling was not much more than a biggish hall with a few wooden desks and beds arranged along its walls.

In fact, back in those days in 1982, all the buildings of MIJ were rather, ummm... utilitarian. They did not have the distinctive style that is necessary for an institution to be taken seriously by the world at large. The way you dress creates the first impression on those who hold the keys to all the goodies in life. MIJ certainly did not look like it met people's expectations of what a major business school should look like. Nor did it have the necessary spark that creates a major brand.

The Boys' Hostel in the neighbouring block reminded me of army barracks, built so spartanly that it kept everyone alert and on their toes.

'If you do not feel comfortable and relaxed, you will learn to be a fighter. Luxury will dull your desire to excel.' This was what my father said every time I desired but was denied something that was even remotely classified as a luxury.

MIJ operated on the same philosophy. The Boys' Hostel had a grey exterior which made the dull red brick façade of the Academic block look cheerful by contrast. The white-washed rooms each had a bed, a small cupboard and a desk with a rather uncomfortable chair for each occupant. Plastering the walls with posters of Olivia Newton John and Rekha had done little to diminish the overall bleakness. The beds were made of what appeared to be bandages, woven together like a chessboard on a wooden frame. Inevitably, these sagged so low we felt as if we were sleeping in a hammock. Any sense of luxury, however remotely evoked, was certainly not intended.

The teachers at MIJ all lived in the 'profs' quarters, just behind the library. The quarters were designed to look more or less like the Boys' Hostel, but for the rows of trees and bushes which had been thrown in to create a 'more homely environment' in which to shape minds. The quarters were the only place MIJ couples would go for walks, away from the curious eyes of the sickos in the Boys' Hostel. But, getting caught by the profs was not a good thing either. Discretion was the key; couples were not expected to display any affection in public. If occasionally some weak-hearted fellow was caught holding hands with his lady love, he would immediately be reprimanded by a prof (or the prof's spouse) for wasting time in faltu activities and not concentrating on studies.

'Your parents are spending all this money to send you to the number one management institute in the country to study and get a good job and look after them. Not to enjoy life.'

What was THAT all about? Was holding hands meant to suggest that they were enjoying life while the rest of mankind was suffering. Whatever this meant, couples took enormous pains to be heard discussing academics each time they passed a prof going for a post-prandial.

Another integral part of MIJ was the chapel in the administrative block. If you spoke to Father Hathaway, a Scottish priest and one of the original Magnificent Seven who built MIJ, literally brick by brick, this is what he would tell you:

'I came to India with Fr Beez and five other priests, in 1945, with a common dream. Two years later, MIJ was started in a small room of Hotel Bistupur in

Bistupur Market of Jamshedpur. Those early years were a challenge. Within three months of coming here, one of my colleagues died of malaria. But we were not disheartened. We knew a free country like India would have a great need for trained managers. In those days, most companies, like the Steel & Iron Company (SICO), were labour intensive. So there would always be a demand for personnel officers. The first batch of MIJ had only six students. Over the years, the foresight and hard work of both the teachers and students have paid rich dividends and the present campus is testimony to the esteem in which the corporate sector holds MIJ. The chapel was built by us when we started this institute; we needed to get god to sign up for this project of making MIJ India's best institute for learning management! Theek bola?'

Father Hathaway, at this point, usually lapsed into his heavily accented Hindi or Bengali or Tamil or Oriya, depending on who he was talking to. Dean of MIJ and Professor of Organizational Behaviour (referred to as Orgy Behaviour by most and 'OB' by the respectful), the man had over the past four decades untangled miles of bureaucratic red tape to obtain licenses, permits and certificates that kept the babus in the education ministry at bay and built an institute that now had forty to fifty thousand applicants for its fifty odd seats. He had successfully fended off pressure from the rich, the famous and the powerful and ensured that the limited seats they had, went only to the deserving. Affectionately called Haathi, Father was one of the most popular figures in the region. He knew virtually everyone in Jamshedpur, from the CEO to the fruit vendor in Bistupur, and he addressed them all by their names. He also remembered every student who had passed through the portals of MIJ. How did he do it? None of us dared to hazard a guess. He was not only one of the best loved teachers, he was also a guide, architect and visionary all rolled into one. Fittingly, in deference to the regard he was held in, MIJ-ites down the generations have shown great respect for everything Scottish—especially Scotch.

The girls in MIJ swore Father looked like Gregory Peck. Haathi invariably brushed off the comparison, blithely remarking, 'I must see a movie starring this chap who claims to look like me.' At the age of sixty-five, Haathi rode a Royal Enfield motorcycle as if he were on a Grand Prix race track. Anyone who hitched a ride with him to Bistupur swore never to repeat the mistake. He wove through the traffic at top speed, chatting non-stop with the pillion rider even as he waved furiously at acquaintances and shouted greetings at friends, careening along to the increasing horror of his passenger. He still played basketball with us every evening, and gave the students an inferiority complex with his skillful shooting.

Because of Father Hathaway's charismatic personality, fund raising campaigns for MIJ always exceeded their target, and through this, he had been able to finance his dreams of improving MIJ's infrastructure. At every alumni meet that I have attended over the years, the conversation inevitably turned to Haathi. These were all words of praise; everyone professed only undiluted admiration and respect for him, including the students who had received lousy grades in his classes.

Another aspect of campus culture: the original building of Hotel Bistupur where MIJ first started off now houses a popular bar. This is why, according to Boys' Hostel folklore, every MIJ-ite is 'bar-coded' and hence destined to be a confirmed boozer. 'Win or lose, we must booze' was the unofficial motto, especially when we played our football matches on Saturday evenings against the local engineering college—and usually lost. MIJ's official motto, 'Enter to learn, go forth to serve,' was modified to read: 'Learn to enter; Go forth to serve,' on the bathroom walls of the Boys' Hostel. Certainly, it reflected our point of view and desires more accurately than the official motto ever would.

Our batch, that of '82, consisted of eight girls and forty guys. Not a happy ratio, I thought, as I made a quick mental calculation of the probability of success; hopefully, I looked up the names of girls who would be my classmates for two years, off the list of Juniors. Our senior batch was worse off—they had only one girl in their batch, the sole fantasy of forty-four depraved young men. In their eyes, our batch, with eight 'babes' had made a huge improvement on the Quality of Life Index. We got no sympathy from them when we cribbed about the adverse boy to girl ratio. But we thought differently; we felt a law should be laid down to restrict guys to pairing up with girls from their own batch. Any Senior caught glancing lustfully at the girls of another batch, especially ours, ought to be hanged, surely. In the absence of any such legislature, our Seniors took it as their natural right to make amorous moves on the girls in our batch. It was all grossly unfair.

So were a lot of other things in life, I realized for almost the first time, when we began applying for summer trainee assignments. I was very impressed when I heard this statement at a Pre Placement Talk (PPT in MIJ lingo): 'We offer a career and not a job.' All companies declared they were looking for leadership qualities, motivation, dynamism and excellent communication skills. They all wanted someone who liked to work in a fast-paced environment and loved challenges. When asked what the promotions and increments were based on, every company had the same stock response.

'Ours is a meritocracy. At the end of the day, all that matters is who got us results and who didn't.'

So, when I attended an interview on campus for a summer trainee assignment with a company that manufactured a very popular brand of cough syrups, I was determined to impress. I was also sure that honesty was the best policy. When their director of personnel asked me why I had chosen Personnel Management as my specialization in MIJ instead of marketing, the more glamorous option, I could have lied through my teeth and said something untruthful like: 'Right from my student days, sir, I noticed that the one factor that makes or breaks a company is the quality of the people it has. Every organization can buy the same machines that its competitor buys. Every product can be copied but what cannot be duplicated is the collective set of skills that its employees possess. It is the business of the personnel department to ensure that every employee uses his potential skills for the benefit of the organization and helps it to transform from ordinary to exceptional ...' etc.

But stupid me, I decided to tell the truth.

'I don't know, sir. Getting into MIJ and this course on personnel management was all just one big act of serendipity.'

I did not get selected for the job. The bonehead who interviewed me didn't care to know the truth. All that he had said in his talk at the Pre Placement Talk, about looking for a person who would be smart enough to take over from him in five years flat, must have been just that—all talk.

I was upset and angry. Had I not been selected just because I had failed to tell the usual story? It was so unfair! I decided to boycott the cough syrup for the next two months, even if I ended up sounding like a foghorn. I also went around telling people to avoid the brand because it contained harmful drugs—my very own smear campaign against the mighty corporation. It was my way of saying, 'That's what you get when you fool around with a loyal customer... even if he wants to apply for a job.'

Noticing my rather peevish behaviour, my friend Rusty said to me one day, 'Abbey, who on earth asked you to use that word "serendipity" in an interview? And what does it mean, anyway?'

'Serendipity is the trick of making fortunate discoveries accidentally,' I replied, innocently.

'I know what serendipity means, Abbey. But I bet the guy who was interviewing you didn't. That is why he didn't select you. Nobody likes a smart aleck in the workplace. They make difficult subordinates who are likely to overshadow and expose the ignorance of their bosses. So no manager will ever employ anyone smarter than himself, assuming, of course, that you are smarter than him.'

I ignored the sarcasm. 'But Rusty, this guy declared during the PPT that he was looking for a subordinate who could take over from him in five years so that he could retire and spend time doing social work. He said he was looking for somebody who would be better than him in all respects.'

'You are such an ass, Abbey, you'll believe anything. The PPT is a courting process during which you want to entice the applicants. So it can't be the time for honesty. Both parties, the company and the students, garnish the truth. Only after the appointment letter is received and accepted will an employer reveal his true colours. By that time, it's too late. You understand? What that fellow was trying to do was get enough suckers to apply for the job so that he could take back a stack of resumes and show his boss what a great job he had done building the company's brand at MIJ. Then he selected the dumbest, not the smartest, candidate as his assistant. So that, by sheer contrast, he would appear to be a genius, indispensable to the company. Then he would continue to drop hints to his own boss about taking early retirement and also mention in the same breath how fresh and inexperienced the new recruit was. This would make his bosses paranoid about losing an experienced hand. They would give him a big raise and a generous bonus and request him to delay his retirement plans by just a few months more, till they manage to train the MBA they hired from campus.'

'But how do you know all this, Rusty?' I interrupted. After all, he too was a fresher like me.

'Forget it, da. I'll tell you some other time.'

How he knew something about everything, did not matter. What did matter was that talking to him had reduced my embarrassment about not getting selected. I was easily convinced that it was because I was smarter than my potential boss. It was amazing, the number of guys I was smarter than!

In any case, it was never difficult to believe Rustom Topiwalla, Rusty for short. Though he could sometimes be a pompous ass, it was generally agreed that he was the most corporate-savvy person in our class. People called him 'Rascal Rusty' behind his back, I didn't know why? No one knew anything about him. He was an enigma. A loner, he generally avoided the Hostel crowd, and never joined us when we went out to eat Chinese at Franks. He was always dressed in a pair of jeans and a black shirt. I secretly admired his 3C appearance—his Cool, Calm and Collected manner.

Rusty was a teetotaller and made being one sound like a virtue. When he was in his room, he usually sucked on a pipe. There was rarely any tobacco in it, and I don't remember seeing any smoke coming from it. He just liked to hold it as he scanned the business magazines, looking scholarly and professional. He hardly ever spoke, except to make very profound sounding statements every now and then. Unlike most of us in the junior batch, Rusty spent a lot of time in the library, reading annual reports of companies and *The Economic Times*. Then he would impress us by quoting from them. His knowledge of the world of management and of how corporations worked, made even the Seniors ask him for advice—for a fee of course.

We discovered that Rusty had a Bachelor's degree from Loyola College in Madras. He had started his own company, which marketed 'education for busy executives,' and had already been a CEO—even if it was of his own start-up. He had been at the pinnacle of power for five years before succumbing to his 'thirst for knowledge' and joined MIJ, unlike most of us who were fresh off the Bachelor's degree assembly line. Rusty invariably came up with solutions to every problem and short cuts for every task. He had a fair number of disciples who turned to him in a crisis, and helped anyone who came to him for succour, but made sure he extracted his pound of flesh first.

Rusty once sold me a list of references for the price of his haircut. Another time, he offered to help me write a term paper for Haathi in exchange for a month's subscription to *The Hindu.* Paying for that newspaper subscription meant giving up smoking for a week. And Rusty noticed.

'You have a problem, da?' he asked me.

'It's not easy for my father to keep me here in MIJ, yaar. I have to remember that and not overspend.'

After that day, Rusty never charged me a copper for anything. I must have touched a chord somewhere. He decided to take me under his wing and became a mentor of sorts. As he initiated me into a completely unfamiliar world, he was always there to steady me when I stumbled. When someone referred to him as the local Shylock, I rushed in to defend him. I swore never to betray his confidence.

With every other person in the boy's Hostel, however, Rusty was strictly professional.

'Consultancy fee,' he said, as he waved a half-used bottle of Brut aftershave.

'Who did you get this from, Rusty?'

'Consultants never talk about their clients.'

While he bailed out anyone who was in a tight spot, he got them to pay for some expense or the other. But he always negotiated the deal up front, before extending his services. That he once broke up a fight on the basketball court and got both parties to pay for a month's subscription each to *Business India* speaks volumes, in terms of his business acumen.

'How do you manage to advise them, yaar, when you are a fresher like us?' I asked Rusty out of sheer curiosity, for his grades were just about average.

'Practical experience, that's what matters in life. Most of our Seniors only know what Kotler has said about marketing. They have no clue how it translates to designing a marketing plan for the district of Shimoga. I know what works in the marketplace. Kotler is bound to agree with me.'

'Who is Kotler? How does he know about Shimoga?' I asked, clueless.

'The guru of marketing, Abbey,' Rusty explained, so briefly as to just escape sounding patronizing. I flushed. But then he went on. 'Philip Kotler's *Marketing Management: Analysis, Planning, Implementation and Control* is the most widely used marketing textbook in B-schools worldwide. The guy has a PhD in Economics from MIT, has done post-doctoral work in Mathematics at Harvard, and in behavioural science at the University of Chicago.'

'Do you know him?'

'We are not best friends or anything like that. But yes, our ideas have frequently struck a common chord. I too have spoken about decision making and planning models in marketing. As in life, in marketing too, planning is everything.'

'But yaar, in my experience, serendipity rather than careful planning has brought me here, to MIJ.'

I repeated my catch-phrase, now somewhat self-conscious.

Rusty snorted. 'I bet that you are here because some Professor called Sarin took pity on you—was Sarin *di* pity as the Punjus would say?'

'But it is the truth,' I insisted, as Rusty rolled over with laughter at his own wit. He had a strange sense of humour—and a thing for oxymorons.

Unlike Rusty's carefully planned and well-timed approach to life, there was nothing planned and executed in mine. I just kept stumbling into different rooms down the corridors of life, stopping briefly like a travelling gypsy before moving on.

My father had been with the Indian Railways for thirty years. We lived in the Railway Colony in SP Marg in Delhi, and all of us kids hung around the Railway Officers Club. It was all I knew about the world, curiously ill-informed about anything beyond the local railway station. But it did not matter then. The world of private sector companies and multinationals was alien to us. They did not influence our lives, except perhaps as consumers.

After finishing school, I went to SRCC (Shri Ram College of Commerce). Like a typical Delhiwallah, I was in the habit of abbreviating names. There I signed up for the Economics Honours course. I had accompanied my neighbour from SP Marg—Vikram Gupta and merely followed what he did. I found it very difficult to make choices; I had no burning ambition to achieve greatness. I was happy with life as it unfolded. It was much easier to emulate someone who was often cited at the dinner table in our house as a role model. Why? Vikram Gupta planned out everything ahead of time. He always knew what he was going to do in the next hour or the next day or year. While we sat gawking at life passing us by, he read the *Competition Success Review* and *The Economist.* Fortunately for me, both of us were admitted to the BA Economics Honours course. I was relieved. No more decision making, at least for three years, I thought. I could sit back and just follow the marked out course without taking any responsibility.

But after attending classes at SRCC for two weeks, Vikram announced that he was flying to the US to do his undergrad at the University of California. I felt very let down. After all, the only reason I had signed up for Eco was because he was doing it. If he was abandoning it, maybe I should follow suit. The response to this suggestion at the dinner table was not encouraging, to put it mildly. I dropped the idea of following Vikram Gupta all the way to the US. I would have to find someone else to emulate.

Delhi University (DU) and SRCC offered me the luxury of spending my time and energy chatting with friends in the college canteen, learning to play the guitar, starting a literary magazine no one read and going from college to college attending inter-collegiate competitions and cultural festivals. The prize money funded my endless cups of coffee and cigarettes. My classmate Sanket Narain, alias eccentric Sanki, taught me to smoke cigarettes and sharpened my public speaking skills. He encouraged me to run for the post of Cultural Secretary of the Students' Union. Unshackled by any academic ambitions, I devoted all my attention to 'cultural activities' in college.

Most of us in DU were not really sure what we wanted to do in life, professionally speaking. We attended rallies and meetings, where we debated the need to make 'laissez-faire' the dominant approach to government. What we had been trying to do, I realized in retrospect, was to recreate the insouciance of campus life for the rest of the world. Take away ambition and the need for action from any part of the world and what you have left is life as I experienced it in my three years at Delhi University.

And this is why I was quite unprepared for the rigour that MIJ demanded of me, to keep my nose above the academic poverty line. In MIJ, everything was different. Every student was ambitious and wanted to run the world, or at least a part of it. The toppers set standards everyone tried to beat. Almost everyone was determined to work for a multinational or at least the private sector because that was where meritocracy reigned—or so we believed. Anything to do with the public sector or government service was considered infra dig and if you opted for a job in either, you were a loser. I harboured no such prejudices. Frankly, I did not see anything wrong with these options. Coming from a background where writing the entrance exams for the Civil Services or for jobs in the public sector seemed to be the sole object of one's life, I could not understand why they were anathema to MIJ-ites.

One day, while he was glancing through an issue of *Business India*, Rusty asked rather dramatically, 'Abbey, imagine I am interviewing you for a job and I ask you to name five companies you would consider as your employers of choice…'

'That's easy,' I responded casually, turning my gaze from the smoke ring heading for the ceiling, and rattled off, 'Tata, Bata, Birla, Sunlight and HMT.'

Rusty burst out laughing. A minute later he sobered up and explained to me a very important fact of life.

'Abbey, Tata and Birla are both large business houses with several dozen companies in different sectors. They are not a single organization. Always be specific. Sunlight is not the name of the company. It is just a brand, Abbey, a brand. Hindustan Lever is the company that owns the brand. They make different things like vegetable oil, animal feed, detergents as well as the soap that you and I use, and sell each product under a brand name, like say, Dalda. Dalda is a brand. Different brands are meant for different markets like... heck man, why am I taking a Marketing class here! You've paid MIJ to teach you all this.'

I realized how little I knew. But Rusty never made light of my queries, which often reeked of ignorance.

Rusty also spoke of 'Nusli Uncle' or about the times when 'Dhiru Uncle' and his sons Anil and Mukesh had stayed in his uncle's farmhouse near Madras, frequently. I had no reason to wonder whether he really knew all these people, for I genuinely believed he was very well connected.

One day, while having breakfast, he told me Ratan was going to take over from Jeh as the head of the Tata group.

'Who's Ratan?'

'Ratan Tata, you idiot. Don't you ever read the papers? He is going to be the head honcho of Tatas after JRD retires. JRD is affectionately called Jeh. I used to call him Jeh Uncle but then he insisted that I call him Jeh. The word uncle makes him feel old, he said.'

'Ratan Tata? Wow. That's a lot of companies to inherit. Ratan will be a rich man.'

'He will RUN these companies, *da*, not inherit them. Privately held companies can be inherited, publicly held ones are managed either by members of the family, or by professional managers. That's what you and I are here for. To become one of those managers who will run these companies. Get me another cup of coffee, will you?'

I did not like being ordered around, not even by Rusty. But the thrill of getting an insiders' scoop into the life and career of Ratan Tata was worth it. I pretended to get a refill for myself, then discreetly put the cup next to Rusty.

A few days later, I found an old issue of *The Illustrated Weekly of India* with a photo of Ratan Tata standing behind a seated JRD on the cover. Inside was an interview with JRD in which he had named Ratan his successor.

I charged up to Rusty's room. 'Rusty, you rascal, you read about Ratan Tata in this issue of *The Illustrated Weekly* and passed it off as first hand information?'

Rusty merely shrugged and said, 'Well, *The Illustrated Weekly* and I have the same insider as the source of information ...'

'Insider? Where?'

'In Jeh's office. Both of us said the same thing, didn't we?'

What could I say? I went back to my magazine. Every issue had a few pages, my favourites, showing women who found the weather too hot for clothes. But that was not the only reason why I read the *Weekly*. I loved Khushwant Singh's editorials. I did read them. A few of them. Very few. But I never missed a single word of the comic strips, especially the adventures of *Phantom—the Ghost Who Walks*. I was an authority, like most of my generation, on the Phantom, the jungles of Denkali that he lived in and his sidekick Guran.

Phantom was my hero. I wished I too could be like him—so cool in his purple coloured skin-tight body stocking and the revolvers in his holster. Phantom was unflappable in the face of danger. He had no problem thrashing the bad guys and leaving his trademark skull and crossbones imprinted on their jaws. And there was another side to Phantom. He had married his long time sweetheart, the voluptuous Diana, an employee of the UN. That was in the year 1977 and some time later he became father to the twins Kit and Heliose. Phantom remained a role model for many of us who grew up reading those Indrajal comics—at least when it came to success with women.

Chapter 2

I could have hammered a few bad guys myself—especially Professor Tathagato Chattopadhyay or 'Chatto', as he was called. Chatto taught us Quantitative Techniques or QT which was anything but cute—neither the subject nor the Professor. This course was earlier called Advanced Statistical Concepts and was renamed QT in the late '80s. He was known more for his strange dress sense than his impressive academic credentials. According to the MIJ prospectus, he had a PhD in Statistics from the prestigious Indian Statistical Institute, Calcutta, and a Masters' degree each in Psychology and English Literature. That itself was enough to convince us that he was crazy. But we were told when it came to QT, he reigned supreme.

He was short and walked with an air of confidence which comes from the awareness of one's powers. He knew when to drop the guillotine and no, he was not known to have mercy on the hapless. When he walked into the class in white pants, a large floral printed shirt (Alps AKA Alpana said it was probably made from his living room curtains) and addressed us in a squeaky, high pitched nasal voice in a strong Bengali accent, he instantly became the subject of mimicry among the back benchers. But none of us dared to make eye contact with him as he peered at us through his thick glasses, for we had been warned by every senior that Chatto was the ultimate king of sadism. Batch after batch of MIJ students had been the victims of his terror tactics. His accent and marking style were both unique. He had unleashed a reign of terror in MIJ from the time he joined the faculty. For, to get to the final year at MIJ, one had to have gone through the Chamber of Horrors known as Chatto. There was no escape. Two papers in QT-1 and QT-2 had to be cleared in our first year in MIJ.

The first day he entered the class, Chatto introduced himself and the course he would teach.

'I am Professar Chottopadhyay. While my Masters' thesis was on Crowd Dynamics, which can be defined as the staady of how and where crowds form and move above the creeticaal density of more than one person per square metre. Baat my real laabh is the study of Waarld Literature. I have been caallecting the complete waarks of every nobel laureate in Literature obhaar the years. You are welcome to come home to borrow my books for nine days. That is the time it takes for a literary book to be read and understood by a person with more than fourteen years of education. Not retaarning my books in nine days will result in a strong extraneous variable being introduced in my marking of that student's QT paypaar. Just a joke ha... ha... I will be teaching you quontitative takeneeks. I would request you all to be attenteeve, as this is going to be a deefficult paypaar for saam of you. You must be all expaarts in the basic statistical concepts. So we weell start off by doing a small review queez on the concepts of Mean, Median and Mode. You maast have dunn those for yeaaars now. So let aaas staart the queez.'

Like several others, I too was delighted at this opportunity to demonstrate my prowess in QT. We had all studied Mean, Median and Mode for years—since school to be precise. Doing the Review Quiz in concepts would give me an opportunity to impress this Prof with my brilliance in Statistics. I think every single student in the class had the same thought. We were all looking forward to starting off at the head of the class with a straight A+. But as Chatto handed out the question paper, I watched the expressions on the faces around me change from confident and eager to frowning and in some cases positively bewildered.

This did not augur well at all. I wondered what could be so complicated; these were basic concepts. Maybe I was the only talented soul around. I was sure I would not even need the full thirty minutes for this simple quiz. Chatto's squeaky voice broke into what proved to be a brief spell of delusion.

'You can start the queez. I weel ka-lekt the test paypaar after thartee mineets.'

I looked at the first question.

You walk into a watch shop and notice that most clocks show a time somewhere in the range of 5:50 to 6:00pm. Which statistical measure, i.e. Mean, Median or Mode will give you the best estimate of the actual time. Why? And why would the other two measures be unsuitable?

What? My forehead creased in a hundred furrows.

Who came up with this shit? What was this man's intention? What knowledge of QT will he measure by this absurd question? Who cares to use Statistics when you are in a watch shop? You simply buy the bloody watch and get the fuck out. And why would you care if different clocks in the shop showed different times.

I told myself that I would come back to this question later. But I could not get the first question off my mind. *Wouldn't you just calculate the mean of all the different times and come to the conclusion ... wait ... it must be the Median ... oh, I know ... no ... Okay, move to the next question!*

I moved to the next question. And the next. They were no better. The class had suddenly gone quiet. Chatto seemed to have grown a few feet taller in the last half hour. When he collected the papers, I thought I had managed to put up a semblance of a fight.

The next day he came back with our answer sheets and started distributing them, calling out our marks in that squeaky, feminine voice:

'I like to poot everything in order of mayreet (merit). In my subject, understanding and application of mathematical concepts is important. The class marks have all been arranged in the form of a normal distribution curve that fits the trends of marks distribution that I had already estimated using basic models of Statistics that we weel larn about next week. I have arranged the marks in ascending order. So the laytaar your paypaar ees the baytaar your maarks are. The parson who scored the least in my queez is Joyonto Ganguly. He scored 0.86 followed closely by Horpal Singh who got 1.38.'

Jayant Ganguly alias 'Joy' and Harpal Singh alias 'Hairy' led the funereal march. Only Mozart's *Requiem* was missing as the background soundtrack for this mourning. In a moment, the mood of the class became one of the total fear Chatto evoked for the rest of our stay in MIJ. The slaughter continued—I got 2.73.

2.73 out of 10? What a nut case, giving marks in decimals. *'Couldn't you have rounded them off, you weirdo?'*

The top of the heap was Sethu. He had scored an unbelievable 9.8, which forever established him as the brain of the class. A title which was never contested during our two years at MIJ because Sethu was always three miles ahead of the nearest rival in every subject. But his quiet and easy demeanor made it very difficult to dislike him, even though he was a topper.

That day, however, we were awestruck by the fact that Sethu had got a near perfect score—9.8 out of ten—until Chatto announced that the marks were out of 100.

'We assumed the marks were out of 10,' said Jayant Ganguly, in a rather hurt voice.

'Whane you ASSUME without checkeeng, you are makeeng an ass of you and me. That is why in my class, nayvaar assume anneetheeng.'

Chatto wrote the equation on the board: ASS+U+ME = ASSUME.

After this first instance of academic disaster, Chatto had our undivided attention and undiluted respect, two qualities which slowly turned into resentment as the two years went by.

Late that Sunday night, I went over to Joy's room to bum a cigarette off him. I noticed that he was glued to the QT book and desperately trying to figure out some complicated difference between Type I Error and Type II Error. This was a faint effort at fortifying oneself against the massacre scheduled for the following day's quiz. What a way to screw up our weekend! The sight of Joy chewing the end off his pencil inspired me.

'Joy, *you* are studying for Chatto's exam at this hour! Forget it, yaar! It is 2:30 a.m. Go to sleep now or you will be snoring during the QT class.'

'No Abbey, I have to work for it. It makes a tremendous difference. I did not study for the first quiz and I got 0.86. Then I slogged my butt off for the second quiz last week and my marks had improved dramatically. I got 2.17 out of 100. Studying for QT helps, I tell you.'

Like me, Joy too was having a bloody awful time. No matter what we wrote in which subject, the professors made our answers look like Swiss cheese. This resulted in an instant bonding between us. Moreover, both of us were from Delhi and therefore labelled despicable 'Northies' by Gopher, the leader of the 'Southie' gang. In MIJ, anyone who was not from the south of the Vindhyas was classified as a 'Northie' in any case, East and West be damned. It was assumed that they were loud and aggressive.

Occasionally, the guys from Bombay or Poona would protest at being clubbed with the North Indians. They wanted to be in a different category.

'Why are you Bombay types so touchy about being called Northies? Is it a bad word or what?' I asked Francis Fernandes alias 'Fundu'.

The wise man replied, 'All Northies are stereotyped as crude, arrogant and violent, unlike us polite and well-mannered Bumbaiyyas.'

And so we unfairly maligned Northies had to stick together.

'Isn't it strange that the North–South divide should be present amongst the students at MIJ? You know what Chatto would say?' asked Joy, and then imitating Chatto's squeaky voice continued, 'MIJ represents a "random sample" drawn from all parts of India. So all socio-economic and political issues bothering the country would be present in MIJ as well.' Switching to his normal accent, he went on, 'Abbey, this power of statistics to predict with damning accuracy both impresses and saddens me. Institutes of higher education seem to be no different from the Indian Parliament!'

Joy was like that. He could get downright earnest at times. But I had more immediate concerns.

'Joy, how does one get through these frigging QT quizzes? I just don't seem to get it. More importantly, I do not think I will get it in future either. I am unlikely to get a kick out of figuring out the difference between a Type I and a Type II Error. Frankly, I just don't care.'

'Neither do I. But Chatto does. He has been sent by god to wipe the smiles off our faces. Now, do you want to have a chhota rum? Maybe that will improve our understanding of QT.'

Joy stored the rum in a shampoo bottle in his cupboard, behind the shirts (to safeguard it from curious eyes of fellow hostelers). I sipped the bitter stuff, then gulped it down. Joy's father was an officer in the Indian Air Force and Joy had thoughtfully swiped a few bottles of fauji XXX Rum from his Dad's bar. This act had made him very popular in the hostel. One thing Dale Carnegie seems to have missed, in his *How to Win Friends and Influence People*—the one book I had read from cover to cover.

After a few sips Joy said, 'I have figured out this place, Abbey. Smart guys like me and you,' he added hurriedly, 'will always suffer in a system that assumes people have nothing better to do in life than study QT till 3 am. Chatto is such a sadist, he knows we are all terrified of his marking and yet he will not make it any easier,' and proceeded to explain to me what Professor Suri would term as 'Consumer Insight' about the MIJ grading system.

'In MIJ, every subject is graded on an 8 point scale. An A+ in a subject gets you 8 out of 8. So if you get an A, it means 7 points out of 8 and B+ is 6 out of 8 and so on. Right? If you get less than 6 out of 8 grade points, you are no longer looked upon favourably by the profs. Which means that when companies come to our campus with job offers you won't be considered—at least not by the good companies. So you cannot afford to get less than B or B+ in any subject. If we slog hard and get a D in QT, which is most likely an optimistic hypothesis, then we have to keep praying that we get an A in several other subjects to make up.'

The marks system in MIJ seemed completely crazy to me. The focal point of our life was to worry about our CQPI (Cumulative Quantitative Point Index) and to ensure that we were scoring at least 6+ on an 8 point scale. Every three months we had to wrestle with six new subjects and as many professors. Each prof assumed that we had no other occupation in life but to work on term papers, quizzes and other trivia, in his or her subject. Every second day we were subjected to 'surprise quizzes' that proved, much to our surprise, how little we knew about anything, especially when taken by surprise. Every prof had his or her own set of favourite weapons of destruction. Having been schooled in the august, less strenuous tradition of Delhi University, I was a stranger to studying six subjects every day and still getting lousy marks.

When I was doing my BA (Honours) Economics at SRCC, my presence in the classroom versus the canteen stayed at a steady 1:6 ratio. I would buy the course syllabus and text books a month before the the exam schedule was announced. Despite this act of arrogance I cleared the exams, not with flying colours perhaps but honourably enough. My previous life certainly suited my temperament more than the current avatar at MIJ.

Father Beez's weapon of choice was group assignments. The assignment was to be done by a group of students chosen at random from the class. I inevitably landed up in a group where half the guys were free loaders and had no interest in contributing to the assignment, perfectly content to share the marks the other half managed to obtain. Since everyone in the group got the same grades as the others regardless of their effort or contribution to the end result, a lot of friction was generated. The Free Loaders, referred to as FLs since they just tagged on to the dicks who worked hard, loved it and the studious ones hated it. I was not sure whether to work hard on a group assignment and keep my conscience clear or to be an FL. A clear conscience demanded a lot of hard work. I was instinctively drawn towards the FL camp, courtesy my three years in DU. But I decided to ask the man himself for some insight. So one day I walked up to Father Beez, the Scottish priest (and another member of the Magnificent Seven who started MIJ), who taught the paper on Group Dynamics and asked him why he gave us group assignments. He was reading a book on Greek Mythology and had the word 'Pygmalion' written on the small blackboard next to his office desk which was littered with books and magazines. Mythology seemed to be this guy's fetish. I made a mental note.

Beez pushed the reading glasses down on his nose and looked up at me. 'I always believe that you should apply theoretical principles in real life situations. Group assignments are the best way to learn my subject. The idea of a group assignment is for the studious few to figure out how to make sure the free loaders work as hard as themselves. It is an opportunity for everyone to use the principles of group dynamics in reality. Here's your chance, my boy...'

In my naïveté, I said, 'But, sir, what will the free loaders learn in the process?'

Beez merely gave me a go-figure-it-out-yourself look.

Everyday we would get a bunch of marks and all of them conclusively demonstrated what an idiot I was. This daily revelation had certainly bruised my ego. How the heck was I going to 'Keep it above C level' as Joy had so sagely advised? I began to nurture secret doubts in my mind; had there had been a major mistake in my getting selected for MIJ in the first place? Was I the only one who felt this way? I knew that Joy had similar doubts. Hairy ought to feel the same, as must everyone else, especially each time Chatto returned our papers.

I remember how I had strutted into the club in our good old Railway Colony at SP Marg and announced that I had been selected by MIJ. I had a huge feeling of superiority about my academic prowess.

'Must have been a tough exam, na beta? My son was telling me more than 30,000 students write this exam every year. Is that true? Ek anar tees hazaar beemar!' said Mr Samtani—the club secretary, adding his own version of the Hindi idiom to the English sentence. He invariably did that and then translated it for the listener's benefit. 'One pomegranate and 30,000 patients.'

Faking modesty, I replied, 'Actually uncle, 40,000 aspirants try for the fifty seats at MIJ. But at the end of the day, I would certainly say it is a very simple exam. You just need to know what they are looking for.' Then after a deliberate pause, I added, 'If Divya wants me to coach her, I will be happy to give her some tips.'

Divya Samtani, a year junior to me at SRCC, was the snootiest thing in our colony. Her claim to fame was that she had been voted 'Miss Beautiful' by her college. Well, she was cute, and I had been eyeing her ever since she moved into our colony the year before. But she didn't even say hello to me. Must be under instructions from her Dad to avoid all the guys in the Railway Colony, I figured.

'Do you want me to come over later this evening and talk to her about how to prepare for the MIJ entrance tests?' I repeated.

'Nahi beta. Divya has already joined Skillful Tutorials. Anyway, congratulations. I am very proud that someone from this Colony has got into MIJ.'

'Uncle, I am sure Divya will be able to get into MIJ as well. And even if she does not manage to get in on the first attempt, she can always try next year. After all if I could get in, anyone can.' I loved this last bit.

Now that I was in MIJ, the story was quite different. The marksheet for each subject seemed to prove that I was anything but the brain I had been momentarily deluded into thinking I was. Each quiz was a disaster. If this was an indication of the times to come, I was sure that by the end of the first trimester, my self-esteem would be like a stubbed-out cigarette butt.

While I was trying to absorb Joy's advice about getting a decent grade, we were joined by Joy's roomie, Gopher.

Gopuram Ramesh was called 'Gope R' or 'Gopher' for short. I had taken an instinctive dislike to him.

Gopher get up at five in the morning and went for a jog. When he used to came back he would pray aloud for half an hour and emerge from the room with his forehead smeared with ash. Then he would head for the library and read for an hour before getting into class. Joy swore Gopher studied until midnight regularly, even on weekends. He always had the right answers to the prof's questions. After the class was over, he would walk up to the professor and ask him for clarifications. Once he was past our line of sight he would help carry the prof's books to his office. He specialized in running errands for them. If the hostel did not have so many curious pairs of eyes, I bet Gopher would have gladly taken the professor's dog for a walk or done something crass like that too.

Obviously, Joy and I hated Gopher. He made us feel inferior, like academic dimwits. He would ask us what we were talking about and then feel obliged to offer his two paisa bit of wisdom.

'Ei O Yabbey! You better work harder, da,' he chirped. 'Three Ds in your grade sheet and your stay at MIJ is over. For that matter, getting two yeffs has the same effect. MIJ is naat like your Naarth Indian colleges. In the South, our Universities are much more demanding. Getting a 55% there is like getting 80% in any other place, da.'

The condescending manner in which Gopher spoke got my back up.

'Just shut the fuck up, Gopher,' I retorted sharply. 'Do you even know how tough it is to get marks in

Delhi University? I barely managed a second div in my Bachelor's. Even Joy got only a 55% in his B Com. If we had studied in your college, we would have had first divs for sure. Anyway, you get grades in MIJ because of your ACP (After Class Participation—normally done by sucking up to the prof after class). So don't kid yourself into believing you are a bloody genius.'

This was not a smart thing to do, I realized. I did not need advice from the ACP Champ but I need not have expressed my opinion so bluntly. Rusty had warned me that Gopher was a slimy kind of a guy who could start an active whisper campaign against you and prejudice the profs when he indulged in one of his frequent ACP sessions.

All the ACP-types like Gopher were disliked by the anti-establishment crowd I was part of. In the Boys' Hostel, if you scored less marks than the guy doing ACP, you ascribed it to unfair advantage. If you got more marks than the ACP whiz, then you just felt sorry for the poor guy instead, in a fit of generosity.

Doing ACP was not cool at all. The Unwritten Dictionary at MIJ defined it as 'a subtle form of sucking up to the professor to stroke his or her ego with the ultimate objective of gaining a good grade.' Unlike 'maska maroing', ACP required a certain degree of finesse. Every batch of students very quickly identify the ACP types, of which there invariably are many. But the ease with which Gopher accomplished his agenda earned for him the title 'King of ACP.' In fact a new phrase, DCP, was added to the Unwritten Dictionary at MIJ by our batch to describe Gopher. DCP stood for Desperate Class Participation. What Gopher would typically do is walk up to Father Beez just as the class ended.

'Father Beez,' he would begin, 'late last night, while I was preparing for this morning's class...'

Beez's ego is massaged. He says to himself, *'Hmm, my subject is significant enough for the students to come prepared!'*

Gopher continues sucking like a vacuum cleaner. 'I tried to read the article in the *Harvard Business Review* that you were referring to last week and I had a very fundamental doubt ...'

Beez says to himself, *'This fellow not only listens to my lectures, but also takes pains to read the articles I have mentioned. Must give him a decent grade in his Term Paper. He obviously understands the importance of my subject.'*

At this point Beez, completely taken in by the boy's earnestness, says, 'Son, why did you not come to my office to ask me about the doubt that bothered you?'

With an ingratiating smile, Gopher moves in for the kill. 'I did not want to ... It was late ... about three in the morning, Father. I did not want to disturb you.

If you have a few minutes, I could accompany you to your office and pick up a copy of the article you wrote for the Journal of Group Dynamics… I want to be like you…'

Game, set and match to Gopher.

No wonder Gopher got A+ while I was awarded only a B+. But that insight still did not solve the problem of our poor grades. Joy sounded really worried as we compared our Mid Term marksheets. We both had Cs in almost all the subjects except one, where we had a D. That honour was obviously given to QT.

'Abbey, let's plan this better. We have to reserve at least two of the three Ds for Chatto. I am sure QT I and QT II will take care of the two Ds. The trick is to work hard and get all As … I know that is not going to happen. We have thirty six papers to go through in MIJ. Why did I ever want to come to this place?' Joy mixed a strong glass of Old Monk rum with a little Thums Up as we stared out of his window and contemplated the unfairness we had to live with.

'How does one manage with this restricted quota of Ds and Fs? Isn't that against our fundamental rights or something? I mean, they are taking away your choice to work hard or chill out. This restricted quota makes for a very high probability of disaster. Two Fs or three Ds means we will get kicked out of this place before the end of the year, man. This is only the first term here and already we have one D each. What is the probability of our surviving the two years at MIJ?'

'I don't know Abbey. If I did, I would not be drinking like this.'

I went back to my room, slightly inebriated, worrying myself sick about how to juggle Ds and Fs and stay alive in this madhouse.

Chapter 3

'Language is not only a means of communication, it is also a method of creating a bond within a group. Jargon and phrases and nicknames all serve to create a bond within a group but at the same time, could work to alienate some. Each generation creates its own set of terms as a legacy for the rest of the world. As managers, the only thing that will determine your success is how skillfully you learn to communicate. When you write anything, remember that the reader is not interested in what you have written. You have to *make* it interesting for the reader. The listener is not interested in what you have to say unless you say it in a manner that makes sense to him or her. How far up the corporate ladder you manage to climb is an index of your communication skills. The best leaders are all great communicators.'

We were learning about communication in Father Hathaway's class on Organizational Behaviour. We

ORGANIZATIONAL BEHAVIOUR - II
THURSDAY 18 AUG 83
UNDERSTANDING SELF
FR. E. HATHAWAY
ID, EGO & SUPEREGO
Describes YOU
Baser instincts He he he!
Balances
SELF
SOCIETAL EXPECTATIONS
DIED OF BOREDOM?
No lack of Sleep
RIP 1983 ABBEY
so sweet
Looks so much like Gopher. Amazing... Down to the tail
What time are we going for the movie?
8pm
Me!
One flew over the Cuckoo nest? SHRI JACK NICHOLSON
1 flew over the Kaku's nest
Seen the FLIX poster?
Some crazy firang film is on CZECH it out!
HUNGARY for more?
Let's POLISH it off.
Am I RUSSIAN into judgement?
LIMERICK OF THE DAY
Ayesha has pretty brown eyes
Always leaves me with a surprise
She just hates her nose
When I kissed it she froze
So tonight for Abbey there's no prize
- POET LAUREATE - ABBEY.
Animesh would make the perfect Big Chief in the Indian version of 1 FLU over the KAKU'S nest. (Bengali version)

sat spellbound as Father Hathaway explained how a group created and used its own language or code to distinguish between the insiders and the pretenders.

Father Hathaway was certainly the most effective communicator I had seen. He could say the most hurtful things without humiliating you. There was something so endearing about the way he huffed and puffed and modulated his voice to tell us about the importance of communication. Organizational Behaviour was a combination of Psychology, Sociology and mimicry. Haathi would imitate different accents, suddenly walking up to an unsuspecting student and talking directly to him or her while addressing the rest of the class.

Once he came up to Joy's desk and stood in front of him for full five minutes before Joy woke up from his mid-morning snooze and wiped the little pool of drool that had formed on his desk as he snored, far away from the complicated world of bad grades and cruel professors. Having woken him up, Haathi decided to ignore the lad and continued, 'Sharing a common vocabulary and language is one of the strongest methods of bonding among people. Every cohesive group will have its own jargon, its common jokes and nicknames ... the double meaning and winks and nudges are all indicators of bonding in a group. When you meet an MIJ-ite for the first time, you relate to the person the moment you realize that he or she talks the same language, laughs at the same jokes and possibly shares the same worldview as you. There is a nice German word for worldview—Weltanschauung.'

Haathi would keep everyone riveted by changing the pace and pitch of his voice, sometimes whispering in a conspiratorial tone and at other times laughing loudly at his own joke. We watched, mesmerized. He would break the trance by jumping off the table on which he sat and addressing the class.

'Humour is a significant part of the bonding process. Think about the typical humour MIJ-ites share. The nicknames you have for each professor ... I know you call me Haathi ... Professor Chattopadhyay is called Chatto. Harpal Singh, who is sleeping as we discuss all this, is called Hairy. This is part of the experience of being in MIJ. Have you noticed how your language changes when you meet other MIJ-ites?'

Haathi's classes always left me fascinated and full of insights about human nature. I loved this subject, the one and only—'Orgy' Behaviour. But the class was divided in its opinion on OB. All those who loved quantitative stuff (not QT—no one liked that) and the like, were appalled by the very notion of a subject as abstract as OB.

'Unscientific mumbo-jumbo,' they said dismissively.

But what Haathi said was so true. MIJ had its own version of the English language, full of acronyms and words that were part English and part another language. If you did not know the lingo you would miss out on half the conversation. The first MIJ phrase one learnt was 'JLT,' which stood for Just Like That. It usually referred to something (or someone) without any purpose or meaning.

'It's like chumma in Tamil. It means random, indifferent or anything else that you wanted it to mean, *da*,' explained Gopher.

'Anything without substance is JLT, right?'

'Orgy B is a JLT subject. You can write anything in it and get a good grade. Anything can be JLT. So the weekend was spent being JLT. I just ate and slept,' said Sethu.

The steps in front of the Mess were called the JLT steps, to account for the many man hours wasted JLT at that sacred spot, especially in feminine company.

MIJ phrases took birth usually by shortening a phrase or noun beyond easy recognition. The way Organization Behaviour became Orgy B or Father Beez's classes on Group Dynamics was called 'Dyna.' You often heard someone rushing out of the Mess with a slice of bread hidden under a mountain of jam shouting out, 'Talk to you later. Got to go for Dyna.'

Many a naïve fresher has wondered who this Diana

babe was, until enlightened, 'Beez is teaching Dyna just now. You are late for class. Run!!'

Every MIJ nickname had a rationale and story whether one knew it or not. These names became such a common currency that one sometimes had to stop and think what the person's real name was. There were several categories of pet names. The simplest ones were truncated versions of the original. Hence, David Chemmanoor became Chumma. Viswaranjan was Vishy. Alpana was Alps. Hathaway became Haathi.

When there were five Venkateswarans floating around between the Senior and Junior batches, the shortened version of the name had a prefix attached to it. So, instead of demanding impatiently, 'Which fucking Venkat are you talking about?' we referred to them as—Junior Venky, Senior Venky, Mess Venky, who was our Mess Secretary, and Curly Venky because of his frizzy hairstyle. Only one guy had the honour of being addressed as plain and simple Venky.

Balvinder, for a while, had been called Balls, until we began to call him Ballu; Nikhilesh was Nicky. Ratina Pillai preferred Tina to 'Rats', obviously, though some names were just easy game. Sunaina was originally called Naina (her suggestion); later this became Nanny, because of her habit of mothering others. But some names stuck; Tathagato Chattopadhyay *had* to be Chatto because he really *chatoed* our brains.

The origins of some nicknames were unknown or mysterious, as in the case of Pavanpreet Kochhar, a full blown Surd who was called Tin Tin. Phanibhushan Grover was initially called 'Tiger' but was later dubbed 'Funny'. Some say it had something to do with his constant use of the term bhayncho which he used to complete every sentence. Manjusri Gaekwad became Mona-darling. The Manjusri to Mona bit is easy to figure out, but Mona-*darling*, that was a mystery.

Arunesh Nanda Abhayankar had a raw deal. His nickname was created with his initials, 'ANA,' and so he was Ana and occasionally called Annie, affectionately. He tried very hard to wipe it out but never managed. The more he squirmed, the more convinced we were that we had stumbled upon a goldmine of perennial excitement. The more it hassled him, the more determined the boys were to call him Ana, a 'top of the mind recall' (to borrow Professor Suri's jargon). Arunesh would often, out of frustration, physically assault the fellow who dared to call him Ana. He was a good 6 feet 3 inches tall and very aggressive—with a nick like that you have to be. But half an hour later, everyone would forget all about it and restore the status quo.

Doing well academically—at least in most subjects was all about 'Pshosha'—pronounced as shosha. Especially applicable in case of Dyna. Pshosha is what will make a difference between a B+ and an A in the Dyna term paper.

'So isn't the "P" redundant in the spelling?'

'Exactly! The redundant "P" itself is the Pshosha.'

I was picking up the lingo thanks to the coaching I received from a Senior—Posh. His name was Tapas Misra. Chatto pronounced it 'Taposh Miss-row', which soon became Posh, in true MIJ tradition. I had been a willing customer for his old textbooks. He sold them to me at half the price. Once he got the money, he even threw in a bonus; he gave me a copy of the November 1979 issue of *Penthouse* and a bunch of term papers written by MIJ-ites over the years in different subjects.

'What would I want to do with this shit?' I asked Posh.

'The *Penthouse* is worth its weight in gold.'

'I know. I was referring to the term papers.'

'I got them from someone who was here five years back. You know what that means? You can use these as handy references, especially when Beez gives you term papers to write. Just mix and match the stuff, change the sequence of the paragraphs. But always add your own pictures and illustrations. Beez hates people cogging pictures. I don't think he reads the shit we write anyway. I am a great believer in recycling knowledge.'

I offered some cash for these treasures in my attempts to end this discussion. I was already itching to spend quality time with the *Penthouse* centre spread. But Posh had turned woozy, three quarters of an Old Monk bottle inside him, and wanted to talk. Magnanimously, he declined the offer of money for the term papers.

'There is no charge for term papers, Abbey. This is part of one's obligation to one's Juniors. Give back something to others ... Anyway, fuck all this acad stuff. Do you want another drink ... or should I polish off the bottle?'

He was beginning to slur. Finally, Posh fell asleep on the floor and I scurried off to my room, the treasure tucked under my T-shirt.

Posh was right. I learnt soon enough that the difference between an A or an A+ in Father Beez's assignments on Dyna depended on the pshosha one put in. So, I started reading *The Illustrated Weekly* even more regularly to look for pictures to paste in term papers. There was a visible improvement in my grades at least in Father Beez's class. I often wondered what Chatto would give me if I pasted the *Penthouse* centre spread in the QT assignment. That was a possibility worth exploring.

But I had his weekly quiz to prepare for and desperately needed a cigarette before I sat down to study. I looked at the strange stuff written in the QT text book lying open in front of me and instantly felt very sorry for myself. I would have to endure this torture as long as there was QT in this world and a sadist like Chatto teaching it. A growling stomach did not make things easier either. I would have loved to have a bite. But that meant eating the horrendous mess food again. I banished the thought even before it settled.

Hum tumhe khana-e-mess khilayenge…

Nahiiiiiii…!

Why is it that food in every Hostel Mess has to be just that? A staple of watery daal with rotis that would decapitate a pig—if thrown at the correct angle, was what we got at every mealtime. Plus, there was the glob of sticky stuff that went by the generic name of *sabzi*. Every day a daily menu was put up on the door of the mess, giving 'the glob' a different name to compensate for the lack of taste. One day the sabzi appeared as Alu Gobhi, the next day it would show up as Gobhi Alu. On some days, when the red chilli was too much for the average commoner to handle, the Menu would term it Shahi Gobhi, meant only for the aristocrats!

On Mondays and Fridays we would get a 'Non-Veg' dinner. Unless you snuck out of the class and grabbed the good stuff early, you would have to deal with long queues and a potentially 'no chicken left—only curry' situation. Most of us felt there was nothing so sacred a Prof was going to tell us in the last fifteen minutes that would compensate for the loss of a succulent piece of chicken. When in a Hostel, he who doles out the pieces of chicken has the power of life and death over you. And our Basanto, Senior Bearer of the Mess, was a king on these occasions. As we stood in line, salivating over the likely size of the chicken that would be ours to chew, Basanto would find a way of shattering our hopes. We outdid each other in putting on the most pitiful expressions as we stood in line, holding our steel trays with a lump of rice soaked in yellow liquid that passed off for dal, the blob of *sabzi* in one compartment, willing Basanto to dish out a generous helping. But I was at a distinct disadvantage. My body contradicted my authentic poor boy starving, so-far-away-from-home look. A hungry stomach in a healthy body evokes no sympathy.

Basanto would dive into the container of oily gravy and scoop up a ladle full of the red stuff, a little piece of chilly floating on it.

'Basanto ... give me a piece of chicken...'

'I have. See this?'

'Oh! I thought that was a chilly.'

At this point, Basanto would pull off his famous 'Five Rupee' trick, which all MIJ-ites were well aware of. He would very slowly search for and come up with

Basanto doling out chicken

a real, generous piece of chicken and whisper within earshot,

'I needed to repair my cycle. Can you loan me five rupees?'

'Yeah sure ... can you add another piece of chicken? Just a small piece.'

Within minutes of my getting back to my room I would hear the dreaded knock on the door. It was payback time, as the godfather said. Basanto would take my precious five rupees, with the look of an agent collecting his share of sales tax on behalf of the government and waiving the penalty for late payment. Greedy dog. Exploiter. Must report him to Haathi... would always be my first thoughts.

Rusty had a different point of view.

'Think of it, Abbey. You pay him five rupees twice a week. That works out to forty bucks a month. I give him twenty bucks occasionally. Maybe every three weeks. It is cheaper and the controls lie with me, not him. I keep him guessing when I will bless him next. In turn, he is always trying to please me. He gets my breakfast tray to my room on Sundays. So I don't have to wake up early just to eat on weekends.'

'But isn't that against the hostel rules? Food is sent up to your room only if you are sick.'

'I am a sick person, Abbey!'

I tried to follow Rusty's advice. I stayed off cigarettes for three days and parted with a twenty rupee note. Basanto did not even look surprised. He just took it as if it was his due and walked away.

The 'Five Rupee Trick' was repeated the following chicken night. I was puzzled.

I confronted Basanto in the kitchen when no one was looking.

'Why did you ask for money again when I had given you twenty rupees yesterday even without you asking for it?'

'That was not your money. It was Rusty Babu's. He told me you owed him money and that if I could collect it, it was mine. You gave me a loan of five rupees. Is it too much to ask for?'

'Rusty! You unscrupulous dog,' I exclaimed. 'Never again will I trust you.'

I looked out of the window of Room 208 of the Boys' Hostel in MIJ. It overlooked Dadu's Dhaba. How much better life would be if Dadu would ask his son Niranjan to deliver stuff to the Hostel Rooms! Dadu's dilapidated dhaba was the source of tea, cigarettes, snacks and credit. Not necessarily in that order. Though housed in a temporary structure, Dadu and his dhaba had long been a permanent fixture in the lives of all MIJ-ites. Dadu had, what in today's world would be described as a home office! The dhaba was where he lived with his wife and two young sons—Niranjan and Monoranjan, fourteen and twelve, respectively.

I often wondered if Dadu paid Basanto to serve bad food in the Mess so that we would be compelled to eat more often at his dhaba.

Chapter 4

Just as Haathi was responsible for the existence of MIJ, so was he responsible for Dadu's presence on the campus. In a characteristic act of charity, he had permitted Chittoranjan Das to stay there, but only temporarily. The story goes that Father Hathaway had gone to the hospital to pray for a patient who was dying of kidney failure. Just as he had said 'Amen,' he found a pair of dark eyes willing him to look their way. It was Chittoranjan Das's wife, Debi. She pleaded with him to come to her husband's bedside for only one minute.

Father Hathaway stood by his bed and asked, 'What is the matter?', repeating it in Oriya probably to make him feel comfortable. 'Ki houchhi?'

Chittoranjan was too embarrassed to ask a stranger for help. But his wife's insistence—'Always the gora sahibs are the people who helped the poor. They had been the rulers of this country after all'—and poverty, which does strange things to people, gave her the courage to explain his plight to the gora sahib.

The rains had failed for three years in a row. Chittoranjan Das had been forced to sell off his land to the moneylender and walk to Berhampur railway station to catch the train to Kalimati town. His wife and their two little boys, the younger one barely a year old, had sat on the painted tin trunk, on a hot and crowded platform for almost six hours. Debi kept looking at her husband and wondered if he would find a job in the Steel Company. She thought of her land and her eyes filled with tears. In response, Chittoranjan would silently light a bidi only after he had spent two to three hours chewing one end of it. That made the bidi last longer.

The train reached Kalimati station the following day. Chittoranjan and his wife stood outside the huge factory gates, looking for work. After five days, he found work as contract labour in the blast furnace area of the Steel & Iron Company. A month later, just as they were settling down, he slipped and broke his thigh bone. He had been in the hospital for a month now and the situation was getting desperate.

'Hai bidhata, when will all this suffering and misery end?' was the summary of his question to Lord Jagannath. God responded to his plea. He sent a silent message to Chittoranjan's wife.

'Talk to him. Tell the gora sahib about our fate,' she had goaded him.

Chittoranjan could not get himself to ask for help. But Debi was desperate and prevailed on her own. She explained as best as she could. Father Hathaway heard her out.

'Listen Chitto-run-john,' he said. 'I will give you a shelter in my institute. But remember, this is only a temporary arrangement. You cannot stay there forever. The moment you have earned enough to pay me back and buy your family a return ticket to Orissa, you have to leave. OK? Bujhi gela?' With this, Father Haathi loaned the man ₹ 100 to set up a tea stall.

The rest, as they say is history, at least for us.

The long hours and hard work made Chittoranjan look so much older than he was. He and his wife stayed up till well past midnight every day, making tea for the night birds in MIJ. By 5:30 am, the couple was up again making tea and coffee for the early risers. Debi encouraged him to keep adding new stuff to their menu. One day she made ten samosas. The students loved them.

But Chittoranjan was the Quality Control guy.

'Kharaap na... Not bad!! Needs to be crisper,' was his verdict. His best compliment was '*Kharaap na...*'

When Debi made jalebis, they were devoured by the students in no time. The eternally hungry and ever appreciative students kept encouraging her to try something new. Since we had limited influence over the mess food, we concentrated on getting Dadu to extend the menu beyond samosa and jalebis and start serving the recently launched quick noodles someone had picked up on a trip to Calcutta. Dadu was not in favour of the suggestion. But Nanny was very persuasive and managed to hold cooking demos for Debi. She agreed to make them for us. But Dadu was unimpressed when Nanny handed him a plateful of steaming hot noodles, garnished with some peas and fried eggs. Dadu refused to touch the plate.

'How can you eat that stuff?' he sneered. 'It looks like a plate of earthworms. Only, these worms are white and they don't wriggle.'

Nanny almost threw up and I went off noodles for a week.

But ultimately, no matter what Dadu's Dhaba made, it was a huge improvement over the mess food. More importantly than that, Dadu's Dhaba was a place for students to hang out at, to get away from it all and relax, sip chai and listen to Dadu play the flute. The Dhaba was a witness to heated discussions and debates, arguments and confessions. It even featured in Professor Suri's class as a case study. I still remember how vividly he explained the concept of how to 'Expand the Market by Redefining the Customer.' His article had recently been published in our very own *Marketing Trends Journal* and Rusty said that a sure-fire way of getting an A+ was to quote a line from it while answering any of Suri's questions. So I paid attention to the lecture.

'Dadu's Dhaba struggled to create a niche in this market which had a limited customer base. The only form of advertising he had available was word of mouth. So what did he do? Jayant, if you wake up and pay attention, even a person like you will understand how Dadu's marketing plan worked. The place was a hangout for only boys initially, but he figured out a way to get the girls there as well. This entrepreneur had noticed perhaps that boys spend more when there is a girl around. The ultimate mark of consumer confidence was demonstrated when couples started making Dadu's Dhaba their preferred hangout. Dadu cashed in on the popularity by extending the product line—from just tea to samosas and jalebis—to keep up with evolving tastes. Slowly it has grown to be the preferred location for a lot of activities. When the students go there to celebrate—and you all know what that means...'

We all nodded and recalled Father Hathaway's first address to the students on the day we joined the institute. We were sitting in the auditorium listening to various professors introduce themselves and the subjects they were going to teach. Father Hathaway then proceeded to explain to us what was expected of us as students of this hallowed institution.

'There is a strict code of conduct applicable to all students of this Institute. Let me start with the academic requirements. Any student who gets three Ds or two Fs at any time during the two years will have to leave the Institute. Any student caught using unfair means will be asked to leave MIJ the same day. We all live in the same campus. We expect you to be sensitive to the presence of the professors and their families as well.

And then in a firm, warning tone he said,

'Please remember the three Ds banned from the Boys' Hostel. No Drinks, no Drugs and no Dames. If I catch you drinking in the Hostel, you will be dismissed instantly. No amount of pleading will make me change my mind.'

Our faces fell, but our Seniors were unperturbed. 'All it means is don't make an ass of yourself after you drink. Drink discreetly in your room and never sing loudly when you are boozing. When you want to have a wild booze party, go to Dadu's and freak out. That is technically not part of the Boy's Hostel. So Haathi's law does not apply there.'

How Chittoranjan became 'Dadu' and his wife, 'Didima' over the years remains a mystery. Dadu became a permanent fixture in the life of every

MIJ-ite, and his wife their affectionate and doting grandma, indulging the eternally hungry students. Lovingly, she would give us tea and cigarettes on a never ending line of credit. She also had blind faith in all her grandchildren—even though they were usually broke. Naturally, the students loved her and appealed to her every time Dadu refused to extend them credit. Invariably, Dadu had to relent, but not before expressing his fears.

'What if the fellow runs away before returning my money? Every week he says that his money order is coming in the next Monday. I don't trust him.'

'Of course he will pay. I trust him,' Didima would reply.

She was right. How could you cheat someone who trusted you so much? Generations of MIJ-ites would return to Jamshedpur months after getting their first jobs with gifts for Dadu and Didima and cash to settle their debts at the Dhaba.

Posh took me for my first cup of tea at Dadu's and opened up my 'account', which basically meant that I could buy tea and cigarettes on credit during my stay at MIJ.

'Chai and cigarettes for both of us.' Posh ordered.

'No more credit for you until you settle the ₹ 117 balance on your account,' Dadu declared, after squinting at a small red diary.

Posh looked a little embarrassed. Denial of credit in front of a Junior was a huge insult. This had to be fixed. He had to be discreet.

He walked up to where Dadu was sitting on a charpai under the neem tree and pleaded his case.

'The postal system is to blame, Dadu. My parents have already sent the money order. You will definitely get it by next Monday, Didima, please, why don't you tell him? Have I ever …?' he whispered.

There was a deathly silence as Posh waited for the verdict. All that could be heard was the hissing of the kettle as Dadu's wife added a fistful of tea leaves to the brew. Then she walked up to Posh and handed him a cup of tea and a Navy Cut cigarette.

'Let me open an account for your friend. He will need it for the next two years,' she smiled and said. 'You can pay your dues next week.'

Posh's self-esteem had been salvaged just in time. He walked back to me and victoriously handed me the chai and cigarette.

Just then, a few more MIJ-ites arrived at Dadu's Dhaba. The Seniors who accompanied the freshers were all given a complimentary chai, courtesy Dadu's wife. There were no prizes for guessing who was the popular one at Dadu's; Didima not only supplied endless cups of tea and snacks, she often stopped by to ask after someone's health or about their girlfriends.

Dadu's relationship with the students was different. He had an amazing gut feel about the corporate sector, even though he had never read a book past class two in his village school. He had a one line summary of each company that had ever employed an MIJ-ite. The companies were divided into two categories—the good companies and the lousy ones. Most people seemed to respect his sometimes unconventional advice. Posh told me about the time when Dadu had 'counselled' a student against accepting an offer from a fairly well-known textile company, saying that the company did not pay its employees well.

'That Pinto fellow in Room 305 took eight months to settle his account with me even after joining that company as an officer. Would that have happened if he had a well-paying job?'

It was difficult to disagree.

For every MIJ-ite, Dadu's Dhaba was an affordable alternative to the tasteless mess food we had no choice but to endure for two years. But it was also much more than that. It was a place to seek the wisdom that comes from quiet introspection. The tea and cigarette often led to gossip sessions and confessions when Dadu took a break and joined us for a smoke. As he poured the chai into the saucer and drank it in slow noisy slurps, he enquired about our grades, our confrontations with the professors and our love lives. He knew how

I was struggling with QT and how miserable I was in Chatto's classes.

When I told him, 'Dadu, I will never be able to clear these two papers on QT,' he said, with not a hint of sympathy—or ridicule—in his voice, 'I have seen students stupider than you, yet all of them are now doing so well. I see no reason why you will fail.'

For a moment, the remark hurt—Stupider than you?—then, it became a comforting thought.

Another time, when I was particularly down in the dumps, I blurted out, 'I hate this place, Dadu. I hate this city. I hate MIJ ...'

Dadu just guffawed and said, 'That's simple. You need a girlfriend.'

That statement set me thinking. What were my chances of finding a girlfriend here? Would I actually get lucky?

Several weeks had passed since college had started and things were changing. From being part of a galaxy, we had all formed our own little solar systems. Mine consisted of Joy, Hairy, Arunesh, Chumma, Pappu, Fundu. Even Rascal Rusty became part of our group. There were some who had hung around us at first but gradually drifted off to form their own orbits. Sethu was like a satellite—he thought we were too JLT for him to belong, yet he couldn't peel away. Of the girls, Ratina, Alpana and Sunaina also became part of our group by virtue of doing four group assignments with us. And of course, there was Ayesha who believed that she was the centre of every solar system, which was true to some extent, for some of us. Gopher tried his best to join in but the decision to keep him out was both conscious and unanimous. Initially, everyone had some reservations about Rusty. I had noticed Alps and Nanny were more guarded in his presence. But eventually even he managed to earn his membership by his sheer ingenuity; simplifying assignments, dividing up the tasks and then adding some unique insights that would get our group a special mention. Through all of this, Rusty became a necessary part of our group.

Dadu's Dhaba was the venue of our drinking binges on weekends as drinking liquor was prohibited in our Hostel. Dadu loved the boozing sessions and our WC-DMR (Pronounced WC-Dimmer and stood for Who Can Drink the Most Rum) contests but hated our collective efforts at singing, which was the highlight of each such event. On these occasions, we would pool our resources and buy a few bottles of Old Monk rum and pour it into a large drum that was permanently kept at Dadu's. Dadu would be given the honour of declaring the bacchanalia open. He would collect his share of three mugs of rum all at once and then gulp them down in large eager swigs. Mug after plastic mug (a precautionary measure to prevent injuries from broken glasses!) would then be dipped into the drum and emptied hurriedly. This would go on until elbows became immobilized or the liquor ran out.

And then Dadu would ask us to sing—a request he would regret as soon as he had made it. Sometimes he would try and accompany the singers on his flute but the English songs we sang were alien to him. That would make him grumpy. He would mutter something about tuneless foreign music, curse us all, then roll on the floor and fall asleep until his wife dragged him in. Occasionally, he would get up from his drunken stupor, damn us to hell for our off-key singing, then go back to sleep before completing the slurred sentence.

These booze sessions usually ended up with a bonfire and all of us, softened up by all that liquor, would sing our favourite Dylan songs. Bob Dylan was our hero; he wrote and said all that we wanted to. Then, after the initial spell of drunken choral singing, we would hand over the stage to Arunesh for some professional grade music. This was the moment he loved and gloated over. For, if you wanted him to sing a specific song, you had to address him as Arunesh—never Ana or Annie, and ask for it in a suitably reverential tone.

Everybody, without exception, agreed that Arunesh played the guitar as well as Dylan. There was a certain magic in those starlit nights as the moonlight shone on his black Yamaha acoustic guitar. He caressed each note off the nylon strings and shiny frets. He once wrote the lyrics of 'Blowing in the Wind' for us on the blackboard. We all memorized the words and thereafter we sang it like it was our anthem.

'How many roads must a man walk down, before you can call him a man?'

It was not sung like a drunken sailor's song, but like a man's plea for an answer. There was something in that song that made me pine for Delhi one helluva fucking lot more than what I was capable of handling emotionally. All that rum inside me did not help either. For some strange reason it reminded me of Priya and I missed her. I felt sorry for all the times I had hurt her with my stupid comments.

Did that mean I loved her? NEVER! She is not my type. You know that, don't you?

I would stop talking to myself and quickly skim over the ache, concentrating on the rum and the music.

Arunesh did not only depend on Dylan for songs. He was equally at home singing Kishore Kumar numbers, complete with yodelling and all. We all thought he sang Simon and Garfunkel, Beatles and Cat Stevens just as well. Besides this sort of mainstream music, there were rugby songs that were especially requested for during

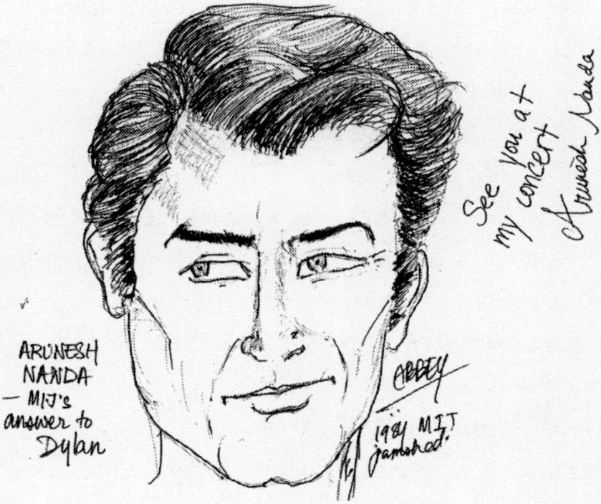

our all-male singing sessions. Our eternal favourite was 'Diana's Song':

Diana, Diana show me your legs
Diana, Diana show me your legs
Diana, Diana show me your legs
A foot above your knee.
Rich girl rides a limousine
Poor girl rides a truck
The only ride that Diana gets
Is when she is having a F…

A few more glasses of rum and he would egg us on to greater heights, 'Who wants to sing the German Soldiers' song with me? It goes something like this:

The German soldiers went to hell Parlez-vous
The German soldiers went to hell Parlez-vous
The German soldiers went to hell
They screwed the Devil's wife as well,
Inky pinky parlez-vous.

Once Chumma had gotten technical, 'Machan there's a technical praablem in this saang. If they say parlez-vous, it hassz to be French soldiers, da and not German. I did French for eight months at the Alliance Française.'

A yell from the crowd followed by a volley of abuse that can only be politely summarized as, 'Who cares?' but the exact words that were used… you don't want to know, *da*.

This and several other songs had been handed down over generations of MIJ-ites. Often, the singing continued till the soft rays of the moonlight gave way to orange hues in the eastern sky. Some of us would wake up to the sight of Gur going for his daily run while others would quickly get back to the Hostel, avoiding eye contact with Haathi, who would be reading his Bible as he walked briskly along the cobbled pathway that led to the Boys' Hostel.

Watching the sunset along the banks of Subarnarekha was a universal favourite activity. The sight would fill us up with wonder and amazement at the spectacle nature could paint for us. Sometimes the colours were so vibrant that the scene looked unreal. If Arunesh joined in with his guitar and sang the soulful, '*Kahin door jab din dhal jaye...*' or '*Woh shaam kuchh ajeeb thhii...*' we would sit there mesmerized. The only challenge was to prevent some of the others, especially Chumma, from joining in and ruining the moment. The weak Chumma would get himself into an emotional knot—invariably Joy would then politely remind him about a pending assignment. This would keep him silent and withdrawn until we returned to the hostel.

Chapter 5

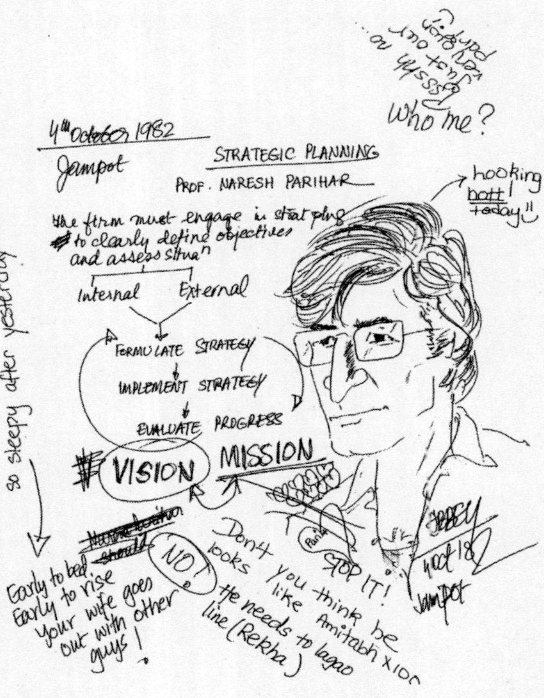
Who me?
4th October 1982
Jampot
STRATEGIC PLANNING
PROF. NARESH PARIHAR
looking hott today!!
The firm must engage in strat plng to clearly define objectives and assess situa^n
Internal
External
FORMULATE STRATEGY
IMPLEMENT STRATEGY
EVALUATE PROGRESS
VISION
MISSION
so sleepy after yesterday
Early to bed
Early to rise
Your wife goes
out with other
guys!
NO!
Don't you think he looks like Amitabh x10
He needs to lagao line (Rekha)
STOP IT!
Parihar
4 Oct '82
Jampot

Professor Naresh Parihar was explaining the intricacies of Strategic Planning for business. He taught us a paper titled Business Policy. Professor Parihar (called 'Pari' for short) was a most unlikely teacher figure. He was about forty and looked thirty. Always nattily dressed in a pair of faded Levis jeans, a crisply starched, white, full-sleeved shirt and trendy Ray Ban Aviator glasses perched precariously on his thick mop of hair, he looked like an action hero from Bollywood rather than a Professor of Management. I had not infrequently noticed Nanny and Tina throwing lustful glances at him. Only Pari was oblivious of them.

'Must be a homo...' hypothesised Nanny.

'Maybe the guy who stays with him in the Profs' Quarters is his lover and not his cousin brother as he claims,' was Tina's frustrated rejoinder.

'He may just have better taste than to lech at you,' retorted Hairy.

'I agree with you. God created three kinds of beings—men, women and MIJ girls ... Ouch Nanny! Joke yaar! Don't hit so hard.' Joy jumped up clutching his stomach.

Pari's colleagues all hated the way he flaunted his money and his jaunty single man's status. He drove to the MIJ Academic Block from the Professors' Quarters, a distance of about 400 metres, in his shining, new Fiat Premier Padmini. Chatto's old Standard Herald looked even more run down when the Padmini was parked next to it in the Professors' Car Park. As Pari got out of the car, he would shut the door without even turning back, straighten the imaginary creases on his shirt, light up a Marlboro and stride towards the Academic Block. Of course, he extinguished the cigarette before he entered the classroom. He had a deep baritone that made the girls swoon. Most people agreed that he sounded like Amitabh Bachchan. Once Nanny even called him up at home (from a shop in Bistupur) just to hear him say 'Hello, Dr Naresh Parihar's residence…' A satisfied Nanny disconnected the phone and savoured the moment by having another Thums Up. Pari was a man of few words, yet he had the ability to explain esoteric stuff like strategy in words that got everyone hooked on the subject. Naturally, the students were in awe of him while the profs, well, their attitude was reflected in this statement by a colleague, 'Typical—all style and no substance.'

Pari's unconventional manners and lifestyle had created this impression of him. But we knew soon enough that such a remark only came from the green-eyed monster. Pari was much sought after as a consultant in the industry. In addition, he had authored a bestseller on *Research Methodology in Developing Markets* which was on every MIJ-ite's bookshelf and on the desks of the top executives of the industry. The royalty he earned went a long way to support his style, they said.

I thought Business Policy was all about making sense of oxymorons. Rusty's favourite example of this figure of speech had to be 'Military Intelligence' or maybe 'Civil Engineer.'

'Ever seen one?' Rusty would ask as he cackled insanely.

As far as I was concerned, even 'Business Policy' or 'Strategic Planning' were oxymorons.

Pari started off the class by saying, 'Business Policy teaches us to focus on the basic question: Why are we in this business? What is the business we are trying to carry out?'

He gave us an example of how the American Railroads Company had nearly gone bankrupt because they believed that their actual business was the railways.

'And what was wrong with that?' I asked Rusty in a whisper.

He was taking notes and ignored my question. I looked to my left and thought of questioning Joy next. But he was in raptures, drawing nudes, and was oblivious to the lesser pleasures of Business Policy. I tuned back to Pari's baritone.

'And what was wrong with that assumption?' Was Pari a mind reader or had he heard my query?

No. It was Pari's teaching methodology. He asked the questions and then after a pregnant pause, answered them himself.

'Everything. A very narrow definition of your business will make you myopic and stop you from looking at changes happening in the world. On the other hand a very loose definition of your Business Policy will prevent you from focussing.'

Great! Damned if you do and damned if you don't. So how had the American Railroads stepped out of the doggy do? As expected, their angel came disguised as a wise consultant.

'Wise consultant! Another oxymoron for your collection,' I muttered to Rusty.

We were waiting, with bated breath, to find out what great idea the consultant had come up with.

'The consultant changed the focus of the American Railroads Company by making them realize that they were in the business of transportation. This was the insight the consultant made the client understand. It was done by asking the critical question: What business are you in?'

What was the difference? Being in the transportation business seemed to me to be the same as being in the railways business. Weren't the railways a form of transportation just as much as bullock carts were? They both took you from one place to the other with almost the same level of efficiency—and sometimes in a similar time frame. So what did the consultant do that impressed Pari so much? Pari was animatedly trying to explain the correlation of some obscure variables (which I could not figure out) by drawing graphs on the board. Pari's eyes shone as he imparted this great aha experience which he expected us to absorb instantly. But I did not get it.

Later, on that evening, I walked into Rusty's room, looking as always for answers.

Rusty was lying on his bed and listening to Pink Floyd's 'Wish You Were Here' on his swanky Sonodyne music system. Rusty was the only one in the Hostel who had a proper music system. Must be part of the consultancy fee some sucker had doled out, I assumed. A few of us had small mono players. So I had to listen to 'proper music' either in Rusty's room or in the Hostel's Music Room. I lowered the volume to get his attention.

'Rusty, what was so smart about asking that single question? A consultant gets paid for saying that kind of shit? I always thought a consultant has to be a smart guy, Rusty. He comes in completely unaware of what is bothering the client. Then he gathers all the info that the client has, asks the client for what could be a possible solution, then puts it all together in the form of a massive report and leaves the client to implement the recommended solution. Simple, all of us in MIJ could become consultants.'

'Sure. Beez gives us enough practice in writing crappy reports with no substance. Maybe I will be one too. Who knows! Maybe even you will, Abbey...'

'I will be happy if I get a good summer training assignment in a good company. That's what I am worried about now.' I added a practical angle to this esoteric conversation.

Before Rusty could say anything, Funny burst into the room. 'Hey guys, bhayncho, chalna hai kya, bhayncho, to Franks for Chinese? Bhayncho Alps is treating...'

'What? Why?' I interrupted.

'It's her birthday yaar! It's the first ten guys who sign up. Be at the Music Room in 30 seconds.'

The rule at MIJ was that if anyone offered to treat you, you just ran and ate first, then asked questions if needed. Rusty rolled over and continued to listen to Floyd.

'Aren't you joining us Rusty?'

'No Abbey. I am trying to find the hidden meanings of the lyrics in this album.'

With Rusty, one never knew whether he was being serious or frivolous. But when he said no, he meant it. I was his friend but not such a good one that I would sacrifice a Chinese meal for his company. When I reached the Music Room, I found fifteen greedy souls there already. In a fit of generosity, Alps agreed to treat all of us to fried rice and chilly chicken, and we prepared for a feast.

First, as per our time-honoured ritual, we went to the Sardarji's shop in Bistupur for cold coffee. I watched Satwant Singh talk to each of his customers as if they were his long-lost cousins. He would take their orders for coffee, pour the sugar syrup and then add some milk into the mixer. Next, he would add coffee powder and a handful of ice cubes. When he pressed the 'start' button, the turbulent mixture turned to delicious cold coffee. Whenever we went to his shop, the Sardar invariably gave us an extra glass for free. It probably came from the generous chunks of ice that he had added. But we did not care. That day, Alps got the extra glass since it was her birthday.

Even before we had savoured the coffee, Funny said, 'Bhayncho, I better go ahead and keep a table for us at Franks.'

'Don't act like a despo, Funny. We will all go together. As long as we reach there by 10 pm, that sucker is duty bound to serve us. Venky, hurry up. We don't have all day.'

At Franks, we dug into the chilly chicken and fried rice, and there was chilled beer for all.

Alps raised a toast, 'For those unfortunate souls in MIJ who were condemned to eat the mess food tonight. May god give them courage to face this great loss.'

I instantly thought of Chumma who was, at this point of time, slaving away in the library. I told everyone. 'Chumma wanted to join in, but he is working on a term paper for Beez. He has to redo the last one. He forgot which group he was assigned to. So his name did not feature in any.'

'Gopher must be reading up *Research Methodology in Developing Markets* for the second time this week in a desperate effort to impress Pari. Why does he have to be such a dickhead always?' wondered Joy.

'What's the point in impressing Pari?' asked Vishy.

'Simple boy. If Pari is impressed his Summer, Placement is assured in Balwan Papers. If you do a summer job there, your final placement is guaranteed. Boss, this is called forward thinking,' said Sethu.

I could not help envying guys like Gopher. They know exactly what they wanted out of life. They made out a game plan, weighed the options, decided on the best course of action, systematically implemented the project plan and then threw a champagne party when they achieved their target. Some guys even put together a 'Plan B' for every moment of their lives, just in case the first plan cocked up. Maybe this is why I disliked Gopher and his kin so much. He made me painfully aware of my lack of direction in life. I did not understand how anyone could plan things to that extent. It must make life very boring, I told myself confidently. The more I thought about it, the more convinced I was that I did not want to be like any of them. I did not admire them. I despised them. Probably because I couldn't ever be like them, even if I tried.

When we returned, I went straight to Rusty's room to give him an update of the dinner treat.

'Rusty, you missed something, man. The chilly chicken was unusually good today. Not to mention Alp's knockers. She was wearing a real tight T-shirt. Looked as fake as the consultant's advice to the American Railroads Company.'

Rusty did not show the slightest interest in Alp's assets. Instead he passed me a book called *Lateral Thinking: Creativity Step by Step*, by someone called Edward de Bono.

'The consultant was right, you know,' he said to me. 'Linear thinking can produce limited results when the problem is undefined. I had once read about a great example of lateral thinking. You want to know what it was?'

Of course I did—it would save me the bother of reading it for myself. When you are used to being spoon-fed as we are in our education system, predigested mush is always welcome!

Rusty explained, 'A hotel had a major problem. The guests constantly complained that the hotel lifts were too slow and they had to wait endlessly to go from floor to floor. What would you suggest, Abbey, if they had called you in to solve this problem?'

'That's a no-brainer. The speed of the lifts would have to be adjusted so that the frigging lifts move faster. The lift mechanic could have told them that,' I replied glibly.

'Now that is a classic example of linear thinking. You would never cut it as a consultant, Abbey. Listen to this. The consultant who was brought in suggested something truly amazing. He got the hotel to fix massive mirrors in the waiting area near the lifts. Within no time the complaints stopped. Why?'

I pondered over it for a moment. 'Why would you want to fix mirrors near the lift? Some kind of optical illusion?'

'Hmmm ... yes and no. But mainly no, da. The mirrors gave the hotel guests something to do while waiting for the lifts.'

'Yeah, I know that one. The mirrors let them make last minute surveys of themselves—check if hair is in place, and zip up fly before stepping into the lift. Since they were occupied, they did not notice how slow the lifts were ... Hmmm ... Now it figures. That's what Pari meant when he said we should look for the real problem and not the symptoms.' I felt enlightened.

I was determined to test this theory. I made it a point to walk into the lobby of Hotel Bistupur the following week and did not believe what I saw.

Even this hotel had mirrors. I noticed a fat man in a light green safari suit waiting for the lift, looking at himself in the mirror and admiring the gold chain he was wearing. After he had had his fill of fiddling with the chain, he glanced surreptitiously at the girl at the reception desk and caught her looking at him. By the time he decided upon what interpretation to put on that look, the lift happened. Fatso waved a casual smile in the general direction of the reception and stepped into the lift.

They say no woman could pass a mirror and not look at herself. I think one should change that to no one, man or woman. Sure enough, I myself checked to see if my hair was in place and if my trousers were being rude. The girl at the reception desk was rather cute, too. When I went back to the hostel, I told Rusty that there was some truth in the mirror theory.

Rusty just raised an eyebrow and said, 'Abbey, always remember, differentiate the problem from the symptom.'

Rusty was so good at using these clever phrases. Once, during a case discussion in Professor Kamini Mishra's class on Industrial Relations, we were grappling with the problem of how to bring down absenteeism in a troublesome plant. The discussion was getting completely out of control. Each one tried to outspeak the other. Ballu talked about militant trade unions. Vishy suggested opening a counselling centre for the workers.

'Let us get professional counsellors to hear out the workers' grievances,' echoed Tina.

Nanny chirped, 'Vinaya Jaggery in Rajahmundry had an identical problem. When I was visiting my uncle's factory…' Nobody was interested.

'Absenteeism can be solved only by changing the patterns of indebtedness among rural migrant labour.' We all turned to stare at Joy with a look reserved for the giraffe in the zoo. He shut up.

Rusty, who had remained silent all this while, said in a quiet but confident voice, 'Let us ask ourselves if absenteeism is the problem or the symptom.'

As soon as he said this, something happened in the class. Professor Mishra's face glowed with the pride of a master whose puppy had just been toilet trained.

She walked up to Rusty and said, 'It is surprising that only one person in this class was able to demonstrate managerial insight and acumen. As managers, we have to first learn to segregate the problem from the symptom. Absenteeism is the symptom.'

She awarded Rusty an A+ while the rest of us remained stupefied. In MIJ, where every student fancied himself or herself a Mensa member, such appreciation of someone else's cognitive prowess instantly brought to the surface waves of jealousy.

'What did Rusty say that was so clever?' asked Nanny, leading the charge.

'He just figured out a smart phrase to cover up his ignorance. Evidence that he will be the first one from this class to become a consultant.'

'Sure,' said Nanny sarcastically. 'He has already become the "con" part of consultant.'

The catty remark took everyone by surprise. Rusty just bit his lip and pretended that he had not heard her.

Rusty did not join us for lunch that day. I knew it had something to do with Nanny's sideswipe. It had been a bit below the belt, I thought, with a strong urge to go and kick Nanny in her mean little ass. I felt sorry for Rusty. He had been really decent to me. He had helped me get over the culture shock of living in a hostel for the first time in faraway Jamshedpur, of studying in MIJ and its difficult courses. He had also taken it upon himself to groom me for the corporate world.

All afternoon, Rusty locked himself in his room and sucked at his pipe, and scribbled away in a grey leather diary. A few days later, when he was out, I tried to sneak a look at what was written in the diary. It was all in Greek. I recognized some of the letters like sigma, omega, pi, etc. Those symbols instantly brought to mind the torture of Physics and Statistics lessons in school. I closed the diary and looked up to see Rusty watching me, his head cocked to one side.

'Abbey, you sneaky bastard! You are trying to read my diary. You won't succeed. This is all in Greek. Everything there is in code.'

'Why in Greek? Why not French?'

'French is for sissies.'

'So what is this great secret?'

'I am writing a book called *Selected Oxymorons for All*. This diary contains the final draft. A publisher in the US has offered to publish it and has given me an advance on the royalty—that's how I bought the Sonodyne music system. The idiots in our class won't understand that I am different. They are only good at being petty.'

'Don't feel bad about Nanny's remarks. She is a stupid nut.'

'I don't care, Abbey. Envy arises out of one's own sense of inadequacy. If you want to level with someone Abbey, there are two ways of doing it. Either you rise up and become as tall as the other person or else pull him down to your level. Obviously, the easier route is the preferred option with most people. I understood the case-insight before they did. So, they needed to cope with their disappointment at being beaten. They did it by calling me names!'

He paused. When he saw my almost admiring expression, he continued, 'I have never called Nanny and Tina names when they tried to suck up to Pari during the entire term. That's because I do not feel threatened by their incompetence. They were just trying their best to figure out what would work for them—but they failed. Let's face it, Abbey. You can't deny that I read a damn lot more than all of you put together. I don't con anyone. I know what my strengths are and I leverage them. I concentrate on finding ways to understand the system and then explore ways to do that with least effort. There is no law in the world that says one should not try to take the easy way out if one can. To do well in life, you have to understand what is the system you are a part of and then figure out how to beat it.'

He paused, picked up his pipe sucked on it, unlit, for a couple of minutes, and waited for me to say something.

'Go on Rusty, You were saying ...'

'Yes ... You are somehow different, da, that's why I am telling you all this. Abbey, each prof is like a customer. In marketing terminology, it's called "having customer orientation." For instance, if you did a term paper for Beez, you would write it differently than the one you would do for Chatto, right? You stick pictures that you cut from magazines when you write a term paper for Father Beez. But you would get the royal boot if you put anything besides your hard-working ass into Chatto's papers. Does that make you a con artist, haan?'

I shook my head. It was the first time I had heard Rusty explain himself. He wasn't angry, just a little hurt, I guess. I didn't know what to say. Something Professor Suri had said in class came to mind.

'Customer orientation seems to apply in all walks of life, right Rusty?'

Rusty smiled. 'The rules of the game are different for each system. If you play cricket the way you play rugby, that's curtains for life! You are doomed, Abbey!'

Chapter 6

Being in MIJ was not good for my ego. Within a few weeks of coming here, I was assailed by grave self-doubt. I knew I was not brilliant, but then I had written the entrance test, cleared the interview and been selected by this premier institution. Granted, I had not been a hundred per cent sure I'd make it. When Jayprakash, the postman who had been delivering mail to us in the Railway Colony for the past million years, handed me the letter bearing the official stamp of MIJ, I almost fainted. He had looked very worried and asked me if everything was all right.

'Looks like you got bad news...'

'Oh no! I have been selected to MIJ. This must be a mistake,' I said in a voice choked with emotion.

'Is that good news?'

'Yes and no, Jaypeeji,' I laughed, almost hysterically.

Shaking his head uncomprehendingly, Jayprakash went away, completely confused. I stayed that way for a long time.

How had this happened? Maybe I was not so dumb after all—or had they made a mistake while tabulating the marks? Alternately, did this prestigious institute in fact have pathetic standards? If I continued to think this way, I would have no confidence left in myself at all.

My mother came into my room, pretending to look for something. She had noticed that instead of spreading joy all around me I was lying down on my bed listening to the Beatles sing '*Yesterday … all my troubles seemed so far away. Now it looks as though they are here to stay …*'

She sat on my bed stroking my hair, and said, 'You must be very proud of yourself, Chhotka. I was absolutely sure you would get selected to this management college.'

'Ma, it is called the Management Institute of Jamshedpur. There must be something wrong in their selection process … I never thought I'd …'

'But you got admission in Shri Ram College, that too for Economics Honours,' she interrupted. Before I could say anything deprecatory about myself she continued, 'Chhotka, you are going away soon—far away … I won't be there to tell you this, but always remember one thing—if you do not value yourself, nobody else will. Aim high. Try to get right to the top. Work for it. There's nothing wrong in being ambitious. If there is stiff competition, don't get discouraged. And most important, be proud of what you have achieved. Never treat it casually.'

The three years in Delhi University, from 1979 to 1982, were wonderful. All I had to do was to land up in college and float around the college campus. Sit in the SRCC canteen and sing songs, discuss the demerits of capitalism and smoke endless numbers of cheap cigarettes. Occasionally, we would turn up for the screening of the firang films by the university's film society, called Delhi University Film Fraternity (or DUFF). You can figure out what the members were called. These were our best bet for seeing flesh other than at the film festivals, where one had to suffer two hours of gibberish for a three second reward.

Occasionally, the big question popped up in my mind: What will I do after my graduation? Then I would rephrase that question.

Where would I be able to continue this lifestyle? Rather, how could I continue to have this lifestyle for some more time?

I thought of the options. Doing an MA in Economics from the Delhi School of Economics seemed too much of a price to pay for staying on at Delhi University. The coffee and sambar vadas of the D School canteen were great, but the course was too tough. If I joined up, I would not have the time for the sambar vadas. Besides, MA Eco was not really my scene; I probably wouldn't have been able to cope with it, even if I tried.

When I got to the final year of college, this question seemed to come up more often than I could conveniently handle. I spoke to a few guys around the college, seeking different perspectives. Some of them were lucky and had a ready-made family business they would enter seamlessly as soon as they graduated. This was not an alternative for me.

It was my friend Kapil who suggested I should seriously consider writing the Civil Services exam. Most of the guys from the University—especially the Eco or History types, were heavily into pursuing that greatest of national pastimes. They had no problems at all answering the question of, 'after graduation, what?'

The Civil Services seemed like a worthwhile option. I read the *Competition Success Review* for possible tips on writing the exam. They always had the standard advice: 'Work hard and success will be yours.' (Unstated: And read *CSR* regularly!) The magazine had published statements and interviews with the toppers of the Civil Services exams. All of them sounded ever so smug and always so predictable.

'I have always dreamt of serving the country. Of working in the villages of India and making this a better place to be in. *Competition Success Review* gave me the right kind of guidance.'

Can't get away from that 'a word from our sponsors...' bit. Even potential Civil Servants had to do that, I guess. I did not know it then, but later when I met Rusty I would add to his list of oxymorons—Civil Servants. Ha!

Kapil tried to paint a pretty rosy picture of the life of a sarkari babu in his special brand of English. 'After you are joining the Civil Services, you will be getting the first posting into the interiors and life is very tough there, baba. But you get jeep, bungalow and lots of servants. Civil Servants are also getting good dowry in the *marrij* market says my Mamaji. It is the job that has lots of power and status.'

Kapil's description matched the popular opinion held by Delhi University students about life in the Civil Services. I decided against it. It seemed like too much hard work. I wondered if there was anything wrong in being labelled 'unambitious.'

Until I found a satisfactory answer to the question, 'beyond undergrad what?' I was quite happy to be travelling by the U-Special buses that plied up and down from various locations in the city to the University Campus. I was also quite satisfied with the progress I had made in my life in college. In my first year, heeding the advice of my Seniors—that if you got elected to one of the Students' Union posts, attendance requirements for classes would be waived—I worked very hard towards becoming the Secretary of the English Debating Society.

I was elected unopposed, because nobody else cared to contest. My duties were to organize one major debate competition in college during the year. Organizing the debate was easy. One intense-looking guy in khadi kurta signed up as a speaker against the topic: 'The hands that rock the cradle, rule the world'. The difficult part was getting at least one speaker for the motion. Mr khadi kurta suggested that I take on that role instead of wasting energy and time looking for other speakers. So one fine afternoon, the debate was held. Professor Vinod Kumar, our English teacher, was the judge. I came second. To celebrate the success of the event, all of us went to the college canteen and had coffee and burgers sponsored by the English Debating Society.

Solidly encouraged by my success as a debator, I started participating in other college festivals. I applied the simple law of probability; if I signed up for every debate in every college festival, there was a great possibility that I would win some prizes somewhere. And it worked.

With a string of 'cultural' achievements to my credit, by the time I was in the final year of college, I was well qualified to contest the elections for the position of Cultural Secretary of SRCC. I celebrated my success with Kapil, who had been elected President of the SRCC Students' Union. Both of us agreed that by all definitions we were hugely successful in life at a rather early age.

Being the Cul Sec meant taking on the responsibility of organizing Crossroads, the Inter-collegiate 'Cul Fest' of SRCC. Every college had its own college fest. Stephen's had Winterfest, Hindu College had Mecca, Lady Shri Ram College had Tarang, Jesus and Mary College had Montage, IIT-Delhi had Rendezvous, BITS Pilani had Oasis and so on. These and some others were the prestigious festivals to attend if your reputation mattered. Then there were the other not-so-hip ones which were given a miss by the majority of the snooty competitors. One stood a greater chance of winning prizes there. Of late, cash prizes were in vogue and that helped improve one's financial status greatly as well.

Crossroads was also a great opportunity to legitimately work on improving one's hitherto non-existent love life. So I decided to figure out how we could use Crossroads as an excuse to get to know some of those Pretty Young Things from the all-girl Jai Mata College, our dream destination. I went to meet Kapil in the Students' Union Office and seek his cooperation as the President of the Union.

The Office was bare except for a large desk with aggressive phrases painstakingly tattooed into the wood with ink. Uncalled for phrases like 'Fuck you' or thought-provoking ones like 'Suparna has nice tits' (who *was* Suparna?) or more immediate bon mots: 'Call Mamta at 228699 for a screw.'

Kapil sat behind the desk and pecked away at a typewriter that looked like it would disintegrate at any moment. But sending letters on the Students' Union letterhead was a good thing to do. So Kapil was concentrating on locating the letters that seemed so arbitrarily arranged on the keyboard. He was clearly busy. Here was an opportunity to check out Mamta. I mumbled some excuse and walked out to the payphone near the water cooler, desperately trying not to forget 228699.

I dialled the number and wondered who this mysterious Mamta was. Could she be someone from our college? A student trying to make some extra cash perhaps?

'Hallow Mamta Hardware Store.'

Aw fuck!

I had been conned. Some sadist's idea of a joke. Who would associate Mamta and screw with hardware? I looked around to see if anyone had been witness to my embarrassment. The college compound was deserted. I walked back to the Union Office and pretended that

I had gone out for a smoke. I needn't have bothered; Kapil hadn't even noticed my absence.

I looked at Kapil Aggarwal: fat, well-oiled hair and obsequious mannerisms. Perfect material for President, Students' Union. Not part of the hip Economics crowd of SRCC, bright like most B Com types, but distinctly uncool. Despite all this I liked Kapil. He was a sincere, well-meaning guy.

Kapil was academically brilliant, but had to deal with two major challenges. One was losing weight. The other, talking to a girl. In the presence of a woman, the Neanderthal in him would surface. If he was not suddenly afflicted with Alzheimer's, or simply tongue-tied, he suffered from the foot-in-mouth disease.

Whenever he found me in conversation with a PYT, he would straighten his shirt, flick back his hair, waddle up to us and introduce himself. 'Hello Bhabhi-ji! Myself Kapil—President, SRCC Students' Union. If anyone looks at you with evil eye, just let me know. After all you are our Cultural Secretary's *ispesal* friend (wink, wink, nudge, nudge). Both of us are having lot of pull in the hostel and will beat anyone who is bothering you, Bhabhi-ji. Abbey is just like bada bhai to me you know...'

This would shatter any hopes I may have nurtured about taking this relationship somewhere. But Kapil saw nothing wrong in what he had done. As far as he was concerned, any girl I spoke to was a potential wife and hence his bhabhi. He would make it a point to inform everyone that this girl was 'off limits' for them. I often threatened to kill him if he ever tried to help me again, but Kapil was incorrigible.

'There are so many luchchas in college, you have to be careful. It is my duty to protect her and you from jealous fellows. But I am telling you Abbey, you are not to worry. If you zenuinely take liking for a girl, just let me know, I will talk to her parents and explain. If necessary I will ask my Mamaji to speak to her parents also.'

Kapil had started sprinting when I had not even begun to walk! 'Don't even think of doing anything like that Kapil. If I need your help, I swear I will ask you. Just don't fuck it up any further for me, boss.'

What Kapil and I did share was a common dream of organizing the ultimate college festival in the history of SRCC. We would sit down in the canteen and make grand strategies about how to raise money from different companies to sponsor Crossroads.

'Okay Kapil, any ideas on how we to create legitimate opportunities to socialize with the JM college babes? Please try and be clever and don't suggest anything stupid.'

'Organizing an event jointly with an all-girls college would be an ideal opportunity to know many more girls. There will not be any competition also from any boys.'

'How clever! I would have never figured that out!'

'Don't be sarcastic, Abbey. I am only trying and helping you with my ideas, naa. We must organize the best Cul Fest DU has ever seen. Yaar, if we plan the SRCC festival at the same time as the Jai Mata College festival Vintage, maybe we can jointly hold some cultural events like Poetry Recitation Contest etc. and share the costs among both the colleges.'

'This is called grabbing an opportunity with both hands and rushing off to the window to throw it out. Organizing a joint event with JM college is a good idea. But we can't waste it on some silly frigging poetry contest. You know what, Kapil? Let's get Shiva, the rock-band from Calcutta. Shiva will play at Crossroads first and then at Jai Mata's fest. It will be their first show in Delhi. We will need to have lots of meetings with the JM college girls who will be involved with this great joint venture and ...'

'Then some of the ladies of JM college will surely fall in love with you while dancing to the music of Shiv-ji.' Kapil finished the sentence for me, retaining the essential idea but screwing up the presentation.

Bright idea in mind and a prayer on our lips, Kapil and I sought an appointment with the supreme powers of JM college. Sister Gopalan was a rather stern looking woman who inspired fear in my heart. I was worried that if she could remotely read my mind, she would never agree to the proposal. I carried a copy of Paul Samuelson's book *Economics*, published first in 1948 (as incomprehensible then as it was to me that day). I had written up the plan in my best handwriting and stressed on the benefits to JM college a couple of times. It was either the well-written proposal or the sight of Samuelson that thawed the ice maiden.

'You are also a student of Yikonomics? My fyaavrit subject. So you want to worganice this jointly with JMC? You have to ask Jespreet, our Students' Union representative if the students would agree to this. The yidea is good but I know nothing about these Shiva fellows.' I was a little taken aback by her strong accent.

'This will be a good opportunity for your students (I avoided the term 'girls') to build their leadership skills by organizing such an event,' I volunteered.

'We do not need you to teach leadership to my college gerlz,' she snarled.

Kapil piped in, 'Madam, if two colleges are putting joint show together, then all costs are half for both colleges. You can also have a nice function with low cost.'

I kicked him under the table. Kapil looked at me and kept quiet.

Then we heard some music, 'If there is no coast involved for uzz, then I yam willing to grant you permission.'

I jumped in to clinch the deal and said, 'We will bear all the costs. You just give us permission for Shiva to play in your college.'

She finally smiled and nodded and said, 'So remember ... no coast for JM college.'

Kapil was about to clarify the bit about sharing of costs, but another sharp kick silenced him. It took me a huge amount of self control to not kiss the lady in question. I wanted to jump up and kick my feet in the air and shout. But I did nothing of the sort. Until I was out of the JM college campus and at the bus stop.

I was delirious, 'Kapil this is history in the making. We will be collaborating with JM college to organize a rock show. Now we can go to their college every day and meet all the babes that we want to. It is all official.'

Kapil was not all that ecstatic, 'But why you are not telling that Gopal Madam that we would be sharing the costs fifty-fifty? This way they are getting benefit of our effort at no cost to them. This is bad bijness decision.'

'Consider that a star negotiator's style. You think she would let us go to JM college every day if she had to pay for this shit? Look at it this way. We would have spent this money anyway. We are just extending this as a gesture of goodwill towards the girls. Case closed. I have to run out and buy some nice aftershave. Remember, we will be meeting the JM college babes every day. Our lifestyle has to change to reflect this event. What do you recommend I buy?'

'Buy Charlie perfume. My cousin gave me one bottle. If you want I can buy for you also.'

'Nah, I will buy a bottle of Brut. Drives the women crazy I tell you, Kapil! They can't keep their clothes on when they smell Brut on a man.'

So, Shiva came to Delhi to perform for the first time. Their band members Douglas, Jeff, Nelson and PC had a whale of a time flirting with all the PYTs from JM college and went back with an even larger fan base.

And yes, I too got to know a few PYTs, especially Jaspreet Kaur. She was the Event Coordinator for JM college and the cutest sardarni I had met in my whole life. We met every day for a month, and she spent the three days of the Crossroads festival with me. I borrowed money from Kapil and promised to pay him as soon as I won a prize in the next Cul Fest, then went and bought a small perfume bottle for her. I still remember the name of the perfume—Desire. Jas had the cutest dimples when she smiled and said, 'Thank you, Abbey.'

We would sip coffee as we sat around the bonfire in the centre of the football field of the SRCC Hostel. Shiva played on the open-air stage. They drew loud cheers from the crowd when they played cover songs from Floyd's latest, '*Brick in the Wall.*' The crowd sang along, '*We don't need no ejukayshun... we don't need no thought-control...*' I held hands with Jas and wished time would stop.

It did. The good times stopped.

I tried to call Jas at home. She picked up the phone, said 'Wrong number' and put the phone down. I called again.

This time a gruff male voice said, 'If you call my daughter *one* more time, I will call the police, you fool!'

I tried to meet Jas in the JM college library but she was very cold and formal. I asked her why she did not want to talk to me on the phone.

'We had to work together on a project. It was nice working with you, Abbey but now the project is over. I see no need to keep meeting you. You are a nice guy, Abbey. Now if you will excuse me I have to go back for my classes. And one more thing, Abbey, please do not come to the college to meet me. It is very embarrassing. The lecturers have already started asking me why I need to keep meeting you even though the festival is over.'

'This is a college, Jas—not a school. That Gopalan woman cannot decide who you will or will not meet and why. *You* decide that. I will respect your decision.'

'If you really respect my wishes, then please do not meet me or call me. Bye.'

That was it. My love affair had ended. Even before I got to kiss her. I mean she would have surely let me if I had asked her. But what the heck, how *do* you ask someone permission to kiss?

Excuse me, Jas. I want to kiss ... no ... I need to kiss you ... OK how about ... May I kiss you?

They all sounded equally stupid and fake. Maybe I should have just taken a chance anyway. I could not figure out why this perfectly charming girl, who had let me hold her hand at the concert, who I thought was deeply in love with me, was backing off like this.

I decided to confide in Priya, my buddy, and get a Psychology student's insight.

'Maybe you had a crush on her and she just did not want to spoil it for you during the festival.'

'This is not some silly crush Priya, I am in *love* with Jas.'

'I am sure Jas will call you once she has sorted things out. Love is such a confusing feeling. People react differently to this emotion. She seemed like a sweet person. I am sure she knows how much you love her. You are a very caring person, Abbey.' Priya tried to cheer me up.

'What's the point being caring if no one loves me? All my life love has been a one-sided thing. I seem to love all those people who never love me back.' I was nose deep in self pity.

'Happens to all of us Abbey,' Priya held my hand and comforted me like I was her puppy. 'Love is a strange thing. The more you chase it the more elusive it remains. It is like a guest who you expect to turn up any day and it doesn't. You wait and you wait until you are ready to quit. Then one fine morning it knocks on your door and is there to stay. I don't mean to be personal, but did Jas ever tell you that she loved you? I mean, I know you said it to her. But did she...?'

Fuck! I never thought about that. She had never said a word. She was probably too embarrassed. Maybe she meant to at some appropriate moment later, but no, she actually never had. Oh shit! Was it all one-sided? Again?

'Can't be. She behaved as if she liked me, that's for sure... And then again...'

Nothing is more pissing off than arguing with yourself and still losing the argument.

Priya was very sympathetic. She bought me coffee in the canteen and even gave me a packet of Dunhill cigarettes that she had smuggled out from her Dad's cupboard while I was struggling to crawl out of the depression pit. The SRCC canteen tradition dictated that coffee was drunk by those who had class; the others chose tea—and Priya knew I had class!

Kapil was deeply concerned that my love life had not taken off, despite my concerted efforts.

Moreover, I was convinced that I could not sustain any PYT's interest beyond a few hours because of my limited financial resources. My father was definitely unaware of the cost of living in the campus. Whenever I broached the topic of a hike in my allowance, he would tell me how he used to get just two rupees a month when he was in college. I tried explaining the concept of inflation, which I had learnt about in my Eco classes, but he remained unmoved. Mom was the only hope. Occasionally I wheedled her into giving me a bonus. On those occasions, I smoked a slightly better brand of cigarettes and ordered coffee in the canteen instead of tea.

Once I told her that I had to buy a log table for my Math class. She gave me fifty bucks to get a nice one that would last me at least three years. I did not have the heart to tell her what a log table really was. But I kept the money.

The only way of rising above the poverty line was to participate in all the college festivals, as they offered cash prizes. Besides, speaking extempore and acting and drawing cartoons seemed infinitely easier than attending classes.

I felt rich during the last quarter of the year. I had made quite a killing in the previous term, winning the debates and impromptu skits competition at Winterfest. The ₹ 150 prize money got me *Abbey Road* and *Best of Doors* LPs. As I listened to the Beatles on my dad's old HMV record player, I felt like a king!

After that there was no looking back. I participated in every event where there was a cash prize. I tried my hand at drawing, theatre, singing, creative writing, water-drinking competition—you name it, I tried it, provided the rewards were in cash. With each success came the prize money and the opportunity of impressing the vulnerable. I soon felt rich enough to invite any PYT who would to join me for coffee in the canteen. But there were no takers.

Kapil suggested that I offer a more romantic setting than the SRCC canteen to the next PYT who gave me the hots. That meant serious sums of money.

'Abbey, the girls are always wanting to see your earning potential before they are offering their own hand in marriage to any boy.'

'Going for coffee with a girl does not mean that I am going to marry her, Kapil. Why don't you understand that I just want someone to talk to? And as the song says—"I have a lot of loving in my heart." If my love life continues like this, I will only be taking my hand out for dinner for the rest of my life.'

Kapil gave a nervous laugh but continued to be helpful, 'Even for kayzual romance, choose decent restaurants, yaar. Maybe you can take the girl to that coffee sop at the Taj Mansingh—what's it called, Machan, or something.'

'That is a five star hotel, stupid. Just cold coffee and burgers will cost a bomb. And if the girl orders anything more expensive than burgers, I will have to wash dishes. Nah, suggest something sensible.'

'But you are winning so much of cash prizes during festivals. Don't tell me you are already spending all that money... How many girls you are inviting for saring your diet, Abbey?'

'I am not sharing any diet. I bought some great LPs with it. I am the proud owner of eight albums of the Beatles, one of Grateful Dead, four of Pink Floyd and one of Jethro Tull. I had sixty-five bucks left which I used to settle my dues in the canteen.'

'You are such a chutia, yaar. No money sense. Now you are having no choice but to listen to pink and green floid and remain a bachelor. No girl will put her future at stake with a boy who has no bank balance. Only Priya Bhabhi is such a tolerant lady.'

'Who, Priya? Bhabhi? Are you hallucinating? She is crazy. She spends half her time reading stuff on Psycho instead of books on Accountancy. Whenever she sees me she asks me to fill out some weird questionnaire. You know, Kapil, all the girls who do B Com from our college eventually go for the CA types. I have seen that.'

Priya Patel was a student of our college. She was more Kapil's friend and I had got to know her because of him. And though she was an all right sort, she was not the kind I could vibe with. A bookworm type, with whom one could only have a conversation on personality, Freud and other psycho-babble. She had vaguely heard of the Beatles and had never heard of The Doors before I spoke of the song '*Light My Fire*.'

'Kapil, even *you* knew about The Doors.'

'Oho, that is because you are always singing that song, yaar. Priya Bhabhi is a very nice and homely girl, Abbey. I know she loves you. I can make out from her eye language. She is best choice for you. Even though she is in B Com, she is always staying in Eco class just to be close to you. She was the only girl who remembered your birthday in first year and second year and bought you gift in both years also. You only will always try to break her heart by doing line lagao to the other girls and that too in front of her eyes. No other girl will tolerate a husband like that.'

'Kapil, there is a world of a difference between what you look for in a wife and what you look for in a girlfriend. She is not girlfriend material, yaar. A girl has to be either cool or hot. Priya is neither. Priya is not my type.'

I saw the expression on Kapil's face and knew that I had fucked up.

Priya stood there. I had not noticed when Priya had arrived. She stood there, just behind me, looking through her thick glasses and said cheerfully, 'Abbey, you were talking about me! How sweet. What was he saying Kapil? Tell me na, please…'

Priya always brought out the cruel streak in me.

Before Kapil could say something polite but untrue, I said, 'I was just telling Kapil that boys don't make passes at girls who wear glasses.'

The quote from Dorothy Parker was completely uncalled for. But it was too late.

Priya was wearing a pink salwar kurta and had a Gurjari folder in which she kept her illegibly scribbled notes, taken from *Psychology Today*. Her well-oiled, shoulder-length hair did not look too bad though. She seemed frozen for a moment, too stunned to react to my senselessly rude remark. The sunlight made her glasses look even thicker and her eyes bigger and more stricken. Straightening her shoulders, she turned and walked away very slowly at first. Then I heard her running off into an empty classroom, as soon as she was out of sight.

Kapil was shocked. There was a kind of chill in the room. Then Kapil did something I would never have expected him to. He kicked my shin.

'You are really a kutta, saala. Made Bhabhiji cry, na. What you got out of this? Just because she is showing love and affection for you, you are being rude to her all the time. One day you will cry for holding her hand and it will be too late. At least tomorrow when you see her say sorry and see how her face will light up like the moon...'

I had been terribly mean to the girl, I realized. But while I liked Priya as a friend, I did not like Kapil's assumption that I had fallen in love with her just because I chatted with her sometimes. Now though, I had to make my peace with Kapil.

'Okay, brother! I will apologize to Priya when I meet her next. I don't know why I feel like being rude to her. She is always so sweet and nice, I can never find fault with her. Maybe that's what pisses me off.'

Priya accepted my apology in her characteristic sweet way. She tried her best to cheer me up, going as far as to say that she would introduce me to her best friend Sylvia who had asked her a hundred questions about me. Politely, I declined the offer.

The next day Priya handed me a card that said, 'I will always be there when you are feeling down, to kiss away the tears if you cry.' I presume she was quoting from the song. Stupid girl, didn't she know that boys did not cry! I looked at the card and smiled at her. It was nice to know someone cared. But the tragedy was that the one who cared did not matter. Those that mattered did not care.

Chapter 7

It was a cold November morning in 1981. Delhi University was just coming to life, U-Specials were doing their rounds and dumping sleepy students in front of the college gates. Most of them, like me, got off the bus and headed straight for the canteen except, of course, the Stephanians. They didn't have a plebeian canteen, they called theirs a café.

I am not a morning person. I find it tough to get my engines started in the morning. When the alarm rang, I broke out in a cold sweat, thinking I had gone blind overnight until I realized I had not yet opened my eyes! It was the same every morning—stress, relief and then disgust. Stress at having to get out of bed, relief that I was not blind and disgust at the thought of going to college. I was not what one would call a motivated student. Rather, a lawyer representing me would say I was indeed motivated—to go to college but not the classroom.

My favourite hangout was the canteen. I would sit there every morning, filling a pristine sheet of paper with doodles and random lines of verse, drink cups of tea and smoke. Sometimes guys would join me for an adda session. Adda is not mere gossip, it is far more dignified than that; a debate on the larger issues of life, issues that no one could do much about, like world hunger and poverty or Satyajit Ray's influence on World Cinema vis-à-vis Mrinal Sen's ... Or the one that always evoked sharply divided opinions—are women settling for less when they abandon their professional careers to raise children? Any issue to which an answer could be found was taboo. So mercifully, one's plans for the future were never discussed. Not that having a discussion would have helped since most of us were unclear about anything beyond that evening's dinner plan.

Sometimes I just liked being alone, listening to songs on Vividh Bharati and savouring the taste of coffee, watching people as they flitted in and out, letting the mind wander... That morning was no different. I put my feet up on the table and ordered a cup of coffee and lit a cigarette. Life was unhurried and predictable. Why would one not want it to continue? My eyes fell on the calendar on the opposite wall. It was 16 November.

Aw heck! It was my birthday. But no one seemed to have remembered. Not even at home, where they were all sleeping or oblivious or all of the above. I began to feel very sorry for myself. The words of the Hank Locklin song, '*And I sang happy birthday to me!*' echoed in my ears as my fingers simultaneously scribbled the lyrics on the paper napkin in front of me. The morning took on a distinctly blue hue. And as I had always maintained, the radio did all it could to deepen the gloom. Talat Mehmood wailed '*Jayen to jayen kahan*'. Suddenly, life seemed so meaningless. When they stopped to announce the news, which was another round of undiluted global morbidity, I thought that with another fifteen minutes of this melodrama, I would turn completely suicidal. I stood up, and decided to go to class for a change.

'Happy birthday, Abbey!'

Before I knew what hit me, Priya had thrown her arms around me and planted a kiss on my cheek. I was stricken. What was this stupid girl doing? Did she even care about my image in college? If anyone saw me being kissed by Priya (of all people), it would be curtains for me. But it was my birthday and she was the only one who cared to remember. I couldn't possibly be rude to her today!

I grinned foolishly and hesitatingly took the gift she held out. Tearing the wrapping paper in my impatience, I mumbled, 'Thanks Peeps, real cool of you ... thanks...' Inside the box were a carton of

Benson & Hedges cigarettes and a bottle of Brut aftershave.

Priya was gushing, 'This combination of tobacco and Brut is so sexy. I love it. Come on, let's go to Moet's for fried noodles. I want to spend time with you and be a part of this very special day in your life.'

'Moet's? That will be…' I did not finish my protest for I caught sight of Kapil rushing into the canteen. He was looking quite agitated. Was there another threat from a rival college gang? Did we need to plan a retaliation strategy?

Kapil looked round, saw me and shouted, 'Abbey! Where have you been, yaar? I am looking for you everywhere. Have you filled up the application form for MIJ?'

Oh, thank god, no fights.

'What forms? What is MIJ?'

Kapil was panting.

He grunted in short sentences, 'Management Institute of Jamshedpur. Most prestigious institute in India for doing MBA. November 20 is the last day to submit forms. Have you filled a form?'

I shook my head. 'Kapil, I don't want to do an MBA. Who wants to be an MBA—Mediocre But Arrogant!'

My wit was wasted on Kapil. And certainly on Priya. She looked at Kapil through her thick glasses, trying to comprehend what Kapil was coaxing me to do.

'You should fill the form, Abbey, I'm telling you!' Kapil sounded angry.

'Don't shout at him, Kapil! Today is his birthday.' Priya the guardian angel to my rescue. 'You know he was busy helping you organize Crossroads and that Shiva concert with Jai Mata College. If you were thinking of applying for MIJ you should have got a form for him also. Tell me, how is the form going to reach MIJ in the next three to four days? Can you trust the postal department?'

That was a brilliant kick on the butt, delivered straight from Priya's boots to Kapil's ass.

Kapil pulled out an envelope and said sheepishly, 'I got two forms. That is why I brought one for him Bhabhi. Abbey, please fill it up and give it to me today. My Mamaji's friend is dealer for Telco. He is flying to Jamsedpur today for dealers' meeting. He will submit our forms.'

'Come on, Abbey, we'll help you. Fill it up right away.'

Priya pulled out a pen from her Gurjari folder and started tickmarking some boxes on the form. She would occasionally stop to ask questions.

'What is the pin code of Railway Colony? Isn't that 110021?' Or, 'Doesn't personnel management have something to do with people and all that?'

The rest of my birthday was spent providing all kinds of personal details and answering wild questions. I had a hell of a time trying to write an essay on 'What do I want to do after I get my degree in Personnel Management?' Priya drafted out a neat piece that proved why joining MIJ was the absolutely only logical option for someone as talented as me.

'Priya, you could be put behind bars for writing this piece of fiction!'

'Just say that I have taken some literary license in a few places. If you are going to be modest about your achievements, you will never be recognized.'

'What achievements? I won some debates and quiz competitions in the Cul Fests. That's all.'

'What about your role in organizing Crossroads, especially about organizing the Shiv-ji programme jointly with JM college?' added Kapil.

'Yeah, I almost did not mention that, Kapil. Thanks. But that was done so we could pile on to some PYTs. You can't write that in the form. Kapil, are you crazy? But even that failed... Forget it, yaar.' I sighed as I thought of Jas's dimples.

'But that is a very good example of teamworking,' said Kapil.

'And collaboration... and risk taking... and leadership behaviour,' Priya hastened to add, thrilled with her words of encouragement.

Priya and Kapil had put together a lovely, if fictitious, document. I was secretly pleased, but more than that, I was embarrassed to death.

I felt I had to thank Kapil. I told him he was what a true friend should be. That I was sorry for thinking he had been selfish. 'If I ever make it big in life, I promise I will repay you for this,' I declared in an unguarded moment of emotion.

That was too much for Kapil.

He broke down and confessed. 'Don't make mistake in understanding me, yaar, but I must tell the truth. I had first applied for the MIJ application form for myself. But it never reached because of postal delays. Then Mamaji found out that I was getting late for the deadline. So he telephoned his friend, the dealer in Jamsedpur and got one more form so that I could still apply in time. Yesterday, the postman brought the original MIJ form. That means loss of fifty rupees. How could I tell that to Mamaji? So I got idea. If you also agree to apply to MIJ, then I would give you the form for ₹ 25. You get a new career and I recover my losses. Mamaji always says that if you are making loss then think how you will stop the loss...'

Before he could say any more I pounced on him.

'Kapil, you unscrupulous, profiteering moron!' I shouted and began to tickle him.

Kapil couldn't handle death by tickling, being

particularly vulnerable to this form of torture. He squirmed and wriggled, giggling, screaming, pleading, threatening. 'Achcha Abbey bhai… Sorry baba. STOP IT! Remember, you borrowed fifty rupees to buy scent for that sardarni, Jas? Abbey, stop it yaar…. sach… I also thought of giving this form to you because I also know that you are the kind who will do very well in MIJ. Priya Bhabhi, am I wrong? Please… Ask him to stop.' Kapil was red in the face and sweating.

I gave him a resounding thump on his backside and stopped. 'Kapil! You swine! To think that I was moved to tears at what I thought was an exemplary act of friendship.'

Priya had to offer her sane philosophical explanation. 'Maybe it is destiny. You are destined to join MIJ. I also think you will do very well in an MBA programme. You speak so well. You've won so many prizes at the college festivals this year for debates. I can imagine you, in white shirt and blue tie, going to work. Coming back home and flinging your briefcase and I bringing you tea…'

'And what are you doing in my home making tea for me?'

'Nnno… I meant someone gets you a cup of tea. I got to go for my class. Bye.' and she was off.

I have often wondered if Kapil would ever realize how deeply he influenced the course of my life that morning by selling me his extra form. Who knows if he hadn't done that where I would be today? Probably doing something different, surely something more meaningful than what I do currently. My ending up in MIJ was indeed an example of serendipity at its best rather than the result of some meticulous plan that I had drawn up and executed.

Chapter 8

It was a hot summer day in July, 1982. I was to board the train to Tatanagar, and I stood on the platform, next to me a big black trunk with 'MIJ' painted on it in white, a brand new suitcase and a carry bag packed with food and water. I felt a strange void inside me. With great difficulty I had dissuaded my parents and kid sister Asmita (affectionately called 'Ass') from coming to the station. It was not going to be easy on them, especially my mother, and I was not comfortable dealing with tearful farewells. And as for me, I felt I was finally severing the umbilical cord, not just that which connected me to my family, but with DU, bidding a definite goodbye to an insouciant life and the aimless drifting that I'd experienced in abundance. It was adios to the happiness that comes from living an unhurried existence.

My father had told me what he had to, the night before at the dinner table, 'Study hard. You must get a good job. This course is a really expensive one. If you waste this opportunity by not getting good grades, you will have only yourself to blame. Opportunity will never knock twice on your door. It was only by the grace of God that you got selected by this place. Do not sleep till late. Try and go for a walk in the morning. The fresh air will help you concentrate better in class.'

'Oho, stop lecturing him about studies all the time, na?' Ma cut in. 'Don't neglect your health. No one will be there to remind you to eat your meals. Keep some biscuits in your room. When you are studying late at night, I know you will get hungry. Don't study till late. Get enough sleep... Here, take some more rice... Have curd every day. Have you carried your sweaters? Write letters every week. At least we will know that you are fine. Phone calls may be expensive.' Then she added, 'If you are not well, then call and let us know.'

I protested, 'If I call you and tell you that I am sick what will you do, Ma? Don't worry, I will be fine... No, Ma, please... I am full, don't give me any more rice... I am coming back in a few months. You are talking as if I going for solitary confinement or something. There are millions of students in the campus. If they can survive, so will I.'

My sister pretended to reach across the table and

whispered in a frequency that could only be heard by canine ears, 'Chup ho ja bhai. Shut up! Don't make it worse!'

'You will make a sissy out of him. He is a man and he needs to struggle in life. Stop fussing over him all the time. It is because of you that he has never learnt to do anything for himself.' Dad gave the final verdict.

'You are the only one who finds everything wrong with him. All you are worried about is his studies and his marks. Someone has to worry about his health too. Even as a child when he fell ill, you never...'

This conversation was getting nowhere. I did what always works with Ma, 'Ma pass me some more rice... no not so much, Ma. Ishhhh!! Ki korchho Ma!!!'

'Will you find your way to the station with that big suitcase and your bags?' asked Ma.

'Of course he will. He is going to do his post-graduation. He is not a baby anymore. At this rate, he will never learn to take responsibility for himself,' said Baba, leaving the dining table in a huff.

I reached New Delhi railway station and went to the platform the Tatanagar Express was due to leave from. I was just starting to wonder where my coach would be when I heard a familiar voice calling out. Someone was waving. 'Here, Abbey, your coach is here.'

I should have known it—Priya had come to see me off. She was wearing a black salwar kurta with red tie and dye work. She was looking rather nice in that outfit. Also, soon after I had made that rather rude remark about girls with glasses, Priya had switched to contact lenses and it had made a huge difference to her appearance. Of course, she vehemently denied that my comment had anything to do with it. We managed to put my entire luggage into the compartment, and since there was still some time before the train left, I got down to talk to Priya. She had brought some food, she said, and a going-away present.

'I made some gobhi ka parathas for you. My grandma taught me. Daadima is a fantastic cook. Tomorrow she is teaching me how to make samosas. You love samosas don't you, Abbey? I am so thrilled with myself...'

Priya sounded rather too chirpy and bright. Was it because she was happy to get rid of me? I would prefer to believe that it was just a cover-up for some deeper emotion. Rather than get into a situation I would not be able to handle, I busied myself with the gift instead. It was a book, as I'd expected: Hugh Prather's *Notes to Myself*. Inside, she had written, 'It is enough that I matter today. Tomorrow does not exist. And neither do I—Priya.' I noted that she had avoided or maybe forgotten to add 'with love' before signing her name. Hmmm...

'I'm parched. Want a coffee, Priya?' I asked. With the 'extra' cash Ma and my kid sister had given me at the last minute, I was feeling rich.

The conversation was an apology for an exchange of thoughts and ideas, a stilted dialogue bordering on the mundane, for the better part of the hour that Priya and I spent together.

'You have some weird co-passengers, Abbey.'

'Yeah ... There has to be someone who will remind me of you!' I said in my feeble attempt to make her smile.

Priya returned the verbal punch with a physical one. I ducked out of the way and spilt the scalding coffee on myself.

Suddenly, Priya got senti. 'Abbey, will you think of the time we spent together?'

'Of course I will, Priya. I will miss having you around. You stood by me every time some crazy girl walked out on me. You were there to jump to my defence, to cheer me on. You have been a good friend to me, Priya. Though I am not sure I have been one to you. I was caught up in my own world. A world where there was no time for sensitivity and kindness. A lopsided world in which there has been place only for I, me and myself.' This was the first time I was speaking to Priya with such gentleness and I was surprised at myself.

I had always taken Priya's friendship and presence for granted. Much later, when I looked back at the way I had treated her, I was amazed that she still cared for me. I had always known that she did.

'Don't be so harsh on yourself, Abbey. You are what you are. If you were kinder, more sensitive and loving, you might be a better person, but it would not be Abbey. You have a million other qualities that so many people would die for. Above all you are my best friend. I will miss you, Abbey,' she said and gently punched my arm.

And then she simply put her arms around me and sobbed into my shirt.

'I have to learn to live without you, Abbey. That will be impossible. Write to me as often as you can, OK? Write to me twice a month.' Her voice was moist with tears.

For a brief moment, I was afraid I was going to cry too. It happens to me. If someone weeps so heartbrokenly, one could ... I mean I don't but ... one could, you know get all emotional and squishy.

'I will miss you, Priya,' I heard myself mumbling, swallowing hard.

When the guard finally blew the whistle, I knew it was time to leave it all behind. Giving her a quick hug, I turned and boarded the superannuated coach of the Tatanagar Express.

As the train began to pull out of the station, I heard Priya shout, 'Write once a day, Abbey, please! Every day ...' And I thought my mum was being unreasonable, expecting me to write every week!

For a long while, I stared out of the window, watching the familiar sights of Delhi fade away. My mind was a blur of emotions. It would take a while for me to calm down. I spread out my bedding and then curled up with the book Priya had given me. Reading in bed was a favourite pastime, made even better by the rocking and monotonous chugging of the train. Before I knew it I had fallen asleep. I dreamt I was climbing a mountain, sweating through the ordeal. Then suddenly I was falling down into a bottomless pit. The frightening feeling of free fall made me wake up in a cold sweat. I gulped down a glass of water and realized it was dark outside and time for dinner. What should I eat? Ma's luchi-tarkari? Priya's gobhi parathas? I settled for the parathas, which were very good. I could not imagine Priya making them.

Was she passing off her daadi's handiwork as her own? Had Priya actually learnt to make them? Wow… these were too good…

A strange feeling came over me. I would miss Priya. I had gotten used to her hanging around, these past three years. I recalled all the occasions I had been so frigging rude to her, and hated myself for it. But after five minutes of castigating myself, I put an end to the self-flagellation and began to make excuses. It couldn't only be me. Priya must have done something to inspire this treatment. Although in truth, I could not think of one thing she had done that justified my meanness. Maybe I should write and apologize to her, in any case. But why? Apologize for what? I too had been hurt by her behaviour on some occasions ... so we were quits.

At ten o'clock, the lights were turned out and soon all was quiet. I surrendered myself to the rhythm of the train and drifted off into a dreamless and often interrupted slumber. Maybe I should say that I slept like a baby, woke up every hour and cried into my pillow. The next morning, I woke up feeling a lot fresher. The terrain had changed. As the train snaked through the thick foliage, which bordered both sides of the track, the world seemed new and untouched. We rattled past sleepy little villages in Bihar, their beautiful adivasi women carrying bundles of firewood and walking along the railway track. Some of them had their goats in tow. Their knee-length white sarees with red borders wound tightly across their slender figures, their hips swaying to some silent melody only they could hear—they would have put any ramp model to shame. As I caught the eye of the last one waiting to cross the tracks, the animal magnetism in her smile dazzled me.

It was almost lunch time and I needed a smoke. At the next station, I stepped out on to the platform and lit up the first cigarette from Priya's packet. I noticed three guys, about my age, watching me curiously.

Then one of them asked, 'Going to Tatanagar? MIJ?'

When I replied in the affirmative, they introduced themselves and we continued the conversation sitting on my berth. They told me that they had been friends since school. Both Harpal Singh and Madhukar Kumar had just passed out from IIT while Jayant Ganguly had done his MA from Calcutta, where his father had settled after retirement. Unlike me, they knew where their lives and careers were headed. These guys had been steered through life to this point, their families in sync.

While my father had left the decision pretty much to me, in terms of the choice of a career, only Asmita had kept pressuring me to take the Civil Services exam. 'It's a good life, bhaiyya, it means prestige and power and a decent amount of money. Will suit you perfectly. You need not do any work if you don't want to. Your gift of the gab will see you through all the endless reports and file pushing… aaaaa owch.'

I had given her ponytail a pretty hard yank and the discussion had ended there. Temporarily. Asmita was smart and cheeky, but what do you expect when she was just a year and a half younger! Known to have all the brains in our family, she was going to be a doctor when she grew up, we'd always been sure.

'So that you can write fake medical certificates for me whenever I want a day off!'

'Bhai, I've told you a million times, I DON'T WANT TO BE A DOCTOR. I want to do Psychology.'

'So you can deal with lunatics all your life?'

'Sure. I have got enough practice with you around... A ou—UCH! Bhai, this is a sure sign that you have a problem—why do you settle all arguments with violence?'

I snapped back to the conversation with Jayant, Harpal and Madhukar. Madhukar drew out a cigarette from a shiny Dunhill packet.

'Wow, you smoke Dunhill cigarettes?' I was impressed.

'Bull, yaar,' laughed Harpal. 'These are Wills Navy Cut in a Dunhill packet. Old trick he learnt at the IIT hostel.'

After some desultory conversation about life in general and our expectations of life at MIJ, I offered to share my lunch with my new found friends. Ma had packed enough luchis and sandesh to feed an army.

'What made you apply for an MBA?' Harpal asked me.

'I have always enjoyed working with people ...' I started but was interrupted mid-sentence by Jayant. He helped himself to the last sandesh that I was eyeing.

'Then you should become a bus conductor. Plenty of people around you all the time.' He said as he gobbled the sweet as if he was doing me a favour.

'This is not the MIJ interview. You can be truthful

with us. I just wanted to escape being an engineer,' said Madhukar.

Harpal added, 'I just wanted to live in a hostel away from home, yaar. There was not much of a career angle to it.'

That conversation left me thinking about why I was spending Baba's hard earned money without having a point of view about what kind of a career I wanted.

The three guys returned to their compartment and I passed the rest of the journey dozing off and reading *Notes to Myself*.

Everyone else in the compartment was entertaining themselves. The couple on the opposite berth were obviously newly married—they were busy cooing and pecking like a pair of pigeons. The gentleman above me seemed determined to memorize the Railway Time Table by the end of the journey. He would announce, to no one in particular, the name of the forthcoming station just as the train left the platform. He would also add how much behind schedule we were already.

Not that I cared. I learnt from his declarations that Jamshedpur was the same place that the Railway Time Table lists as Tatanagar station. I would get off at the different stations on the way and have a smoke. It was fascinating how the snacks available on the platform changed, imperceptibly but surely as we cut across from the North to the East. The oily and spicy jhal-muri available on the Bengal-Orissa-Bihar stretch was perfect. I armed myself with a few packets of the stuff and watched the train rumble past the villages.

At about four in the evening, Mr Railway Time Table announced that the train was running late. I merely shrugged. I was in no hurry. Nor was the train, apparently. As if it was almost reluctant to inaugurate a new chapter in my life.

Chapter 9

On Sunday, 4 July 1982, I officially became a resident of Room No 208 of the MIJ Boys' Hostel. Compared to the campus, which was green and had a quiet air of sobriety, the hostel building and particularly the rooms, were nothing short of dreary. What made it worse was that all the first year students had to share rooms. I was supposed to share my room with some bugger whose name was M. Kumar—according to the list on the Notice Board in the Boys' Hostel.

M. Kumar turned out to be one of the guys, Madhukar Kumar, who I had met on the train.

When I came back to the room in the evening, he was sprawled on the other bed, sleeping as if it was going out of fashion.

That sight was to be the permanent scenery painted in the other half of our room, throughout that first year at MIJ.

Later that night, Jayant and Harpal came into my room, looking for Madhukar.

Jayant prodded Madhukar's belly in a vain effort at waking him up, saying, 'Look at that—he already has the first sign of a successful corporate executive—a beer belly.'

'Madhukar is sleeping. Must be tired after the train journey,' I said.

'Madhukar? Oh, we are so used to calling him Pappu. That's what he was called in IIT,' Harpal explained.

And Pappu he was to remain.

'Then we need to continue calling you by your name from the IIT Hostel—Hairy. Pappu told me your nickname. Kind of goes with your personality, yaar.' Jayant added some extra information to the pool of knowledge.

Hairy alias Harpal grinned sheepishly at this old secret being raked up.

When Madhukar showed no signs of life, Harpal said to me, 'Oye, listen yaar, we will have to drink his share, let's not disturb Pappu,' hoping that it would get Pappu from prone to vertical in a flash.

Jayant opened a bottle of Old Monk rum and poured a generous helping into each of the four glasses he had brought with him. Harpal topped it off with Thums Up. Raising his glass, Jayant said dramatically, 'Welcome to the fine art of drinking Old Monk laced with a dash of Thums Up.'

It was the first time I tasted this concoction, and surprisingly I liked it. It seemed to change the tenor of the conversation.

'So what are you called at home?' Harpal said to me. 'All bongs have daak nams, pet names.'

'I am called Abhinav, pronounced O-Bhee-nabho in Bengali.'

'Oh ya, the Bong alphabet begins with O for Apple,' cackled the surd.

'Very funny! In college I was called Abbey.'

'Abby—rhymes with tabby? Or is it Abbey as in that Beatle's album *Abbey Road*?'

'And you, boss? Are you Joyontoh Gaanguly or what? I love the Bengali language, yaar. Makes everything sound so poetic. What is your pet name?' asked Hairy.

'Um, er, Joy.'

'Ooo! Even if that is the last thing you ever brought! Shit! You spilt rum on my shirt, you ass.'

'Spilt milk, no crying ... Spilt rum different story, yes!'

'Hairy, why didn't you go to the US after IIT?' asked Jayant.

'I prefer desi girls to blondes.'

'Ever been with one?'

'Not with a blonde, even though they say they are better, I am a desi fan. East or West, Dilli di kudiyan are the best. For the moment, I am hoping we can say MIJ di kudiyan are the bast.'

And it continued this way, for a while, before the group dispersed. Tomorrow was the first day and we wanted to be on time.

I was awakened by the sonorous clanging of the chapel bell. For the next two years, this sound was to mark our progress, hour by hour, towards becoming professional MBAs, among other things. From the bathroom window, I caught a glimpse of the Steel & Iron Company in the distance. As we were to discover very soon, there was no escaping its presence. Jamshedpur, with its beautiful parks, clean roads, simple and hard-working people, was an out-and-out company township. Except that at MIJ, they referred to the town as Jampot.

MIJ had a massive marble plaque that acknowledged the Steel & Iron Company's financial contribution to the building of the institute. Inside the classroom, the case studies, which we were given, were based on the steel company's experience. It was the fulcrum of everything in the town.

MIJ was a cocoon set in a lush campus next to the beautiful Bijlee Park. Almost one square mile wide, the park was the city's lungs, protecting its people from the huge puffs of black and reddish smoke the steel plant spewed out incessantly. Every hour, the plant dumped slag into a predetermined area. As the red-hot molten liquid was emptied into the slag pit, it would light up the whole sky. When it happened at night, it was an awesome sight. For a few moments, the glow would overshadow the stars in the sky before letting them do their rightful job again. Throughout my stay in Jampot, I never got bored of that sight and whenever I managed to catch it, the glow would fill up my senses; some of it would permeate my being.

One of my favourite spots in Jamshedpur was the banks of the Subarnarekha, the river that flowed through the town. I would sit on its banks and watch the setting sun transform the muddy river literally into a golden line, as its name signified. The serene patch of liquid gold, the rustling leaves and the cacophony of birds squabbling on their way home was enough to make a poet out of a philistine.

But then, who had the time for such luxurious ruminations, and how often!

Life as a student at MIJ was traumatic. The pressure of academics was killing. There was no respite from term papers, quizzes, presentations. I was fretting about the term paper I had to write for Professor Kamini Mishra's course on Labour Laws. There were only two days left for us to submit our work of fiction and Professor Mishra had warned us, 'I am very clear that I will not grade a paper that is submitted after the deadline has passed. So please make sure you finish your research well in time.'

How original was that! Every prof who taught us said the same thing. Kameeni, as she was popularly known among the students, described her miserliness with grades. Some visiting professor from the US had once mispronounced her name Kameeni instead of Kamini—and the name stuck, at least among the students.

I was sitting in the MIJ library trying to figure out how to write a damn term paper. The topic couldn't have been lousier: 'Definition of Industry under the Industrial Disputes Act.' My worst fears were about to come true. I had no choice but to go through all those dusty volumes of *Labour Law Reporter*; I'd probably spend my lifetime doing just that.

The only consolation was that all my classmates looked equally hassled. What is it they say about misery loving company? Seeing the others in equal, if not greater agony made me feel slightly better. All around me bound volumes of the *Labour Law Reporter* lay open on tables and in front of them sat sweaty students, scribbling furiously as they raced against time. Rusty was the only one who was unconcerned. He was calmly flipping through the 'What the Stars Foretell' column by Peter Vidal in *The Illustrated Weekly of India*.

I used to kind of believe in what these forecasts had to say. Not believe like a missionary or something, but a sort of firm yet casual belief. I would read the forecasts for Scorpio for myself and any other sign as well, depending on the star sign of the girl I was trying to pursue that week.

Until Rusty shattered my faith. One day he told me Peter Vidal was a fictitious character and that there was no astrologer by that name. This was hogwash that Khushwant Singh wrote himself. The readers never knew the difference. In typical Rusty fashion, he claimed to have learnt of it from the man himself. But then Rusty was such a bastard sometimes. Had he lied to me? I wondered.

'When is your birthday, Abbey?' Rusty asked me.

'16 November'

'So, you are a Scorpio? Hmmm ... the forecast for Scorpio says, "You will discover the joy of sex and romance." Lucky sod.'

Rusty's eyes were secretly following Ayesha, seated at the opposite table, like a private investigator. I didn't blame him. She was the prettiest babe in our class. A hot-hoochi-mama for sure. She had a healthy pair of boobies that attracted attention because her shirt always had the first two buttons open, most of the time. Coupled with tight, hip-hugging blue jeans, she was unanimously the toast of our batch. Ayesha was a day scholar and hence a mysterious creature. Her dad ran a slew of hotels in Delhi and Calcutta and was Jamshedpur's star golfer. Every one of us did our best to get invited to Ayesha's home for dinner, in the hope that we would get home food. Anything that saved us from eating in the mess was worth striving for. The fact that she was hugely desirable was an added incentive.

I tried to wave off thoughts of Ayesha which were distracting me like a fly. I reminded myself of the term paper I had yet to write, strengthened my resolve and issued three bound volumes of *Labour Law Journal of India*. For displaying such rare determination, I rewarded myself with one last look at Ayesha's plunging neckline, and dived straight into the deep end of the sewer. I promised myself a look at her for every five minutes I spent reading the journals. And resumed scribbling furiously.

Rusty leaned across the table and whispered, 'Want a simpler way out? Give it to Banerjee Babu. He'll do the term paper for you.'

I glared at him, and sneaked an extra long glance at Ayesha. After all, I would have continued working had it not been for this conversation. But Rusty repeated the suggestion. Was the man mad? How would Banerjee Babu do the term paper for me? Banerjee Babu was the freelance typist who hung around the hostel typing biodatas and term papers, especially for Father Beez's course, where his intervention made the difference between a B+ and an A, no matter how elegant is your handwriting. Banerjee Babu's fees were a princely sum of twenty or thirty rupees per typed term paper. That was what you paid for a whole meal at Franks Chinese Restaurant.

'Shut up, Rusty and let me get on with my work. How can Banerjee Babu do a term paper on "The Definition of Industry under the Industrial Disputes Act" when even I am having difficulty writing this shit?'

Rusty explained, 'Banerjee Babu keeps a copy of each term paper that he has ever typed for any student over the years. He has been typing term papers since the time Kamini Mishra herself was a student here. For a small fee, you could get him to re-type a paper that was graded an A or A+ or B+, etc., depending on what your wallet permits.'

'If I have to engage his services, I may as well pay for an A+.'

'That's not a good idea,' Rusty advised. 'Take one which got a B+. It is safer. Kameeni is such a miser with grades that if she ever gave someone an A+ she'll remember.'

Impeccable logic. But I was still hesitant. 'Then why did you choose the paper that was graded A? Isn't that risky as well?'

'Got to be consistent. Banerjee Babu recommended that one should stick to a single quality of term papers always. All the past term papers I asked him to do were "A" category. Can't deviate now. It will make Kameeni suspicious.'

Thanks to Rusty's policy—'There's got to be an easier way out.'—I got a B+ in Labour Law always. Slowly I extended that ploy to other subjects as well. Banerjee Babu became my saviour. It was better than slogging for hours in the library—there was so much more to life. Of course, it meant that I had to cut corners elsewhere, but what the heck.

Rusty was amazing. He had a new trick for each subject and it always worked. For our term paper on Recruitment Methods, I was going to contact Banerjee Babu but I was told that he had hiked his rates. Money was in short supply, and I took my problem to Rusty.

He said, 'I have stopped going to Banerjee Babu. Everyone knows about him now. Some day, some guy will get caught. Can't do the same stuff too often.'

'So how do I get this term paper going?'

'Look up the *Australian Journal of Personnel Management* in the library. Corner shelf. Choose an issue that is at least three or four years old. Then cog it down straight. Word for word. Guaranteed B+ or A.'

'Why not the *Indian Journal of Personnel Management*?'

'Too common. The prof is more likely to have read the Indian Journal than the Australian Journals.'

I found this section of the library was a virtual treasure house. It seemed to be unused, veritably deserted—except for Ayesha. She was reading one of the volumes of that Australian stuff. I issued one volume and so did she.

'Girls are always more sincere and hardworking than guys—as far as studies are concerned.' I attempted a conversation.

She smiled and said cryptically, 'Guys have other priorities. Maybe some even have too many priorities.'

'If it were not for Rusty's suggestion, I would still be slogging away for this idiotic term paper.'

'You mean the Australian ...? That's what he suggested to me. Fucker!'

I like girls who are expressive. The ones that get embarrassed every time someone says the 'F' word can be a little tiresome to handle after a while. Yet another reason why I liked Ayesha. She was so cool and uninhibited. The main reason was however that she had a healthy body, beautiful eyes and a great sense of humour—a potent combination. We got chatting and automatically walked back from the library to have chai at Dadu's. This was how our relationship began.

The ex-IIT gang on the first floor of the Boys' Hostel were soon keeping a close eye on our growing friendship. It was their particular area of specialization. They would settle down in Joy and Gopher's room, which had a ringside view of Dadu's, and then based on their observations of what each couple was doing, they would formulate their hypotheses.

Especially Gopher. He had nothing better to do. He and his sidekicks specialized in digging out embarrassing details about our past lives. What was worse was that they were usually right. Where they got all these sordid details from was a mystery.

One day, Gopher asked me with a sly wink. 'Heard from that Punjabi girlfriend of yours lately?'

I froze. But with studied nonchalance I asked, 'Punjabi girlfriend? Who are you talking about, fucker?'

Gopher adjusted his lungi and said with a toothy grin, 'You know I am talking about Jaspreet. Does she write to you? At least Priya Patel writes to you more often. She always draws very nice pictures on the envelope.'

'Gopher, you prick, you *have* been looking through my mai! Do it again, you swine, and I will thulp you…' I couldn't contain myself.

'What can I do? When I collect mail from the office for the Boys' Hostel, I have to read who the letter is addressed to, don't I? So what have I done wrong?'

'Who told you about Jas?' I could not help asking.

'I work very closely with the CBI,' said Gopher with a greasy smile. 'But I must warn you, that Ayesha woman really likes you. She is a fast number, da! But she also likes that Punjabi boy—Khosla. He has a bike, remember, you don't.'

Other things being equal, the man with a bike will get the girl—old jungle saying in Delhi University.

I just had to walk away from Gopher and Curly Venky before my homicidal tendencies took over. But in my anger about the unfair competitive advantage a bike had over me, I forgot to ask Gopher how he knew about Ayesha liking me. Too bad and too late.

Chapter 10

When Fr Hathaway used to say 'MIJ is a place where you learn lessons in caring and sharing', some of us thought he should have added the word 'pairing' to complete the list. Because this process had started even before, or at least simultaneously, with the other two.

The first to pair up was the early surd Gurpreet (alias Gur) who got the girl, Neetika alias Neats. They were the perfect 'Made for Each Other' couple. Sometimes I thought they were like husband and wife already. Neats took notes for Gur when he overslept (which was often) and couldn't make it for class. That alone was motivation for me to want a girlfriend. Gur in turn stood in line in the mess with two trays, to make sure Neats didn't have to wait for her dinner. On Sunday mornings, they went jogging together, looking every bit like a typical yuppie Delhi couple in their branded tracksuits. On weekends, they went shopping for odds and ends.

Actually Gur had a headstart because he and Neats had reached MIJ a fortnight before any of us to attend the Preparatory Maths course under Chatto. They had both studied in the same college in Chandigarh, and had studied History and Philosophy. So the priests from MIJ in their wisdom had felt that given their background in History and Philo, they would need help to survive Chatto's version of QT. While it had only a marginal impact on their preparation for QT, it certainly got their personal equation right. As a result, Neats was no longer available in the already restricted female talent pool when the rest of us regulars got into MIJ.

Neats was a very charming person and generally well liked. A great singer herself, she scored high in our ratings because she succeeded in preventing the tuneless and toneless Gur from ruining our musical soirees.

After that evening at Dadu's, Ayesha and I had started spending a lot of time together. She was the only girl in our batch who was not going steady with any bloke within the first month of the first year. In a race, it might be a smart idea to get a headstart over your rivals. At MIJ, Ayesha used a different strategy. She made sure she was never associated with any guy in particular. That kept all the guys ever ready to bend over backwards to help her in any way possible.

Moreover, it took the victim a long time to figure out that he could straighten up, since the target had already moved on to the next victim.

The guys had to use a different approach if they wanted to be successful at the mating-dating game. We could not use Ayesha's strategy; the competition was too strong to allow us that luxury. We had to make a quick decision and then use all of our charm to move ahead of the competition. The unwritten rule was that once people perceived the girl as 'taken' they were no longer in the running for the rest. So, if you dragged your feet and debated about who had better curves or who was more compatible, you'd be so far back in the queue that you wouldn't see sunshine ever again. Even if at a later point of time, some couple broke up and the girl was ready to pair up again, you had a slim chance of catching up to stake your claim.

Being a 'day ski' (day scholar) meant that Ayesha had to have a regular arrangement to shuttle between home and MIJ after class every day and sometimes more than once a day, thanks to our millions of group-projects. Initially, her father used to drop her at the campus on the way to work and then pick her up on the way back from golf. However, as the days went by, the routine became less predictable for Ayesha and her dad got sick of waiting indefinitely. My chivalrous spirit rose to the occasion; I offered to walk her home, of course.

'It is not safe to walk back alone, Ayesha. I would be happy to walk with you. Anyway, I go for a walk every day (lie!) and it is really no problem for me.'

Ayesha was a clever girl. She understood my eagerness.

She smiled. 'I would be honoured,' she said.

So every day after classes ended in the evening, instead of rushing off to the mess like a hungry dog waiting for a bone, I chose to sacrifice my position in the mess queue and escort Ayesha home. I have never been the long-walks type. This trudge was killing. I could not afford an autorickshaw on the way back, but then I enjoyed Ayesha's company so much, I suppose it was a price I had to pay.

Everything Ayesha did had a hint of salaciousness about it. I was driven to despair with lust. The two open buttons of her shirt helped improve my peripheral vision so greatly that I could pretend to look straight and still keep a steady eye on the goodies on display.

One evening, half way to her home, we got caught in a freak thundershower. In no time at all, we were drenched. After an initial attempt to run home, Ayesha slowed down her pace and said, 'Let us just enjoy the walk in the rain.'

But my heart began to thud and I had a hard time controlling my thoughts.

There is something about rain that spells magic. 'Walking in the rain is the most romantic act in the world. It is every girl's dream to do it with the man she loves.' Priya had said this to me once.

Shit, why was I thinking of her at this time?

The mercury vapour street lights created strange shapes in the puddles on the rain-spattered street. The rain lashed and the wind whistled. We did not care. I showed Ayesha how to kick into a puddle and send the water splashing away in a series of disconnected bubbles. We competed in kicking and out-splashing each other. We stopped to admire the raindrops dripping from the mango trees that lined the road. Every flash of lightning lit up Bijlee Park in an eerie, scary way. By the time we reached her house (it was more like a mansion, complete with a pebbled driveway et al) we were soaked to the bone. Ayesha walked into the drawing room. I followed her, leaving small puddles of water wherever I fumbled for a step. It was dark. A thunderstorm meant no electricity for two hours in Jamshedpur. In the dim lamplight, I could make out the shapes of some crystal vases and marble nymphs, even a midget pissing.

'That's not a midget. It is like Cupid or something. That's from my Dad's trip to Brussels. Haven't you heard of that famous statue that everyone goes to see there?'

I sidestepped the midget and followed Ayesha. She opened the door to her room and asked me in.

'Just give me a minute. Let me get a candle. I will find you some dry clothes. Sorry, you got totally drenched.'

The candle threw strange shadows on the walls as I looked around. The room was so different from what I expected Ayesha's room to be. I would have expected posters of rockstars, maybe even Jimmy Connors. Instead, there were four large oil paintings of European landscapes and a charcoal sketch of Ayesha when she was 18. The paintings were signed 'Guddu.'

'This was a gift from an artist in Paris. I had gone there after my school finals to visit my Maasi. That's when I learnt to paint these landscapes.'

'I did not know that you were the soft landscape painting kind of person Ayesha. Who's Guddu—or is that your pet name?'

She did not answer. Instead she said, 'Do you want to change your shirt? It's soggy wet.'

'No, not really. I can just wring it out. That would be fine. Don't bother.'

She smiled. 'Just take it off and give it to me, yaar!' When I had hesitantly peeled off the dripping shirt, I felt strangely vulnerable. Ayesha was her usual imperturbable self. 'Maybe I could lend you one of my T-shirts. Here, take this one, its plain white. Unisex. I can have your shirt washed and ironed and give it to you on Monday.'

'I *cannot* possibly wear that one, Ayesha. It says, "I like 'em Wilde, like Oscar". Guys in the hostel will think I'm a homo!'

She did not answer me. She took my shirt into the bathroom and came back with a dry towel. She wrapped it around my bare torso as I stood shivering in her room in the small puddle that had formed around me, growing warm at its welcome comfort.

When you stay in a hostel, especially a Boys' Hostel, the most innocuous gestures from girls become larger than life. Ayesha rubbing my back briskly with the towel did something to me. I swivelled around, drew her close to me and kissed her lips. But she did not protest. She closed her eyes as we met that evening, like two strangers getting to know each other in great detail. Only no words were spoken.

Chapter 11

A roomie like Pappu can leave a deep impression on one's psyche, especially if you've shared a room for the entire first year. Pappu alias Madhukar Kumar was tall, lanky and more importantly, disorganized, careless, crazy and philosophical.

I never once saw him reading the class notes or handouts but he would routinely be somewhere at the top of the Honours' list when the results came in. When he did attend class he would be sprawled on the chair, chewing continuously on the right tip of his moustache until it was all stiff and pointed, coated with saliva. He gave the impression of being in a perennial reverie. Occasionally, he would break out of the stupor, wipe his specs and ask the prof a question that stumped everyone including the professor.

Pappu could out-sleep any human being on this planet. During the weekends, he would sleep for thirty hours at a stretch. On most other days too, he would come to life well past 10 p.m., take a leisurely bath and then go around to Dadu's Dhaba for a meal. As a result of this debauched lifestyle, I became the single point of communication between Pappu and the rest of the world. Particularly with Ganauri.

Ganauri, the dhobi, was a tiny, wizened old man. When we were casting for the MIJ one-act play competition, I had suggested he play Gandhi's statue. But my choice was vetoed straight off, because universal opinion was that anything other than washing our clothes was beyond Ganauri. When at first we learnt his name and someone hypothesized that Ganauri was probably a corrupted form of the word 'gonorrhea,' I couldn't bring myself to give him my clothes to wash. But after ten days, when the pile of laundry grew larger than what I was capable of handling, I followed Pappu's principle and entrusted my dirty clothes to Ganauri.

Besides taking charge of this unpleasant chore for us, Ganauri had one more claim to fame and popularity. He had recently bought a brand new moped, which he would hire out occasionally to a select clientele. All of us tried to get into this select circle because it was the quickest and cheapest way to go to Bistupur market for a cold coffee at the surd's shop. Ganauri had made it absolutely clear that it was at his discretion who he hired out the moped to and at what rate. And though Pappu was one of the privileged, Ganauri had a problem with him. He could never find Pappu awake. No matter what time of the day Ganauri knocked on our door, Pappu was either in class or more likely, asleep. There was no way he could collect his mounting dues. Thoroughly fed up of this, Ganauri made me an offer. He promised to lend me his moped for one evening if I could collect the money Pappu owed him and hand it over to him. It was, what is called, a symbiotic relationship; thus, I became Pappu's agent.

One day, after much meticulous planning, I fixed up for Ganauri to come in and personally collect his money. Pappu was lying in his bed in his one and only blue silk nightsuit, tapping ash from his cigarette into his sneakers when Ganauri walked in. Pappu reached out for his wallet and pulled out the money. He apologized to Ganauri for not having paid him earlier. And then Pappu said something that only Pappu could pull off in all seriousness.

'Ganauri, have you ever danced? Tum kabhi naacha hai?'

Ganauri smiled embarrassedly and shook his head in denial. Then confessed, 'Just once, the day I was getting married.'

'In that case, you must dance again today. Make this a special occasion.' Pappu was serious.

Ganauri protested for a while, then in deep disgust performed a five minute jig, and said sarcastically, 'Anything more I have to do to collect my dues?'

Pappu got up, thanked Ganauri and gave him a fat tip for his splendid performance. Ganauri left the room with a mixture of emotions.

Over the past few weeks, Pappu had removed the cot from his half of the room and put his mattress on the floor. 'Saves time when you are in a hurry to sleep,' he said. Frankly, I failed to see the logic, but then, who was to argue with Pappu! Gradually, he dispensed with the desk, then the chair and with it the last semblance of structure from his life. He would rush back from class, toss the bunch of cyclostyled class notes on to the floor and change into his deep blue silk nightsuit and go to sleep. I suspect that when Pappu slept, his soul went off into a journey in space. Only the body remained in Room 208. By the time the body sensed the need to wake up for a class, a meal, an exam maybe, it would have made several forays into the unknown.

By and large, Pappu was a fairly hassle-free roomie, compared to some others one could have had. We both admired Rekha, the actress. So every space of wall was devoted to pictures of the sultry siren. The only other women who vied for that prime space were those completely uninhibited *Debonair* centre spreads.

But that is not to say that Pappu was the ideal

roommate. He did have some truly exasperating habits. He used his all-purpose sneakers as an ashtray when they were not harbouring a boiled egg, an orange, a razor. Since that was highly distasteful to me I spent my precious allowance buying a new ashtray every now and then. For, each time we went out for a walk around the cricket field in the middle of the night, he'd carry the ashtray with him. We would sit on the cricket pitch or the basketball court and share some cigarettes. It was a much needed diversion from term paper writing. Pappu would suddenly get up, agitated about the speed with which these precious night hours had passed, and hurry back to the room. Of course, the ashtray was too insignificant to remember when a term paper was waiting to be finished. So we were back to using his sneakers as a repository for the ash that mounted from our incessant smoking.

On the morning of an exam, there would be mayhem in our room. Everyone on the second floor of the MIJ Boys' Hostel would take turns trying to wake up Pappu. People would shout, scream, play music at full volume, but dear old Pappu would sleep through it all.

Only, all the well-intentioned shouting and screaming frazzled me. I could not concentrate on any last minute revision or refresh my memory before the exam. Pappu would sleep on like a baby with not a care in the world until his wandering soul took pity on me and returned home. Then his body would stir to life as his classmates stood around looking like smug surgeons who have brought a patient back from death.

In one continuous movement, Pappu would get up, out of his deep blue silk pajamas and into the pair of jeans that lay on the floor in untidy concentric circles. For the rest of the day, the pajamas remained in blue puddles on the floor surrounded by the sheaves of papers and assorted knick-knacks that made up Pappu's worldly possessions. I had learnt to tell the hour of the day from what was lying on the floor—denim or silk. And I was mostly correct!

On every Saturday afternoon at 1.30 p.m., most of the inmates of the second floor would be found at the windows of the hostel. The windows offered a view of hordes of girls going in to the B Ed college that shared one wing of the MIJ Building. We would stand and wistfully stare at the giggling groups and sigh. If inspired, we would wave out at some of them and hope to catch the attention of some girl in the B Ed class. Then, we thought our chances would improve if we acted less desperate. But it did not work. We felt really sorry for ourselves those days, stuck as we were with our rich crop of eight, while in the B Ed batch, there were fifty girls to three or four men. That to my mind was the closest to having a harem!

Several of us had tried to get introduced to the B Ed college girls but without much success. The B Ed crowd was insular and self-contained (like us at MIJ), and our paths never crossed. We would deliberately stand in the doorway on the way to their classrooms or near the water cooler that they had to pass on their way out, hoping to strike up a conversation with some of the rather attractive girls. But they would walk by in large giggling groups, consciously unaware of our presence. The three or four guys in their batch usually escorted them out. So great was our desperation that we even tried to make friends with the guys in the hope that they would introduce us to their batchmates. But they were not interested.

The thought of writing an end term exam for Professor Naresh Parihar was making all of us miserable. Stress is a strange thing. Without it, I would not feel motivated to even wake up, but too much of it and I went to pieces. It was funny how all the guys studied by themselves for the exams (unless they were trying to copy something off each other), while the girls always studied together. Maybe this was an insight Rusty would some day use to turn a billion dollar industry. The girls in our class would all huddle together in one of the classrooms in the main building and work through the night. Sometimes, they would all take a break to look at the moon shining on the Dalma mountains and go gaga over it for a couple of minutes, before returning to work. All the classrooms had huge French windows through which we too frequently looked at the Dalma range of mountains, albeit less romantically, vast and appearing as a different shade of blue every hour of the day.

I would have smoked a cigarette but the thought of rolling a cigarette discouraged me. This was the standard self discipline smokers are known to inflict on themselves from time to time. The logic being that since the majority of people are really lousy (and clumsy) at rolling a cigarette from tobacco and cigarette paper, it will eventually lead to people quitting smoking. It does not. It only adds to one's frustration and sense of despair.

I was desperate. So I tried to roll one anyway. It did not look pretty at all. The tobacco stuck out like hair from a small nostril. The cigarette paper had been coated from end to end with saliva in an effort to seal it shut and suddenly felt very repulsive. 'Eeks!' I exclaimed in disgust. Pappu was doing a much neater job of rolling one for himself. He ignored my frustration. He was clearly possessed of the hard-won arrogance skilled workers display towards unskilled and temporary staff. He admired the gem he had created, then offered it to me as a true mark of a generous roommate. Then he started to roll the next one for himself.

'Pappu, why don't you roll twenty of these and give them to me. That will save me the hassle of rolling one of those tobacco-in-a-newspaper versions that leave my mouth full of tobacco each time I take a drag...'

'Defeats the purpose of this exercise. The idea is to use the effort as a motivation to quit smoking. Not to make it an incentive.'

'Come on Pappu, be a sport, yaar... while I take these strips of bandage like stuff apart from my bed and fix them back again. The damn thing is sagging so much, I feel like I am in a hammock. What do you call these things... just cannot remember...'

'It's called a niwaar in Hindi. They use it a lot in my hometown. Abbey, oye you've taken the whole damn thing apart...'

'Yeah, if there was a fancy dress party, I could have dressed as a mummy!'

The lint that came into Pappu's eyes did not bode well for any of us. At the end of thirty minutes, Pappu was unrecognizable. Only his eyes and nose were visible. I painted some patches of red on his face to make it look like it was dripping blood. I was enjoying myself hugely.

'Pappu, bugger, you look much better like this, hahhhahha... we must keep you this way,' laughed Arunesh who had stepped in unexpectedly.

'Grrrr,' growled Pappu as he walked out of the room and proceeded to knock on Hairy's door, looking to test market the new look. An unsuspecting Hairy opened the door and let out a muffled scream as the 'mummy' tried to grab him. My sniggers and Arunesh's guffaws gave the game away. Encouraged by this response, Pappu decided to go for the kill. He walked across to the main building, where Alps was leading the study group of girls in one of the classrooms, preparing for Pari's term paper. You could hear a voice:

'To summarize, Strategic Planning is what organizations use to respond to a dynamic business environment.' It was Alps sounding very professional.

'That is used to manage the organization's resources to fulfil the organization's business objectives...' said Nanny—and suddenly stopped.

'What happened? Go on!'

'I must be hallucinating. I could have sworn I saw something walk by.'

'Nanny! What something? Who will pass by at this hour?'

'It I ... looked like a mum ... mummy—you know Egyptian...' Nanny stammered.

'Don't be silly. There is no such thing as ghosts. You know that. Can we just go over the last bit about the difference between vision and mission ... NANNY!

I ... I saw it too ... a mummy. Errr ... Ratina go look in that corridor, I'm frozen ... Oh go on, it's not what you think...'

'Forget it. I'm not going anywhere,' declared Ratina firmly and moved closer to Nanny.

And at that moment, the mummy walked straight into the class, unleashing the loudest collective scream ever recorded by mankind. Pandemonium prevailed as he went to each of the girls in turn—the others shrieking for help all the while. It was the sound of someone wearing heavy boots and running down the corridor that finally got Pappu to rush out of the classroom and head back towards the Boys' Hostel. The heavy boots followed. Pappu turned back just in time to see our very own 'Pocket Bahadur' taking out his dreaded kukri and aiming it at him. Now it was Pappu's turn to panic.

'Bahadur...! It is me! From Room 208... Rakh do, yaar! Main hoon 208 se!'

That Bahadur's knife missed Pappu was fortunate. It was now Pappu's turn to shiver. Suddenly all the lights came on. In the crowd of sleepy, roaring, guffawing, bewildered students stood Haathi in his pajamas.

'Both of you must meet me in my office at 9 a.m. tomorrow, before the exams. Get back to your rooms, all of you.'

The next day, we had to draw upon every ounce of goodwill that we had saved up and appealed to Haathi to forgive us our little trespass. Pappu and I swore never to play pranks again. There was something in Haathi's voice that made it all seem very juvenile and stupid. If I did not do well in Pari's exam, it was understandable.

Chapter 12

Two terms in MIJ did strange things to me. I found myself becoming very competitive, as far as getting Ayesha's attention was concerned. My correspondence with Priya also began to get more and more infrequent.

Priya, however, continued to write very chatty letters. They were massive in volume and usually inane in terms of content. I replied to them dutifully, every once in a while, so as to fulfil the promise I had made.

She once wrote to me seeking my advice on career choices.

'What would *you* want me to do?' she had asked.

I was annoyed. 'Why ask me? Why would I want you to do anything, for chrissakes? It's your call, Peeps. You know how I feel about women who cling,' was my terse reply.

Finally, she had decided to do a Post Graduate course in Mass Communications. Once, she had told me she would love to pursue a career in music, which would fit into this. She had a good voice and had won several prizes in the Inter-College Festivals. Often, she wrote the lyrics herself and set them to music. Though they were generally mushy and slightly tearful, she sang them with a great deal of feeling. I liked to hear her sing. Recently, she had composed a few jingles which had been fairly successful. She sent me a tape of all her jingles and songs and added that she had been interviewed in the Youth Forum programme on Doordarshan. I was impressed. So I wrote and told her it was a good decision and that since she was really gifted, this course would give her the right contacts in advertising and related circles.

There were times when I felt sorry for Priya. She was not bad looking now that she had discarded her glasses and done something to her hair. And she was positively talented. But emotionally, she was a mess. Her father had passed away when she was in school and she had not yet got over the loss. Two cads for boyfriends had not helped matters either. No wonder her poems and songs had a touch of wistfulness and a certain degree of morbidity. She had once written a poem called 'Butterflies.' You know, one of those poems where you basically write one or two clever lines and type them out one word per row. She had dedicated the poem to me.

When I was young
I saw colour in everything
I grew up one evening
When I discovered that
Colour on butterfly's wings
Comes off when you rub too hard

Butterflies

When I was young
I saw colour in everything
I grew up one evening
When I discovered that
Colour on Butterfly's wings
Comes off when you rub too hard

This poem is for you Abbey
Love Priya

It was nice to have a poem dedicated to oneself. Only it was one of those sentimental ones, and though she tried to explain it to me a couple of times, I could not handle the gloomy thoughts it seemed to inspire.

'Write more cheerful stuff, Priya,' I had suggested.

The only cheerful lines she wrote were those jingles. Like the line she had written for a bakery: 'Absolutely the best buns to go for.' Priya did dumb things like this quite often.

One of her most exasperating habits was drawing silly teddy bears and hearts on the envelopes of her letters to me. Didn't the stupid girl know that you didn't do these things when you write to someone in a Boys' Hostel? It just makes the recipient the butt of unnecessary jokes. Her art work put tremendous pressure on me to retrieve her letters from the Administrative Office before Gopher and his gang got to them and started a sniggering campaign. But Priya was utterly predictable. Perhaps her messy personal life had heightened her need to have some order in her existence. She wrote every Friday and posted the letter on Saturday so as to reach me on Wednesday. This caused a mid-week crisis. Thank god Ayesha wasn't around in the hostel or else she'd have thought that I was in love with Priya.

Ayesha, by contrast, was a smart cookie and knew exactly how to get around. In her world, the men had all been assigned various tasks they were only too happy to fulfil. Rusty was supposed to help her out with shortcuts in academics, Khosla was reserved for bike rides and me for company (at least initially). She was a coquette and knew how to maintain a healthy combination of mind and body in our relationship. In a strange way I enjoyed her manipulative behaviour because she had made no bones about it and all of us were willing participants in the exploitation. None of the girls in our class could stand her. Alpana—or 'Twin Peaks' Alps—warned all the girls to keep their boyfriends away from Ayesha.

'Thad female, aanh... she is some sort of maneater. Dainnjerruss!'

Neats was more polite, 'She can't help herself, she is like a butterfly flitting from "phool to another fool!"' she'd say and laugh self-consciously.

Ayesha introduced me to the rich and famous of Jamshedpur. She saw to it that I was invited to all the parties and very soon I ceased to be dependent on the MIJ Hostel for my social needs (or 'affiliation needs' to use the management jargon we were getting familiar with). My weekends were busy, what with lazy afternoons sipping beer at The Steel Club and partying in the evenings.

The Steel Club was an aspirational venue for most MIJ-ites. Three times a week they screened movies out in the open on the lush green lawns or in the indoors badminton court when it rained. Scotch flowed like the waters of the Subarnarekha in spate. Bearers in white gloves and turbans fawned obsequiously on the Bada Sahibs and Memsahibs while Baba-log and Baby-log flirted away in the Billiards rooms. This was a place where most scions were introduced to the pleasures of booze and other assorted delights. The club represented a glimpse of the good life the corporate world offered. Most MIJ-ites were not allowed a sneak preview—except for a few privileged souls like me.

Every year, The Steel Club held a show called The Iron and Wood Golf Tournament. Just as the Royal Derby was not a place to see horses but asses, The Iron and Wood Golf Tournament was not a place to watch or play serious golf, but to see the socialites who turned up with their snooty daughters. This was where the 'glitterati and titterati turned up gland in hand,' as I quipped. Ayesha loved that line.

'You are clever, Abbey. You can be cheap but funny,' she said, chuckling away.

The tournament awards night was to be followed by a dinner and a play staged by a cast drawn largely from the Baba-log and Baby-log. The fawning parents would sit around nursing their drinks and wondering which one of these talented kids would be the next screen idol. The play that was put up on this occasion was usually a bedroom farce replete with double entendres which never failed to draw large rounds of laughter. I had auditioned for and was selected to play a small role in the production that was to be staged that year.

That's where I met Keya. I had noticed her hanging around the B Ed college sometimes and was quite intrigued by her. For one thing, she was stunningly attractive, with a lovely complexion, sharp features and large kohl-rimmed eyes. Her dark hair swung down her back in two long plaits. Imagine my delight when I learnt that she was the heroine of the play and perhaps the only professionally trained thespian in the cast. She had worked with many accomplished stage actors and directors, and was considered a brilliant actress by all. I was told that she had always lived in Calcutta with her grandparents and this was the first time that she had come to stay with her cousins in Jamshedpur in one of the bungalows near Bijlee Park. She had enrolled in the B Ed course after graduating from Calcutta University.

Keya was unlike any girl I had ever met. Impulsive, spontaneous and fun-loving, she had a 100-watt smile that lit up her eyes. It was infectious. Her magnetic charm was hard to resist. Soon after I met her, my commitment to the cause of theatre increased in direct proportion to my attraction to her. I would never miss a rehearsal. I would land up early even though my role started only in Act III, so that I could understand my role in the context of the entire play—or so went the line I put out.

In between scenes, I would talk to Keya. One day, I cracked a new joke, telling her 'I really Keya about you.'

She immediately threatened to stop talking to me if I did that again. 'I have been given a perfectly good name and I do not like anyone taking liberties with it,' she said, her eyes flashing.

After I had duly apologized for the slip, she continued our conversation. She told me she actually wanted to do her MBA but did not know how to prepare for the MIJ Admissions Test.

Imagine the tragedy! She could legitimately have been a part of our batch and I could have spent all my waking hours with her every day instead of meeting her only during rehearsals. On second thoughts, however, I felt it was better she was not part of MIJ. Who knows, if she were one of the eight girls in our batch, some other guy might have hooked her instead. Since she was from the B Ed crowd, she was out of bounds for other MIJ-ites. By the time the play was staged, after two months of intensive practice, we were in love with each other. And I had not even held her hand, leave alone kiss her.

Most of the time, we just chatted about life and times. We would mimic different people and have a good laugh at their idiosyncrasies. Nothing is more soul cleansing than making fun of someone else, as most of us know—it's why we devour gossip-feeding magazines. Keya and I would walk down to the Subarnarekha riverbank and watch the setting sun. I taught her how to play the game of ducks and drakes, by making flat stones skip on the surface of the water. The one whose stone made the most number of skips was the winner. She was a quick learner and I was delighted that she enjoyed what I always thought was boys' stuff. This was probably because Keya was athletic, unlike me. Very often, I found it difficult to keep up with her high energy levels.

But love can make a man do anything. She even persuaded me to trek up to the Dalma hills one Saturday morning. For me, Saturday mornings were intended for sleeping late. I made a feeble attempt at resistance. 'Look at Pappu. What a happy man he is! Never in his life has he stayed awake to experience the rejuvenating rays of the morning sun.'

'What's the point of having more time if we cannot spend it together?' she retorted.

That was a clincher. So, on a Saturday morning, there I was panting and sweating as I struggled up the vertical face of Dalma Mountain. Keya ran up like a fleet-footed mountain goat. Occasionally, she just stood back and laughed at the absence of athletic bones in my body. As I crawled up, I told myself that nothing was worth waking up early on a Saturday morning—not even Keya.

Some evenings, Keya and I would go across to Bistupur to have cold coffee at the Surd's shop or have a Chinese meal at Franks. She once offered to teach me to use chopsticks and then doubled up with laughter when she saw how clumsy I was. I was not just embarrassed, I was annoyed. I did not like being laughed at.

'You must have practised with toothpicks when you were a baby,' I retorted.

Which sent her into renewed peals of giggles. What could one do but see the humour in it and join in!

MIJ had a tradition of FND (pronounced Effendi), short for Friday Night Dance parties—usually held on Fridays, especially after the mid terms and end terms to declare victory of spirit over academics. The first time I invited Keya, she made at least a hundred eyeballs pop. Not only because FND was meant strictly for MIJ-ites but because she outshone any female MIJ had ever seen. Or at least I, with my adoring eyes, thought so. Gradually, as people got used to seeing us as a couple, they did not object to her as my guest.

Keya used to ride a moped—probably because it was against the wishes of everyone at home. After the dinner and dance on Friday night she would insist on zipping back on her own.

I used to worry myself sick about her going back alone at that hour but she just laughed off my concerns and said, 'Even my Uncle does not worry so much about me.' Her free-spiritedness was what made her so irresistible.

The Iron and Wood Golf Awards night and our play were a big success. Keya looked ravishing that night. She went through her lines with the confidence of a veteran. All of us were feeling quite like celebrities, with people coming up to congratulate us. The director offered to take the entire cast and crew for dinner at the famous Highway's Choice restaurant, about thirty kilometres away from Jamshedpur, towards Ghatsila Copper Mines. We were all high with our success. I managed to find a seat next to Keya in the crowded car. The smell of her perfume, the make up still on her face, her laughter ringing through the night, all cast a magical spell over me.

While the cast busied itself with its expensive beers and cheers, we went for a walk outside. The inky sky, filled with a million stars pinned against the backdrop of the Dalma hills, created another kind of stage set. The nip in the air lent just the right amount of shivery anticipation.

We walked silently along the highway. The silence was slit by the roar of a passing truck, but with each step we moved away from the distant raucousness of the cast party. Not so far away, as to not hear it, though the sound provided the reassurance that a blanket provides in winter. You may not use it but you know it is there. We sat close to each other, on a large rock by the roadside, oblivious to the danger of snakes that are so common in this region. With a million stars as our witnesses, we kissed for the first time. Then again and again, until—and without either of us realizing it—we had transcended all the norms of our middle-class upbringing.

Chapter 13

After two FND sessions, where I had Keya as my 'guest,' I told Pappu about Keya. She was the one I loved and there was no going back. We were drinking rum and Thums Up, and smoking a pack of cigarettes that was kept in my cupboard as emergency stock. Both Pappu and I would ensure that between us we would always have one unopened pack at all times.

Both of us knew that this was a serious conversation. It was past 1 a.m. Like a good roommate, Pappu was all ears. He kept chewing the droopy end of his well-masticated moustache and listened to me patiently in a very non-judgemental manner. And then he told me of something I had sensed of late: the growing resentment in the Boys' Hostel about my relationship with Keya. In the eyes of the student body of MIJ, I had a thing going with Ayesha, given that I used to walk her home every day. Since nobody else had any claims to the contrary, it was declared that Ayesha was off-limits for the others, according to the unspoken code of honour in MIJ. Never covet the girl who is 'spoken for.' Now by inviting Keya for the Friday Night Dance parties and worse, openly declaring my love for her, I had committed a grave misdeed, a breach of trust. I had set the speculation machines running again. I suppose if you live in a well, then all the other frogs are entitled to know what is going on in your life.

'But what's wrong with it Pappu? I am not in love with Ayesha. She doesn't have any emotional attachment to me. We are both clear that we are having a good time together. I don't care what anyone else thinks, let me tell you categorically, Ayesha and I are just good friends. I love Keya. Why should it bother anyone here at MIJ? She's not from MIJ. She does not know anyone here and does not want to. She is my friend and do I need to take approval from the hostel before falling in love? This is ridiculous.'

'I know what you mean, Abbey. But bigamy is not tolerated. Once you are seen to be having a special something with Ayesha, stick to that. After some time, people will stop talking and accept your relationship. Look at Gur and Neats. Nobody sniggers and laughs at Gur when he does all those things for her that even husbands don't do! They were in Bistupur last Sunday choosing earrings for Neats. What does Gur know about earrings? But he was there dutifully nodding his head at everything Neats was saying. Anyway ... coming back to your problem, I think you should stop seeing Keya.'

'Pappu, what the hell are you talking about? I don't care who Ayesha goes around with. She could sleep with the entire Boys' Hostel for all I care. In fact, if you really want to know, I think Ayesha has a thing going with Khosla. Have you seen the way she hugs him during the bike rides? Anyway, I love Keya and I don't give a fuck about what anyone in or out of MIJ thinks. Ayesha does not care either who I go around with.'

'How do you know that she doesn't care? Girls can be very unpredictable in these matters, Abbey. Have you actually asked Ayesha that question?'

'No, not in so many words, but I could. Actually, I think I will have a chat with Ayesha tomorrow after class and sort out this mess.'

Pappu tapped the long trail of ash from his cigarette into his sneakers.

'This is a dicey game to play, Abbey. But I understand what you mean. As long as Keya was just another B Ed college girl, it did not matter. Everyone looked at her and sighed. Theoretically everyone had equal chance of impressing her. Then you had the unfair advantage of getting to know her because of that play or whatever. That too happened because Ayesha introduced you to the janta at the Steel Club. You go to the club as

Ayesha's guest and then start going around with Keya, whom Ayesha clearly dislikes. Only a fool would miss the dagger-like looks they were throwing at each other during the last FND, while you were making an ass of yourself, acting all lovey dovey with the "enemy camp" as someone said. No wonder everyone is getting pissed off with you.'

'Who has all these problems? And who decides if Keya is part of the enemy camp—Gopher? I will kick his balls straight up to his eyes if I hear one more stupid comment from him.' I was ready to go and sock Gopher that minute.

'Sit down, Abbey. Don't do anything stupid like that. Don't make an enemy out of Gopher. He may be annoying but as the Godfather suggests—"Keep your friends close but your enemies closer."' Pappu tried to calm me down by offering me a cigarette.

When I went into class the day after that discussion with Pappu, there was a sudden silence as I entered. I felt the temperature drop perceptibly. What was I guilty of that the whole class had ganged up against me? I could sense that my relationship with Keya had been the subject of conversation, but no one would come up and ask me for my take. I pretended that there was nothing wrong and sat next to Ayesha as usual, but she too avoided eye contact. She was taking notes on what Father Beez was teaching us about things that happen

'When a group becomes a mob.' I tried to whisper to Ayesha during the lecture but she continued to take notes. I wrote two lines of a limerick for her as a teaser, hoping that would thaw her and she'd take a stab at completing the remaining three lines.

I love Ayesha's sense of humour
Whenever she hears a nasty false rumour…

'Go ahead and complete the last three lines baby! A challenge from the Limerick Laureate Abbey to his muse.'

It had always worked in the past—in fact this was one of the things that had cemented the friendship between us. We had the same risqué sense of humour and she was as good at double entendres and bilingual puns. But this time, even this failed to fetch me a glance.

In desperation, I passed her a small chit of paper that said, 'I can see that you are wearing black today. Nice choice. Can we discuss that and more after class today ... please?'

It worked. She nodded discreetly, avoiding eye contact with Father Beez.

I went with her for chai at Dadu's. Ayesha was used to people bitching about her and calling her names. Like most good-looking, rich young women, she was the toast of the town when it came to boys and men, but extremely unpopular with the ladies. Ayesha, however, was too confident and self-assured to bother about all the nastiness that she knew went on behind her back.

Jampot is a small town. So small that there are no secrets about anyone's past. Every little detail was known to everyone. That explains why there was no love lost between Ayesha and Keya. They had gone to the same school, apparently, and knew each other's past very well, as inevitably happens in a small town or campus. She thought Ayesha was responsible for affirming, if not actually fuelling rumours about her and a guy called Naved Surti a few years ago. Naved was in far away Chicago, with wife and child and Keya had returned to Jamshedpur hoping to lay that ghost to rest. But she was surprised to find Ayesha still there and doing what she was best at—snitching on other people's boyfriends and then spitting them out when they had served their purpose. No wonder that they meticulously avoided eye contact or at best waved politely to each other and moved on.

I could not have chosen a more disastrous combination of friend and lover! I believed I loved Keya, but I also enjoyed Ayesha's company and there was, no doubt, a very strong attraction between us. Keya had been smart enough to notice and had had her claws out at the last FND.

I'd been on the dance floor with her, sneaking a look at Ayesha who was grinding away in the corner. She had a way of making even a simple dance look erotic. When she winked at me, Keya noticed and throwing me a dirty look, walked off the floor, saying she wanted a glass of water. I stepped out for a smoke. Ayesha came up to me and asked me for a light. The way she shielded the flame by covering my hands as I held up the light for her never failed to excite me.

Matter-of-factly she said, 'So you remember that fashion tip I gave you about wearing black? It must be a special occasion. This black shirt… umm… don't tuck it in … here, let me…'

She proceeded to pull out my neatly tucked shirt and fluffed up my hair. I saw Keya watching all of this with thinly concealed anger. Quickly, I stubbed out the cigarette and returned to the dance floor. Ayesha stayed outside, visible from inside as she continued to blow smoke rings into the dark blue sky.

Keya was giving me the strong silent ones. I tried to ask her if anything was on her mind. One look at her eyes and I opted in favour of silence. Why was she so worked up? I wondered. After all, *she* was my date.

And now here I was with Ayesha trying to understand how she viewed our own relationship. Once I knew where I stood with her I would be able to deal with the accusing looks I was getting from my colleagues.

'It's not that incomplete limerick that you brought me here to talk about, right Abbey?'

I stammered something incoherently. I was not quite sure how to begin. Ayesha took the matter into her own hands.

'It's about Keya, isn't it? Smart little birdy. She has you wrapped around her little finger. What else does she do to you with her fingers, Abbey?'

'That was not funny, Ayesha. Leave Keya out of it. You and I are friends. We enjoy each other's company. Let's keep it at that. There isn't anything more than that, is there?'

'Is that what you believe, Abbey?'

'Well yeah... I mean you are very sexy Ayesha and I love your company and sense of humour. We think on the same lines—you complete my limericks, you see humour which most people cannot, even when we explain it to them, there is a definite chemistry between us, maybe even physics—magnetic attraction etc...' I said trying to lighten the mood. 'But... for chrissake you are not suggesting that I am in love with you, Ayesha,' my voice rose a couple of decibels. 'Or you with me ... that would be worse. You are a clever girl, Ayesha, surely you know ...' This conversation was beginning to feel like quicksand.

'I know you do not love me, Abbey, and never will. But I thought you were different. You don't grovel or drool, Abbey, you are pretty up front about what you want. And you make a girl want to give it to you. That's why it feels awful when you dismiss me as just another body that you have had. But I suppose all you men are the same. Do you ever stop to think that relationships are not just about sex? For all your practical, rational approach to life, you show remarkable sensitivity and romanticism with your latest love interest ...' her voice trailed off.

Fuck, this was great, just great! Ayesha who takes greater pleasure in the pursuit than in the victory, giving me a lecture on relationships!

This was the first time; perhaps, Ayesha had been out of her depth. A tear was slowly trickling down her cheek. The moment she saw I had noticed, she cleverly flicked it away with the tip of her pinky.

'Keya and I love each other. She is a wonderful girl who ...'

'I DON'T WANT TO KNOW ABOUT KEYA.' Ayesha was suddenly very loud.

Dadu coughed and gave me a withering look. So even he thought I was the villain. I could see most of the inmates of the Boys' Hostel standing next to their usual window, pretending to be lost in thought.

Ayesha too was aware of the sympathy she was getting. And in true Ayesha fashion, was cashing in on it. 'Do you know that Gopher and Alps came to me during the last FND and asked me why I had been dumped by you? That is *so* fucking humiliating. And you were making it worse by hanging on to that woman as if she carried your breathing apparatus.'

'But Ayesha, why do you get upset at those idiots' remarks? If they said that *you* dumped me, I would not even flinch. The morons don't know that we are very clear about what our relationship is all about,' I paused, wondering how best to say it. 'What happened that night was great, wonderful. I am not sorry. But it was just one of those things. Nothing more to it. So how can I be accused of ditching you when we were never going steady?'

I took a deep breath. 'Be logical, Ayesha. Did I cheat you into anything, yaar? Have I ever felt jealous when you went for all those bike rides with Khosla?'

Immediately Ayesha retorted, 'See! The very fact that you mention it means that something must have bothered you, Abbey. Anyway, forget about Khosi. About that day, I agree. It was not wrong. I really like you, Abbey. You are a nice guy, but you are not my type. Yet, when you act so bloody soppy with that Keya female, I am jealous, yaar, of course I am. I feel so damned inadequate.'

Then Ayesha did something completely out-of-character. She started to cry.

I did not know what to do. Should I hold her and risk sending the wrong signal to her and the whole world? (Gopher and Curly Venky had a ringside view of this meeting, after all.) So I restrained myself and lit a cigarette instead, to keep my hands busy and out of trouble.

Before I was prompted to say something mean and hurtful or something silly, I checked myself and focussed on this sobbing girl, unrecognizable as Ayesha.

'Geez, I never knew you could cry, Ayesha,' I said in a tone that was part awe and part disgust.

'Who's crying? What are you talking about?' she snapped, tossing her hair back. 'Why are you men so uncomfortable when you see anyone crying?'

I tried to add a touch of levity to the situation and imitated Rajesh Khanna's famous *Amar Prem* line, 'Pushpa, I hate tears!'

'You do not have to *do* anything, Abbey. Just talk to me and tell me that it will be all right. But first you need to acknowledge to yourself that there are moments when no one can help another person in distress anyway.'

Deep Purple singing,

There once was a woman, a strange kind of woman
The kind that gets written down in history
Her name was Nancy, her face was never fancy
She left a trail of happiness and misery
I loved her and everybody loved her…

was wafting in from the Music Room where we listened to music on the MIJ music system. This room also doubled as the dance hall during the FND.

'Ayesha, seriously man, you had me worried with your tears.'

I was about to commit a grave blunder by comparing Keya's cheerfulness with Ayesha's present weepy state of being. That would have been asking for it—inviting death by stoning. Curly Venky and Gopher leading the attack and Ayesha throwing the heaviest rock for sure.

There was an uneasy silence for a while. The song had ended and someone had forgotten to put on another LP. The whole world seemed to be holding its breath to watch me make the next move. Ayesha knew she had the sympathy of the entire MIJ (for a change even the girls sided with her) and revelled in it. I knew I would be made the villain of the piece no matter what I did. I was screwed, either way. Ayesha sat with her head down, twirling her ring on the table. I glanced at her watch. It was well past 1:30 p.m. What would be a smart way to end this impasse? I made the easiest move. The stupidest one.

I stood up and said, 'The Mess will close in another ten minutes. See you tomorrow, Ayesha.' And walked away, as if nothing had happened.

Chapter 14

We were in the last term of the first year. After a desperate struggle, in spite of a few dips and peaks, I had eventually managed a steady average of 6+ on the dreaded 8-point scale.

Over the months, each professor had left behind a dash of knowledge, a bag of jargon and a string of quotable quotes which I used as a fig leaf to cover up my ignorance. Each one had his or her eccentricities. Father Ballantine ('Balla' for short) had his favourite aphorisms.

'Problems cannot be solved. They can only be absolved, dissolved or resolved.'

This was to come in handy during many a meeting later on.

The pipe-smoking Professor Chandran was an interesting sight, with his large build and beard, both of which slowed him down immensely. He felt compelled to consult his beard while talking to anyone and it seemed as if he was trying to coax a response out of his goatee. Professor Chandran may have been slow in his movements but he was quick with his repartee. Like Pari, he too used to drive down from the Professors' Quarters to the institute. In his room, he had neatly organized folders with scripts for each lecture. Each script had jokes and one-liners written on small square grey note paper and stuck at appropriate points in the script. One killjoy from our Seniors' batch actually compiled all these one-liners and marked out the sequence in which they'd appear in the lecture. That sheet was then copied and circulated in the Boys' Hostel.

We were all tickled when in the first session, while taking attendance, Chandran said, 'In a few days I'll get to know who is who and then who is whose.'

Soon we realized that the joke sheet was amazingly accurate. We knew beforehand what jokes were coming our way. So when we laughed, the poor professor thought we were impressed by his wit. Little did he know that we were laughing *at* him and not with him. Pity, because it took away all the joy of attending his otherwise interesting classes.

Somehow we never seemed to see our profs as human beings. They were only profs, not regular people like us. So seeing them do things like sipping cold coffee at the Surd's shop in Bistupur or queuing up to eat chicken rolls diminished their aura in my mind. It was like watching Amitabh Bachchan getting shouted at by the policeman for jumping a traffic light. But that's what happens when you live in a small town like Jampot; the mystique that anonymity brings did not exist. The first time I saw Chatto trailing behind his very fair wife, shopping bag in hand, I was shocked. A bunch of bananas and a head of lettuce peeped out of the bag he was carrying. The groceries made him look positively uncool. I was tempted to help Chatto with his shopping bag, but Keya was there. I didn't want it to look like ACP (the lethal angle to the decision) and after a swift weighing of options, I decided to continue sipping my coffee. It was kind of tough imagining Chatto eating lettuce (or bananas) instead of doing QT. I wondered what kind of conversations he had with his wife. Surely there were intimate moments between them—did he give her his undivided attention or was he preoccupied with figuring out a trick question that would flummox all of us during the end of term exam? Keya did not know and did not care. If she did not care about something, it was probably insignificant anyway.

After seeing Chatto as a vegetable-eating, hen-pecked husband, I was less in awe of his skills in QT. Besides, two semesters of QT I and II were over. I had escaped with minor stripes across my ass. So when Chatto invited Keya and me home for dinner, I was not wholly averse to the idea. Keya was not sure whether she should come with me, but the opportunity to miss one meal in the mess was too good to pass up; I persuaded her to accompany me as an act of courtesy.

On the appointed day, the two of us landed up at Chatto's doorstep clutching a small bouquet of flowers. Chatto's house looked like a cross between a library and an artist's studio. A large canvas was stretched out on an easel at one end of the room. Obviously, his current work-in-progress. It was a study of a woman in the nude. I was caught totally off balance when he sneaked up behind me and asked me for my opinion on the painting. What was I supposed to say?

'Nice drawing, Sir. I did not know you were into nudes. I like the big boobies you have drawn on that woman...'

Instead, I made a noncommittal comment—'Hmm ... Interesting choice of colours'—and let it go. I could hear Keya and Mrs Chatto laughing in the kitchen about something. I got worried, hoping Keya had not said something daft about me that might impact Chatto's opinion of me. But I remembered that Chatto had finished teaching our batch and released my clenched teeth.

After a delicious meal of my favourite, Ilish Macher Jhol we adjourned to the drawing room. Chatto said literature and Indian classical music were his passion. Keya and I flipped through the enormous collection of books. Did he just buy them or did he actually read them all? He actually had books by most of the Nobel Prize winners over the years. Among them I noticed two well-thumbed books—*The Book of Laughter and Forgetting* and *The Unbearable Lightness of Being*.

'Do you like Kundera's work?'

I shook my head like a good Southie would—at an angle which could mean yes, I do or no, I don't. It had taken me a couple of minutes to figure out he was referring to Milan Kundera and not a Bong writer.

Without giving it much thought, I said that I did read some amount but my interest lay more in the movies. This turned out to be one of those foot-in-the-mouth moments. Chatto went off into raptures.

'Czech films are my passion. I loved Menzel's direction in his 1966 classic *Closely Watched Trains*. Milo Forman made this film in '65 called *Lásky Jedné Plavovlásky*. Translated that means *Loves of A Blonde*. The story is about a young woman in a small town who sleeps with one of the band members of a group from Prague.'

The plot sounded interesting. It would go down well in the Boys' Hostel, I figured.

'We should try and get these classics and show it to the MIJ-ites here, Sir.'

'I can talk to their embassy. They will be happy to give the film on loan. It will be free for us. Why don't you form a Film Laavaars Club? The kaalcharal scene here is so dry.'

I had only myself to blame!

Chatto was earnest. He contributed ₹ 500 and started off a club for screening European films called FLIX (short for Film Lovers International Experience). His taste ran the full gamut, including weird and obscure art films. I saw one of them at the inaugural show of FLIX, a Bulgarian film called *Avalanche,* about a bunch of mountaineers who get totally screwed in an avalanche. I felt obliged to sit through the first twenty minutes simply because Chatto would have been pissed off if there were less than three students in the entire auditorium. But after that I just had to get out. It was making no sense to me. Quietly, I sneaked out, smoked a cigarette and went off to sleep.

The next week, Chatto searched me out in the Mess and asked me to put up a poster on Hungarian film history. Who was going to come and see these masterpieces after reading this write-up by Chatto?

> In among the aesthetically inspired Hungarian films, two real masterpieces can be found: Károly Makk's *Love* of 1970 and Zoltán Huszárik's *Sindbad* of 1971. An organic, dream-like visual world comes forth in the following films: István Szabó's *25, Tûzoltó Street* of

1973 and *Tales of Budapest* from 1976. To learn more about such fascinating works, come to the Auditorium at 7:30pm on Saturday.

'Why don't we mention that there will be free coffee? That will ensure good participation, sir. We will serve coffee only at the end. So students will not be able to leave midway either. What do you say?'

'You mean students will not come for their laav of art but their greed for coffee? Surely there are a few like you and Aalpona (oh Alps!) who will be curious to know more about the wonderful Hungarian directors.'

How could I tell him that what is popular is that which appeals to the lowest common denominator? Anyway, I tried to rustle up some excitement in the hostel by spreading the rumour that there were several topless scenes in the movie, carefully adding that that's what I had been 'told,' as a caveat. I did not want to risk the wrath of some drooling MIJ-ite who was sitting through some crazy film only to see some firang chick take off her shirt for three seconds.

I tried to convince Keya to come over but she kicked me so hard I limped back to the empty Audi in pain. Alps was thrilled to see me. Only Alps sat through the entire screening, representing the student population. She came back to the mess and bored us to death with her comments about 'use of the medium' or 'excessive reliance on visual imagery' etc. We watched the Alps heaving up and down as she narrated the insipid stories with great excitement, hoping some of that enthusiasm would rub off on us too. Our interest was more in her than the contents of her speech, so to say. After a while that too palled. But Chatto refused to take a hint. He got Alps to put up posters on the FLIX letterhead. Each time Alps put up a notice on our Mess notice board, some wise guy would extend the base of the 'L' and turn it into a 'U'. That was the level of wit in MIJ! After screening a few Swedish and Italian movies (none of them had any hot scenes either), FLIX died a natural death. And, so, in a sense, did our interaction with Chatto.

Then there was Beez, who taught Group Dynamics II. Father Joe Beez would give A+ to all the girls and an A to the guys who cut pictures out of magazines and stuck them in their term papers. Professor Ranganathan was a sucker for quotes from foreign journals. So for his exams, many of us would write our own stuff and then pass it off as a quote from *Harvard Business Review* and the like. It is one of life's little ironies that some dude makes an absolutely inane statement in a magazine and it gets highlighted, while you could have said the same—well almost the same—thing a million times over but nobody gave a damn. It seems as if it's not the intrinsic wisdom of the statement that is valuable, but the name ascribed to it that adds to its worth.

What I learnt from Rusty was almost as valuable as what the profs taught me. Perhaps more useful and practical. He pointed out shortcuts to writing assignments, strategies to cope with the individual professor's requirements in order to improve grades, and to make group presentations without studying the case.

'Always volunteer to do the introduction or the conclusion of the case. That way you don't have to read the whole damn thing through the night,' Rusty advised. 'Use jokes and funny lines when you have nothing specific to say. People will have a good laugh and nobody will worry about what you have not said.'

I was to discover the truth of what Rusty had said when I started working and was required to attend all those seminars. Most speakers had nothing substantial to say. The smart ones, who got all the attention, had packed their presentations with humour and clever one-liners. As if they too had been coached by Rusty!

Meanwhile, my love life with Keya was placing extraordinary demands on me. We used to meet in the MIJ auditorium because it was safe and conveniently located. It was bang in the middle of the campus, and right next to the B Ed college principal's office, hence studiously avoided by all students. Also, since it was on the way to the classrooms, Keya would just pretend to lose her way back after class. No other couple in

MIJ knew of this place, it was far from the prying eyes of Gopher and Curly Venky, so we knew we would be safe. It was funny how Keya discovered, during one of their programmes, that the door to the makeup room of the audi would open if you nudged it just a little. So she suggested we meet there.

Our rendezvous time was between one and three in the afternoon. It was totally deserted at that time because the whole world was in the mess having lunch. Keya and I would creep into the audi at 1 p.m. Playing Blind Man's Buff in the pitch darkness of the auditorium, we would pick our way through the rows of chairs and head straight for the makeup room. Once inside, we were transported into our make-believe world. We wasted no time and made the most of the privacy this place offered us. And then we would just lie around and stare at the surreal feel of the setting. After a while we would discreetly slip out and walk back to the Library or Dadu's Dhaba, chatting and laughing as if nothing had happened at all.

The only thing we had to be careful about was not to get caught by one of the scores of gurkha watchmen who patrolled the campus all day. They were all called by the generic term, Bahadur. If one of the Bahadurs ever caught a couple in, what is referred to as, a 'compromising position,' you were up shit creek and rowing with only your hands.

We could not afford to forget Father Hathaway's warning, 'In the MIJ Campus, three Ds can get you expelled—Drinks, Drugs, Dames.' You could also get thrown out if you got three Ds in academics, of course.

Keya had become an obsession with me. I had never loved anyone as much as I loved her. The moment she left me, I would ache to meet her again, to hold her and smell the mild perfume of her skin. It was like an addiction. Keya was so different from the MIJ girls. Spontaneous, impulsive, full of laughter, unpredictable, uncomplicated... and also bloody crazy and irrational.

'Abbey, can we celebrate your birthday?'

'Sure we can but not today. It isn't 16 November yet.'

'But I have already bought this book for you and I can't wait for months just because that is when you were born.' She handed me a gift-wrapped book.

I opened the wrapper. It was a collection of poems by Spike Milligan, *Small Dreams of a Scorpion*. I opened a page at random and read the words aloud:

If I could write words
Like leaves on an autumn forest floor
What a bonfire
My letters would make
If I could speak words of waters

You would drown
If I said 'I love you'

Keya was an incurable romantic and transferred some of her romanticism to me. She read out poems from Shelley and Byron. Played a tape of the *Moonlight Sonata* written for the piano by Beethoven, for me. She gifted me cassettes of some of the most well-known waltzes, such as '*The Blue Danube*', '*The Emperor Waltz*' and '*Tales from Vienna Woods*' which were her favourites.

Once when we had gone to see the film *Love Story* at Nataraj Cinema, she told me she was seeing it for the seventh time. We both held hands and cried when Jenny lay, dying of cancer. Our heart bled for Oliver.

A week later, she read the sequel to *Love Story* and was devastated to learn that Oliver had found another woman attractive.

Tossing her two long plaits indignantly, she declared, 'I bet it was just lust that made Oliver look for another woman.'

'Jenny died. Shouldn't Oliver just get on with his life?'

'Why is getting on with life not possible without meeting other women? Oliver should have remained single and faithful to the memory of Jenny.'

Two days later Keya made me promise that if she died, I would not marry again. I said nothing then, but later went back for a clarification: was that a generally binding clause of commitment, to be a one woman man or only if she died the way Jenny had or what?

In sheer disgust, she snorted, 'All you men are the same ...' But a few minutes later, she snuggled up to me, and said, 'Never mind, I love you in spite of that!'

Once, during our afternoon rendezvous in the audi she put her arms around me and sprang back. 'Abbey, you are so hot!'

'Glad you noticed my sex appeal,' I said.

'Abbey, you have high fever! Get off. You must take rest. You shouldn't be straining yourself like this.' She said and shook me off unceremoniously.

I tried to argue about the benefits of this rather unconventional medical path. She just overruled me and ordered me to go back to my room, take a tablet and go to sleep.

I got out of my trance and buttoned myself into a more coherent state of mind. My weak protests were of no consequence and I was forced to promise to remain celibate till my fever subsided.

I went back to the hostel, took a painkiller and tried to sleep. But I was still smarting from her rebuff. She had begun to treat me almost like a husband and that was one definite downside to the relationship. Funny how quickly women can get into the 'house-house' mode, I thought. Half an hour later, I heard a whirr outside the hostel gate. I tottered up to the window and saw Keya getting off her moped. She waved furiously and asked me to get back to bed. I was too dazed to think. So I went back and collapsed into a numb stupor. When I came to, I saw Keya and Pappu sitting next to me on my bed.

'Why did you come to the Boys' Hostel, Keya? You could get thrown out ... actually I will get thrown out of the college if Haathi finds out ... Go away, Keya, don't do this to me.'

Keya waved a piece of paper. 'I took permission from him,' she laughed.

Pappu nodded appreciatively. I noticed he had tidied up the room by moving all his clothes on to one side, and created some free space on the floor.

After hanging around uncomfortably for two minutes, Pappu left us with a discreet warning. 'Haathi may drop in unannounced so be careful.'

Keya glanced at my glazed red eyes and said, 'Don't worry, Pappu. Abbey is too dazed to do anything rash.'

The viral fever lasted for a week. It felt like a lifetime. The medicines made me dizzy. I lost my appetite for food, especially mess food. Or maybe it was just an excuse to get Keya to make sandwiches for me.

'That's about all that I can cook, Abbey,' she said almost apologetically.

Everyday, she would send me a get-well-soon card and a love note tied to a bunch of wild flowers. Pappu cleared some space for all the flowers at one end of the room. The cards and love notes kept piling up like feathers under my pillow. Even when they had dried up I would not let Pappu throw away the flowers. Keya said it made the room look like a grave. One day, I sent word that I missed her, so she sent back a dab of cotton sprayed with her perfume. That must have hastened my recovery.

When I was ill, I realized how lonely it can be if one falls ill in a hostel. For the first week I actually felt that I was going to die. If I survived it was because of Pappu and Keya's constant efforts.

I told Pappu that I felt like a parasite just eating and sleeping all day long.

Pappu was truly surprised at my discomfort.

'What's wrong in that? I would love it if someone were to wait on me day and night. I guess it's my style. If you feel that bad about it, then remember you will be doing just that once you finish this course at MIJ. It is practice for the future.'

The companies would be coming to the campus in a few weeks. Preparations were just beginning.

Chapter 15

There was tension in the air. Campus placements were scheduled to begin soon. Our Seniors were literally walking on eggshells, as they prepared to interview for their final placements, which would make or break their careers. Nobody made small talk with each other. Did that mean friends competing for the same goals do not remain friends? The library was suddenly full of people reading newspapers and business magazines. Not a copy of *Harvard Business Review* and *Business India* was to be had, for love or money. I too felt compelled to lower my ignorance level. But the chasm between ignorance and awareness was too wide to be bridged by this last minute reading.

Our batch was psyched up too. After all, we were interviewing for summer jobs. How to dress right for an interview, to tie a double knot (in a necktie), to behave in front of a panel, but before getting there, how to write a resume. All these questions started bugging us as the placement season drew closer. We had to go and get summer jobs that lasted six to eight weeks. And since they could translate into firm job offers at the end of the following year, we had to choose the companies very carefully.

Thanks to my father being in the government, I had no clue about the corporate world, what the difference was between a public sector job and a private sector one. I had no idea how to write an impressive biodata. Naturally, I turned to Rusty.

Seeing my woebegone expression, Rusty patted me reassuringly and said, 'Don't worry da, Abbey. You have only seen your father and his colleagues who are in government service. Their job is done once they enter the service. You have no idea about the corporate world or what the difference between a public sector job and private sector job is.' After glancing through my life history, he solemnly continued, 'Remember Abbey, companies look for resumes and not CVs. This is more of a Curriculum Vitae. Keep it a one-page, business-like resume and that'll be your USP.'

'What is USP?' I was always one step behind in the world of jargon.

'USP means Unique Selling Proposition. That refers to whatever is special and unique about you. Something that others do not have or will find very difficult to copy. If you don't have a USP, nobody will give you a job. Not even a summer job. Your summer job determines where you'll get a final job offer in the firm year. It's all linked.'

'My USP? Rusty, I cannot see any unique selling proposition for Abbey,' I said, in my customary self-effacing manner.

'All right, let me go through this carefully, da. I am sure we can redraft it. Hmmm... I am impressed, bugger—debating prizes, acting awards and all, eh? Not bad. Hmmmm. We can still make a manager out of you, Abbey!'

'But look at my grades, da.' I had unconsciously begun to use the Southie expression. 'People are hired to do jobs in the corporate sector, not to act in plays!'

'That's negative thinking, Abbey. The future belongs to those who dare. You must learn to market yourself properly. Think of Abbey as a product that needs a good branding strategy.'

'Is this a marketing class or what?' I couldn't help being sarcastic, because I did not have faith either in my merit or in Rusty's offer to salvage the situation.

But Rusty ignored my remark.

He was in right earnest. 'You must position yourself as an all-rounder. Someone who could have been at the top of the class but *chose* instead to learn lessons in leadership and teamwork through extracurricular activities. Getting an A+ in Organizational Behaviour is creditable. Getting an A+ on your term paper on leadership is great. But what use is that if you are not a leader in real life? Who will entrust his sheep to you unless you prove you can lead them in the right direction? As the Cultural Secretary of your college you demonstrated great skills in working across diverse groups when you organized events jointly with another college.'

'But Rusty, that was because we wanted to pile on to the girls in JM college,' I confessed. But such candour was irrelevant in the context, it seemed.

Rusty continued, 'You also have a knack for motivating your peer group to accomplish a task jointly. That's what matters in an organization. You are a reasonably intelligent guy, Abbey and you have the right combination of skills every company is looking for. Any damn fool can get good grades. But it's not a proof of his ability to accomplish anything in an organization.'

Rusty almost made academic excellence sound like a sin that I might have committed, had I been a wee bit callous. This was sweet music to my ears. My shoulders squared involuntarily.

'Look at all the big names in industry today ... like Jeh, or Russi... they were not all toppers, but they had leadership qualities, Abbey, leadership qualities.'

By the time Rusty had finished rewriting my resume, I was brimming with confidence. I walked tall and briskly, with a sense of purpose. Ganauri, who normally looked through most of us, met me in the corridor and saluted me. It was showing.

When I entered my room, I asked Pappu, 'Jeh, Russi and me. What is it that all three of us have in common?'

'Low CQPI?' Pappu answered without thinking.

'Dhat! All three of us were born to be leaders,' I said pompously.

That chat with Rusty taught me that in life, self-confidence is half the battle won. I was not going to be a passive traveller any more. I would be in charge of my life. Rusty had done it all for me. He had briefed me about the intricacies of the corporate world. He taught me all the right jargon. He showed me how to tie a double knot tie so that it no longer looked like something the cat brought in. He conducted mock interview sessions for me. Above all, he showed me how to write bestsellers. These usually float under the term 'biodata'.

Keya noticed the difference and found it hard to deal with the new relaunched Abbey!

'You have changed, Abbey. You are not the same. You were always a bit vain, now you are positively narcissistic!' she said.

I did not bother to reply. I was too full of my new self!

My next interview went off well and I landed a summer project in one of the top edible oil companies of the country. The project required me to be based in Bombay. I was raring to go.

Joy, Harpal, Rusty, Ayesha and even that despicable Gopher were all doing their summer training in Bombay. I found paying guest accommodation in Colaba's Badhwar Park and Ayesha and Gopher were both staying in Badhwar Park as well. The others were in the same area, barely fifteen minutes away from all of us.

I had no intention of socializing with Gopher but I would inevitably bump into him in the lift since he stayed in the flat opposite mine. Just my luck. That creep would show up even at the Badhwar Park Swimming Pool.

Ayesha had a project in the corporate office of the same company as I, but she escaped the horrendous commute I was subjected to each morning. The corporate office was just a ten minute bus ride away from Badhwar Park. I was assigned to do a project in the factory in Sewree—an hour's commute each way. And so, I got my first taste of life in India's financial capital. Bombay was so different from Delhi and MIJ. It was mechanical, impersonal and precise. My routine was to hop on to the 7:48 bus from Colaba, take the 8:13 local from VT station's Harbour Line to Sewree. Invariably I sat in the same compartment with the same travelling companions, spent the same amount of time in the train and was unfailingly amazed by the sameness of it all. The group next to me played cards on their briefcases. Some across the aisle leaned back in their seats and fell asleep by the time the train pulled out of the station. Within minutes, the sound of snoring competed with the whirring of the fans in the hot compartment. This drone had the effect of dulling the senses to a point when an irreversible ennui sets in.

The only saving grace was that every evening when I got back, I would join Ayesha in the club swimming pool. I hated the thought of waddling across the length of the pool in full view of the crowd who had gotten used to Ayesha's perfect bikini clad form. Gopher would bring a book and pretend to read by the pool, surreptitiously leching at Ayesha, though the dog would never admit to it even if the KGB interrogated him.

On weekends, Ayesha and I would go down to Kailash Parbat and have two rounds of pao bhaji and kulfi each. Occasionally, she would invite me over to her room to share a bottle of chilled beer that I would buy. Ayesha believed in living life king size. Having her around certainly made my Bombay life full of fun.

However, the summer project, for which I was in Bombay, was not happening in a big way for sure.

That sucked. The elation of working for the coveted company was quickly replaced by despair. I was eager to work hard and create a good impression so that it would translate into a job offer next year. But I hardly got to meet my project guide, Mr Gowarikar, the personnel manager of the factory. Mr Gowarikar was a short fat man who sweated profusely and could outstare a statue. Having worked his way through the corporate hierarchy, he had a natural dislike for anyone who had ever stepped into an institute like MIJ. I had made it worse by wearing a tie when I went to the factory for the first time to meet him. That encounter with him was indicative of our future relationship.

Before I could finish introducing myself, he glared at me in my crisp white shirt and tie and almost snarled, 'Take off that tie. This is not London… Sit there, on the sofa outside and first spend time observing things around here. How will you learn if you do not observe the culture of this great company? An MBA from that MIJ is useless and will not teach you *anything* that is required in practical life.'

'Sir, what is the project I will be working on?'

'That depends on what you observe over the next few days. When you are ready, take an appointment from my secretary.'

He gave me a look that immediately placed me at the bottom of the food chain, like the worm he had mentally categorized me to be. I took off my tie and sat down on the sofa placed outside his office. A couple of times I was mistaken for his peon. This was annoying, I had to do something about it. And about filling the time 'observing.' Once again Rusty came to my aid.

He had said to me one day, 'Always look busy, Abbey. Nobody will fool around with you if you look busy and rushed.'

So I picked up the house journals that were lying around and tried to concentrate on every word. In four days, I had read every house journal that had been printed in the written history of mankind. But Gowarikar refused to give me an appointment—leave alone a project. So I read the house journals all over again.

They were all the same—boring as hell. All of them spoke about the company going great guns. They carried pictures of people receiving awards for completing their sales targets. A couple of photographs of employees getting married and a few house journals down, the additions to their families.

After some time, I decided to start talking to anybody who seemed to be bored and in need of catharsis. I started with Mr Dasappa, who was Gowarikar's secretary. He told me that these were not good times. There was talk of a lockout. He educated me about Harish Sawant, the Trade Union leader who was holding the company officials by the short and curlies. A showdown was inevitable. Any manager from the head office who dared to visit the factory was pelted by slippers on the shop floor. The tension was palpable. So, I was asked to listen to some of the gate meetings that were held by the Union.

He must have felt sorry for me, having seen me idling away the hours for almost a week, and tried to console me.

'Gowarikar does this to every summer trainee. Nobody wants to come here. Why did you not ask for a corporate office based project?'

'I wanted to learn about the realities of the factory, which one can never learn in the sanitized environment of the corporate office.'

Dasappa gave me a look that was part appreciative and part confused. Gowarikar still did not give me the time of day.

One evening, I bumped into Rusty near VT station. He was talking to an Arab gentleman. The man was lapping up, without hesitation, every word that came out of Rusty's mouth.

Rusty introduced me to his companion, 'Abbey, meet Sheikh Osman bin Haider.'

The Sheikh shook my hand, gave Rusty a big hug, 'Excuse me, I must go now,' he said, stepping into a very fancy car and driving off.

I was most intrigued by the Arab. 'Who was that, da?' I asked eagerly. Rusty ignored my question and changed the topic.

He told me that his summer project was to be advising the CEO of the Arab's company about the kind of HR policies the company should have. Rusty showed me the draft of the HR policy manual he was working on. He was off to attend a meeting with the CEO and his VPs, he said.

I shared my frustration and despair with Rusty, 'My project has not yet started and I barely have four weeks to complete the damn thing, get it typed and make a presentation. You know how easy it is for Kamini Mishra to give me a C or D if the report is not good enough. How do I get that asshole Gowarikar to at least give me a project that I can work on?'

Rusty was in no mood to sympathize.

'Don't just whine and crib about it, Abbey—*do something*. Seek an appointment with the Director of Personnel at the head office to discuss some ideas about how to improve the company's image as a recruiter on the campus. In the corporate sector, a flunkey in the corporate office or headquarters will wield far more power than even someone senior in a factory. In your case, the Director of Personnel is the big boy who will have the power to keep Gowarikar on a leash. So take an appointment with him right now and ask when he would like to see a summary of your project's findings. Then, just before you leave, tell him how disappointed you are at not being adequately challenged during your project. Tell him that no decent student in MIJ ever wants to work in a company that doesn't provide a challenge.'

A day after that meeting at the HO with the Director of Personnel, I was called by Gowarikar to his office. In his best, most waspish manner he said, 'Since you are so keen on getting a "challenging" project, I will personally make sure you have enough of it,' making the statement sound like a threat.

For the next four weeks, I was on what is euphemistically called a 'data collection' assignment. I ran around the factory like a headless chicken pleading with all the staff to fill up my eight-page questionnaire. I had to get 200 such questionnaires filled up, analyze the data and put my findings into a report. There should be a law that prohibits inane summer projects being assigned to MBA students. Is anybody listening?

I criss-crossed Bombay from Churchgate to Sewree, from the head office to factory gates, begging anyone who cared to fill up a questionnaire. But with no luck. Senior Managers didn't have the time. The workers didn't understand it. After my having spent hours trying to translate the questionnaire into words they were familiar with, they would continue to look so blank I would be tempted to kick brains into some of those morons. Time was of the essence. These fools did not realize or care that I just had to get this shit done fast and get back to MIJ. Some of those jerks even managed to lose the questionnaire. Those were the ones I wanted to whip—but the ones that I wanted to slaughter were those who would say the same thing every week.

'When do you want it back? I am very busy this week. I'll mail it to you.'

'Did you want *me* to fill this up or can my secretary do it?'

I cursed Gowarikar to hell and damnation for causing me this mental anguish and suffering. I hope he busts his ass and gets a demotion each year for the rest of his work life, I prayed.

When there were five days left for me to go back to MIJ, I was ready to kill myself out of desperation. I gave Rusty a call. He agreed to meet me at VT station.

'Bring the questionnaires along.'

'All 200 of them?' I asked.

'*Obviously*, da.'

Over a cup of coffee, Rusty explained the do's and don'ts of doing surveys and collecting data.

'There are three basic rules of surveys.

Rule No. 1: Nothing more than one page. So cut out the crap and keep it brief. Preferably no more than 10 questions.'

He sipped the cold coffee that I was paying for and continued, 'Rule No. 2: Tell people, you can't come back and you'll wait while they fill it up. Tell them you'll send them a copy of your project report. That helps.'

He finished the coffee and sucked on the ice cubes before spitting them into the glass. 'Rule No. 3: Don't depend on others to fill up your questionnaire. Do it yourself.'

'What?'

Rusty shrugged.

'But what if someone finds out?'

'Abbey, you are such an ass! Who's going to read through 200 questionnaires? Just give them a summary—an executive summary of the findings. Have it typed and bound so it looks good among the other project reports on the bookshelf. Think of this as a critical term paper. Your main objective is to get good grades—not to discover some brilliant truth which these managers do not know about. Oh yeah, put in a good word about this jerk Gowarikar in the first few pages of the project report, about how he helped you learn so much etc. That will ensure his support during your presentation to the director of personnel on the last day of your project. Tell that Gowarikar or whatever his name is, to grade you on a 4 point scale, A+, A, B+ or B. You will likely end up with a B+. Wear a crisp white shirt and a tie whenever you are in the head office. They will judge you by your appearance, rather than read the shit that a summer trainee has written. Well I must rush ... have an offsite meeting in Goa on Friday ... Got to go and work on my acetates. Good luck, Abbey and thanks for the coffee,' he said, and thumping me on the back, walked away, soon to be lost in the crowd.

'God bless you, Rusty,' I muttered under my breath. When I went up to Gowarikar and told him that the project was ready to be presented to the Head of Personnel in the head office, he was impressed. The report looked pretty, with the fake leather binding I had managed, courtesy Rusty's advice again.

On the day of the presentation, I was distinctly nervous. I bumped into Ayesha on the way to the conference room where I was supposed to meet this mysterious Director of Personnel of the company—the man with the power of life and death over everyone, including Gowarikar. Ayesha said I already looked like a senior manager in my white shirt and tie.

I went into a kind of a waiting room just outside the huge conference room with three other trainees. After almost an hour, six aggressive looking guys in their forties walked in, along with Gowarikar who followed them in carrying all the four project reports that were being presented that day. The big boy, Director of Personnel, was walking ahead, the rest of the pack trying to keep pace.

I want to be Director of Personnel when I grow up, I told myself. He was going to review my project and pronounce judgement on my ability to continue breathing.

I tried to recall my phone conversation with Rusty and his advice on how to handle a project review.

'Reviews are when all mortals have to stand up with the floodlight shining into their eyes and declare that all is well in their tiny part of the murky world.'

Gowarikar had briefed me repeatedly about the etiquette surrounding these reviews.

He was perspiring at the prospect of exhibiting me in front of the Masters of the Universe, 'And no bad news. Nobody wants to hear that. Bad news of any size has the capacity to throw a spanner into the smooth completion of a review. He does not like it. It prevents the brisk flow of the meeting. Don't forget to wear a tie. Everything matters. He notices every little thing.'

Meaning us?

'Go for colour slides, my boy. Print out a copy of the slides on colour paper and put it in a nice binder for Him. He likes colourful stuff. He likes to see hard copies of every presentation.' And finally, 'Don't worry. I will be there!' he assured me.

Gowarikar was a nervous man and he was transmitting that nervousness to me. It was after all his review as well, in a way. I hated that thought.

There were three other summer trainees from another management institute. We were all nervous wrecks and just chewed our nails in silence, waiting for our turn. Every now and then Gowarikar would pop out from the inner chamber armed with snippets of valuable information. He was letting us into a secret.

'He is in a foul mood. He was caught in the traffic jam for forty-five minutes today. We have to make up for lost time. Hurry! Hurry!'

Another time he emerged from the sanctum sanctorum and said, 'He loves chicken sandwiches. I did not know how much we had in common!' He was truly excited that the lord had given him a chance to share this gene with the director.

Again the door swung open and Gowarikar rushed out. He looked in both directions in the hallway as if he was trying to cross the Bombay–Pune Highway and then beckoned for me to go in. It was finally my turn at the electric chair. He stopped me at the door.

'They are running behind schedule. Knock off a few slides from your presentation and stick to the main stuff.'

I reminded him politely that I had only three slides to show. One that said, 'Good Morning.' That was Gowarikar's advice. The last one that said, 'Thank You'—Rusty's counsel. The good news on my project's findings was sandwiched in between these two slides.

Which slide should I remove from His Holiness' view?

My boss merely snorted. 'Keep all the slides but be brief. Keep the pace brisk.'

Throughout my presentation Gowarikar kept winking at me with encouragement or shaking his head to make me pause and think. He silently mouthed words to prevent me from straying and generally tried to put me at ease. I will never know why he was so nervous or why he showed so much sympathy that day.

Anyway, I got a B+ for my Summer Project on 'Perceptions of Union-Management Relations in Sewree Factory.'

I celebrated by taking Ayesha out to a movie. We saw *Masoom* and hummed the tune as we walked back along Marine Drive towards Badhwar Park.

'This is our last day in Bombay, Abbey. Let's celebrate. How about kababs at Bade Miyan's, followed by some vodka and orange juice at my place? Chalna hai?'

'I have a better suggestion. Let's buy some chilled beer and have it before we have the screwdriver. Pun intended!'

We carried the beer bottles, neatly wrapped in old newspaper, and went to Ayesha's room. We drank in true MIJ spirit—with the sense of urgency we had been so conditioned to—drink up the stuff before someone asks to share it.

Ayesha put on '*Nights in White Satin*' and we sat side by side. I held her hand. Ayesha looked at me and smiled.

'I like this city. I like its fast pace, its anonymity. I hate the thought of going back to Jampot. I will never go back there if I can help it.'

'I like this place too, but it is so damn expensive. The room rents are a killer.'

'We could share a room. That would be a good idea. But you wouldn't have the guts, Abbey. You are so middle class…'

There was too much alcohol in us. I was unable to answer her truthfully. I just drew her close to kiss her. One thing led to the other and when I woke up the sun was streaming down into the room. I turned back to admire Ayesha's naked body one last time before deciding to wake her up. She was so comfortable with her nakedness that it made me even more conscious of my paunch.

Chapter 16

July 1983. The summer training was over and it was time to get back to MIJ. We were all fresh from our first taste of corporate life. We had had our share of triumphs and tribulations, but by and large most of us had done well.

Besides in this, the fourth term, life became exciting. We were the Seniors, advising our Juniors about how to tackle the various profs, telling them where to get cheap liquor, offering them feedback on the various companies we had worked with. And then there was the whole new crop of girls—for those still unattached, to try their luck with.

One evening soon after we had rejoined, Rusty, Pappu, 'Fundu' Fernandez (my room-mate for this year) and I were sitting in my room exchanging notes about our respective experiences.

We talked excitedly about the glamorous lifestyles of the senior executives—their fancy cars and chauffeurs, the club membership, the lazy evenings drinking scotch and playing rummy. We thought we had a very good idea now of what to expect out of our lives ahead.

Fundu had been listening to us silently all this while.

Then in his deep and sober voice, he said, 'Guys, we are all students of Personnel Management and Industrial Relations. We are supposed to be interested in people. How come none of you mentioned the plight of the workers in these organizations?'

I opened my mouth to protest, but no words came out. None of us had seriously given this a thought.

After a pause, Fundu continued, 'Did you notice, the workers live in chawls and cubby holes, while our senior managers spend their weekends on golf courses the size of Dharavi? Did any of you ever eat in the workers' mess and notice how different they are from the officers' or managers' dining rooms?'

By this time we were thoroughly embarrassed. Because Fundu was a couple of years older than us and certainly much more mature, we did not tell him to shut up.

Rusty of course tried to explain away some of our collective embarrassment, 'Nature works on the concept of survival of the fittest, da. The senior managers do not do manual labour. It is their intellect and managerial quality that they put in the marketplace. The forces of supply and demand determine what price the market puts on those skills. Elementary, enna da? Whenever a skill's supply is less than its demand in the marketplace, we have to pay a higher price for it. Even nature chooses to give some fruits in abundance as compared to some others.'

'That would be a valid argument if everyone had the same opportunities to start with. The world is not a level playing field. For example, even at MIJ you are likely to find the children of middle or upper-middle class parents rather than an industrial worker's.' Pappu had a point.

Rusty tried to bring some levity in the matter by saying, 'I bet the food in the Workers' Canteen would have been better than what we have in our mess.'

Everyone ignored that statement. The silence in the room was unbearable.

The rum and Thums Up tasted bitter in my mouth. Pappu and Rusty made some excuse and went away.

I stood by the window of Room No 209 and stared out at the sky. The monsoon was at its height. Streaks of lightning flashed through the sky like a careless signature as the rain poured down in a steady stream. It had turned the leaves on the trees a succulent green. The dust on the window panes had collected in large brown puddles on the ground. The Dalma hills appeared a strange shade of grayish blue. Some of the peaks wore a crown of clouds. Somebody had put on a Bob Dylan LP in the Music Room and I could hear Dylan sing:

They stone you when you try to be good ...

They stone you when you're living all alone

... everybody must get stoned.

I lit a cigarette and reflected on my past, present and future. What had the past year given me? Some jargon? A little knowledge of management to cover up my mediocrity. A lot of savoir faire that Rusty had drilled into me along with the million little tips on how to beat, no, cheat the system, the profs and even myself.

I glanced at Fundu. He was quiet and introspective and carried himself with dignity and maturity. He was a diligent student who believed in a regular, almost regimented lifestyle. He would wake up at 6 a.m. and study his previous day's class notes. At 10 p.m. sharp he was fast asleep—a hard act to follow.

Fundu had mentioned once that he had studied to be a priest and then a few months before he was to be ordained he decided to give up his calling. Maybe that's why he had such a clear sense of right and wrong and lived by it.

I was in one sense grateful to have him for a roommate. He would, I hoped, be a sobering, inspiring influence on me.

A wave of intense homesickness washed over me. I missed Delhi, Home, SRCC, Priya... and Keya.

Suddenly it dawned on me that she was the reason for my depression.

Keya.

I had not met or even seen Keya since I returned after the summer vacation. She said she was busy but I got the feeling that she was avoiding me. Why? I asked myself.

'She doesn't need to come to MIJ as often as she had to last year.'

I was talking to myself.

'So what! She could have come to meet me ... She would if she cared...'

'But she did ... at least that's what it felt like when I last met her before I left for Bombay. Leaving her for two months at this early stage of the relationship was the mistake.'

'What should I have done, then? Taken her with me?'

'Be honest, Abbey. Did you bother to call her even once when you were in Bombay? Did you write? Did you even think of her?'

This conversation with myself was getting me nowhere. I decided it was time to go to bed.

Rain had left its tear drops everywhere. There were patches of water on the steps as I walked towards the

B Ed college office next morning and enquired about Keya's marks. I secretly hoped she had flunked the course so that she would have a legitimate reason to come to the MIJ campus for another year—at least till I was around. But I knew Keya was too smart to flunk. Her name was in the honour's list—she had stood fourth in her class.

Discreet enquiries revealed that she was now working in a school as a teacher. Love and romance must have dropped down in her priorities and with it my popularity rating, I thought.

Maybe she had changed in the last few months.

I reflected on the year gone by and noticed that bits and pieces of me had changed too. I had acquired new habits. Some surprising behaviour as well—I had learnt to read the business section of *The Telegraph*. It was a new paper, recently launched and very popular in the hostel. Surely the one whole page devoted to cartoons every day had much to do with it. I had started buying *Business India* to catch up with news from the corporate sector. Occasionally, in the library, I would browse through old issues of *Fortune*. I discovered some great stuff in the *Harvard Business Review*, especially the articles by Peter Drucker.

I thought I would make some allowances for Keya. Not everybody can handle change very well, I told myself rather condescendingly. But that didn't prevent me from dreaming about our meeting after all this while—she would float towards me in slow motion, her hair flowing behind her like in the shampoo ads. Or she would rush into my arms in her exuberant and spontaneous fashion and we would fade into the sunset—that's how it always played out in my mind.

When I had received my stipend, a princely sum of ₹ 700 in Bombay, I bought myself a book that was a bestseller of sorts—*In Search of Excellence*. I never read it. I also bought Tagore's *Poems of Love* for Keya. Then changed it to *The Catcher in the Rye*. I knew she would love it. I wondered how she would react when I gave it to her. Keya did not meet me. For days. Arrogant male that I was, I decided to be macho and not call her either. Probably that's what paid off.

After weeks of playing hard to get, Keya finally called up and said that she wanted to meet me. She seemed to be in a hurry and a little sad. Maybe she had realized her mistake in not calling me earlier.

She was quite preoccupied when we met. I gave her the book.

'How was Bombay?'

'The project kept me very busy. I had this fucker Gowarikar for a project guide. I gave him a hard time. Kept asking him a million questions on the latest in Wall Street and all ...'

She did not respond. Her mind was elsewhere. And her eyes were sad. I continued to talk animatedly, told her how I had a great time in Bombay. She didn't seem to care.

Suddenly she asked me, 'What are the plans, Abbey?'

'Plans? Mine? Regarding work?'

'Have you ever stopped to think of anyone else besides yourself, Abbey?' she asked without any audible trace of emotion. 'Everyone else seems to exist only in relation to you. There's no place for anyone else in your world, not even in your dreams, Abbey. I am going away, Abbey. Leaving. I can't imagine going through a lifetime with you.'

'Do you know what you are saying, Keya? I mean out of the blue, without any reason ...' I was stuttering in sheer disbelief.

'It's not so surprising, Abbey. If you only took the trouble to think and put yourself in my shoes. But then, you men always find it so hard to understand women. Maybe because the word men has *me* as the main part of it and the word women has *we* as the main sound.'

'What do you mean, Keya? You're the one who does not care about anyone else. I've just gotten back after such a long time and you aren't interested in knowing what I did.'

'I am not sure if I am saying it the way I should. Maybe it is not how this was meant to be. But Abbey, I don't want to meet you ever again. I am not angry with you or anything. I still care and probably always will. Don't make it more difficult for me, Abbey. I am too messed up to think straight. Please do not call me again. I want to be left alone. Be happy.'

Keya left me. I stood there, stunned by what she had said. Her petite form receded into the horizon—growing a millimeter smaller with each step she took. She didn't even turn around to say goodbye. Suddenly the two of us seemed like two planets in the solar system which had come close for a moment, only to go away for the next 300 years.

This was crazy.

What had I done wrong? What had sparked it off? Fuck it. I had too many problems in my life to be moping about her. I was sure she would be back tomorrow or definitely by next week.

I looked at her walking away and suddenly felt very alone. Very vulnerable. Very stupid. But there was no one I could talk to, no one who'd hear me out without being judgemental. So I spoke to myself.

'What had happened to her suddenly? She was fine when I left Jampot two months back. She even wrote me a goodbye note then. What could have possibly happened between then and now that caused her to walk away? Had she fallen in love with someone else? Was she disillusioned with the world and men in particular? What did she expect me to talk about when she asked about my "plans"? I hope she did not expect me to talk about marrying her as part of my plans. Or was she jealous because I had had such a good time in Bombay.'

Suddenly it flashed. Gopher had seen me come out of Ayesha's room that last day in Bombay. His smile should have warned me. But I was too euphoric to notice. Shit man! That's what it must have been. He had sneaked about Ayesha and... Hell! These women were crazy. And Gopher needed a swift punch between his legs. I made that an IOU and mentally gave it to Gopher.

I tried to call Keya at home a couple of times but she would not take the call. I dropped in to meet her at home one evening. Her aunt answered the door and gave me a funny look. Blandly, she told me that Keya was unwell and had requested that she should not be disturbed. As a last ditch measure, I tried to contact the school which she had joined. Keya had quit the job. What was wrong with this woman? She had no business walking off like that. The least she could have done was explained things to me. It was so damn unfair...

Chapter 17

After the Keya incident, I discovered that doing a specialized course in managing people had not done much for my ability to build relations with fellow human beings. I still couldn't figure out what had gone wrong with Keya.

But then my rational self took over and said, 'Oh forget it. There's more to life than Keya.'

Why did I have this predilection for getting into relationships which had me doing a balancing act on a tightrope? Jas, Ayesha and now Keya… I would start off with a firm grip, walk along for a while with my arms spread out like wings and then halfway through something would happen to me and I would start swaying wildly. After a while, I would get a severe attack of vertigo and jump off. That was briefly the pattern of all my relationships. To this day, I do not know why Keya behaved the way she did.

My introspection did not provide any answers. Good old Rusty's words of wisdom came back to mind.

'Whenever you screw up something look for someone to share the blame with if you cannot ascribe it entirely to someone else.' That was Rusty's sound advice on how to handle group assignments.

But this was not a group project, da...

'That's the trouble with you, Abbey. The problems are always with the other person when something goes wrong.'

'OK, so the problem is with me, is it? Why? What should I have done? Or not done?'

Why could I not see the relationship through to some logical conclusion? Is there such a thing as a 'logical conclusion' in a relationship? Maybe it had something to do with my 'psychological profile'. I turned to my handouts and books on Psychology to look for answers and theoretical constructs. This was the perfect semester to understand 'Self and Others in Relation to Self.' That was the term paper I had to submit to Haathi the next week. I was deeply into exploring the use of various psychological assessment tools. Each one revealed something distressing about me. I did one test called FIRO-B (short for Fundamental Interpersonal Relationship Orientation). The 'B' stood for Behaviour.

FIRO-B gave you a picture of the extent to which the individual has a need to control others and also be controlled by others. So, if you only wanted to control others and not let them have a go at you, you could be a perfect autocrat. On the other hand, if you let everyone take charge of you without returning the favours, you'd instantly be a big time wimp in the FIRO-B world. FIRO-B would translate all this into numbers on a scale of 0–9 and then we would work with the prof to interpret what the scores meant.

According to the FIRO-B scores, I had a high need to control others but would let only a handful of people control me. Sounded fine to me. Fundu wasn't sure that this was a good thing. He had a major in Psycho before he came to MIJ.

'The FIRO-B also gives you a picture of the extent to which you have a need to include others or be included in their social get-togethers. Remember, that's what Father Hathaway explained that day when you brought it up,' Fundu reminded me.

Fundu and a few of us were taking the special elective course on Understanding Self which Haathi was teaching.

Haathi had said, 'It means that you show more warmth than you actually feel. You really don't want to get that close to people. And your low score on wanting inclusion shows that you don't care if others don't include you in their lives.'

The FIRO-B instrument was quite amazing. It seemed to indicate how one could predict the kind of problems each person would run into in terms of relationships. I had come away from Haathi's class puzzled.

What did Haathi mean when he said that I seemed to show more warmth than I felt? Could that be what happened in my relationship? Is that what Keya meant when she had said 'Everyone seems to exist only in relation to you …' So then have I become self-centred? Or was I always like this and just never knew it? How come both Keya and the FIRO-B scores say the same stuff? Fuck! This instrument is a load of shit.

I desperately needed a couple of Old Monk-Thums Ups to make sense of all that psycho babble and straighten things in my mind. But why did my head hurt and why was I feeling so sick…

'Depressed because of your FIRO-B scores?' Rusty said when he saw my long face and hang-dog look. I was sitting in my room, trying to study for Kamini Mishra's exam the next day.

Thumping me on the back, Rusty continued, 'That's the idea, boss. Who do you think created these tests? The shrinks. Who decides that getting a score of forty in some obscure test means you have the personality of a gecko? The shrink who created the test, of course. He thus ensures that you go to him and he will fix the non-existent problem with your personality. Abbey, can't you see the scam? Never let any test scores bother you. Ka-meanie is giving us an exam tomorrow—worry about that instead of wasting your time!'

He walked away. But the deep-seated loneliness inside me would not go away. In my effort at chasing the mirage of the fancy lifestyle of a corporate executive, I had lost touch with the simple things of life. I hated this town. I hated this institute. I hated the people I was with. I felt like a goldfish in a bowl, constantly being watched and judged. Under pressure to perform. For some reason my thoughts turned to Priya. She was the only one who had loved me in spite of myself. Here in MIJ, I did everything not to appear like an oaf and still everyone hated me. I missed Kapil and Priya's unconditional friendship. I wanted so desperately to be back in the Railway Colony in Delhi.

I missed Priya, even if she was crazy. Hoped she was safe. I prayed that this new guy she spoke of, Neel (henceforth referred to as The Jerk), would have his balls yanked out by the neighbour's dog for making a sucker out of that innocent kid.

I had not heard from Priya for a while. When I had gone home during the last vacations, I had not had enough time to spend with her. But I just assumed she would understand. And be there for me when I chose to write to her. Then I had got her letter. I read those lines again and again…

I was recording the jingle for Sehgal Sarees. Neel is so young and yet so down to earth despite all his wealth and fame. Have you heard of him? I told him that his name sounds vaguely familiar and he was almost offended. He knows R.D. Burman on a first name basis. Calls him Pancham-da. That's so sweet. I will call my kid Pancham. Decided. And final. Don't try to change my mind, Abbey. Neel is a talent scout. He has launched a lot of new singers in Bombay including Vandana. She sounds JUST like Lata Mangeshkar. He says I have more of an Asha Bhosle kind of voice. I will sing you '*Aaiye Meherban*' when we meet next. I have finally got my big break. I will be singing at some of the best hotels in Simla this winter. I am going to be staying at The Cecil there. Mummy wouldn't let me. So I left without telling her. That was an awful thing to do. But Abbey you know I so badly want to be a singer.

Are you happy for me? Are you angry? Please don't be. You know I wouldn't do anything to make you angry. I am fine. Neel is there. He says, if I can make a success of this, the next stop is Bombay. One day I will be singing along with the greats. Will you buy my records?

Study hard and don't smoke too much. Please.

Love LOVE love

Priya

I wrote back right away.

Priya,

This is just a quick note before I go for my Mid Term exam. You are such a bloody idiot. Can't you see you are being used? This Neel or whatever his name is, is no talent scout, he's just another of those smooth talking scoundrels who is just going to use you and walk away. I bet he has never met RD.

Go right back to Delhi. I am sending Aunty your address and phone number. She will have this Neel arrested. STOP being an ass, Priya, and go back home.

Love

Abbey

PS: If you go back to Delhi I will quit smoking ~~for a week~~ forever.

PPS: Are you sleeping with that moron Neel?

I sealed the Inland Letter. I was not sure when it would reach her; letters routinely got delayed or lost in the post, of late. Especially letters to or from this part of the world. Would Priya even receive this letter in time? I was seething inside. How could Priya be so bloody stupid? How could she fall for this rubbish? Someone needed to drill some sense into her head.

There was no further news from Priya. My letters went unanswered.

I felt like killing Neel. Could I hire some contract killers from Bombay to do the job?

Did Fundu know any of them—he was from Bombay after all... Nah, he was not the kind. Stupid girl. Why had she been taken in by this fellow?

To my surprise I found myself praying for Priya.

'God, I am sorry to trouble you. I mean... you know what a simple, foolish girl Priya is. I hope she gets a chance to sing for at least one film. Actually, could I change that to one record contract? But PLEASE PLEASE protect her from Neel and the other lecherous bastards (sorry for my language, boss) you know what I mean—after all YOU are God. Thank you, God. And for myself all I can say is that you know I worked hard for the Labour Law mid term. OK! I COULD have worked some more but you know I did read the notes. Could you please not let Ka-meanie... err ... Professor Mishra ask any questions from the Industrial Disputes Act? That is just too tough to comprehend. Thank you, God.'

I tried to ask myself why I was reacting this way? All these years when Priya had tried to reach out, I had only moved further away. I had taken perverse delight in hurting her. And now that she was walking away, I suddenly felt so possessive, so protective about her.

Why, Abbey?

But that question was too uncomfortable to answer truthfully.

I turned my attention to the thick copy of P.L. Malik's book on Industrial Disputes Act, 1947 and felt intimidated. The talk going around was that Section 22 was a favourite of Kamini Mishra's. It was the section on strikes. I tried to read it a few times over. Then said it aloud in my mind.

22. PROHIBITION OF STRIKES AND LOCK-OUTS—(1) No person employed in a public utility service shall go on strike in breach of contract

(a) without giving to the employer notice of strike, as hereinafter provided, within six weeks before striking; or

(b) within fourteen days of giving such notice; or

(c) before the expiry of the date of strike specified in any such notice as aforesaid; or

(d) during the pendency of any conciliation proceedings before a conciliation officer and seven days after the conclusion of such proceedings.

After trying to make sense of the language by reading it at least twenty-six times, I exclaimed in disgust,

'Who taught these guys English? Why were they not forced to attend Haathi's classes on Basic Communication Skills for All?'

The only consolation was that it would be the last paper on Law I would have to do in MIJ. Unless of course Kameanie had other ideas, i.e. if I did not clear this paper and Kamini made me repeat the year.

The prospect sent a shudder through me. Anyway, I managed a C+ in the end!

Chapter 18

My room had ceased to be the venue for addas since Fundu had become my roommate in the second year at MIJ. Everyone felt a little awkward and inhibited in his presence. Of course, Fundu was not a prude, but he was not quite a dude either. Besides he was much older than all of us. None of us cursed or swore freely in his presence. Thus, Joy's room had become the favoured destination for rum and debate. Especially debates about girls. All of us had our own theories about what led an MIJ girl to pair up with an MIJ guy. Rusty, for example, believed that couples try to make up for their own deficiencies through their partners. And some of us would believe anything that Rusty said.

'That explains why the smartest girls choose the dumbest guys to go around with,' chipped in Gopher.

'Then how come smart guys (like us for instance) usually have had to take our hand out for dinner?' said Joy.

While this kind of conversation was permissible among us, there was an unspoken rule that these speculations were not to be made in the presence of those fellows who were going steady. It was the hypothesis of those with strong arm muscles.

That day Joy had just returned from Delhi, fully charged with patriotism, (and a plentiful supply of fauji XXX Rum) and a fresh look at the prettiest girls of Delhi University. He said that the DU girls were the best in the world. I couldn't let that generalization pass.

'Why do you say that?' I had a stake here and had to defend my turf.

'I don't know, da. The Delhi University janta has, y'know, style. So different from the MIJ crowd.'

'I *know* how much smarter these MIJ chicks are. Delhi University babes were pretty and smart but you know ... not the kind who I would enjoy a conversation with...'

Shit, what was I saying! It was weird how our comments about girls had changed over the last year.

'What rot you talk, Abbey!' interjected Joy. 'DU has the best babes in the world. Don't turn your back on Delhi just because... you know what I mean. These MIJ girls don't know our worth. All they can talk about is the latest case study. Who wants another shot of Old Monk?'

'Listen guys,' Rusty was the only one fully sober. 'Better get back to Beez's assignment. Yes, Joy, sorry to say, it's due tomorrow at 8 a.m. Has 30% weightage...' he said, his words trailing behind him.

I walked back to my room. Joy was biased. Look at Ayesha. I mean she was not just pretty but sexy —that made her pretty sexy, plus she was clever. Manipulative? Perish the thought. And... What else, umm, she knew exactly when to use you and when to discard you—like a cigarette that had been smoked to the butt and then trampled upon. That was Ayesha. Ayesha and me.

What was this relationship between us? Did I care about her? I was not sure. Umm... not really. Maybe a bit. I loved her company. Yeah, more than that I liked the way she flirted with me.

I needed to talk. Fundu had become the natural choice for confessions and confidences—it might have had something to do with his training to be a priest. As usual he had finished his assignment and was ready to go to bed. But I was so distraught that day, I opened my heart out to him. The padre gave his slightly tipsy room-mate a patient hearing.

'Why do you always end up dropping the bird in hand and go chasing after the one in the bush, Abbey? Is that better? Why do you feel a need to flit from one relationship to another? Why can't you stabilize?

There must be a more deep-seated reason. Are you scared of making a commitment? Or are you not ready for a long-term relationship?' Fundu was watching me closely, eyes narrowed, head cocked to one side, as he did when he was concentrating.

'What commitment, Fundu?' I burst out. 'Nobody gives a damn about commitment. I don't. I am not committed to even myself. What does a word like that mean in a place like MIJ? I mean with people in MIJ—whether it...' I blabbered on.

I told him what I knew of Ayesha, of her as a person. She was so used to being Queen Bee, she hated to have attention diverted to another woman. She was trying to do the same thing with Keya and me. Which was silly because though I was attracted to her, both of us knew we were in a relationship JLT. We enjoyed each other's company and shared a common interest; namely, having fun. So it didn't matter when it started or ended. She didn't care—and neither did I.

'That's what you'd like to believe. I think you hurt Ayesha too. I think she really cares for you, Abbey.' Fundu spoke ever so softly.

I paused. But I was too full of it to stop and think.

'Both of us know that when times were bad one had to look around to see who was having a good time, and just join that party. So when Ayesha finds me sulking or moody, she just hangs around with others who are more than willing to make it worth her while. This was something about her I dislike.'

'What we dislike most in ourselves is what we accuse others of being.'

What was Fundu saying? This was not what I wanted to hear; truth is never easy to face. I fell silent. Fundu yawned discreetly, mouth closed. I decided we'd had enough for the day. Besides, I had to work on my assignment and it was already well past midnight.

'It's all right if you want to work, Abbey, don't feel guilty. I am used to sleeping with the light on. My brother used to be a night bird. Good luck with the assignment. Early to bed and early to rise…'

'Haven't you heard "Early to bed and early to rise, your wife goes out with other guys…?"'

CHAPTER 19

During the Christmas vacations of '83, we all went home for a last grab at freedom. I couldn't wait to get back to Delhi. The city looked so good in winter. Home food, my room, familiar surroundings—all gave me a sense of security, comfort and belonging which I had missed sorely in MIJ. The day after I landed in Delhi, I called up Kapil. He was delighted to hear I was back and invited me to his house for lunch the following day. He had wanted both Priya and me to come over before I left for Jamshedpur but somehow it had not been possible. This time, though I was determined to meet him. I had to find out what had become of Priya.

Kapil lived in his ancestral home in Chandni Chowk, next to Parathewali Gali. He offered to meet me at Connaught Place and escort me to his house.

'You're looking smart, yaar, enjoying in Jamshedpur?' was his greeting, as he shook hands with me.

'You are doing well too, I can see. Look at your paunch, Kapil.' I punched him playfully to return the compliment.

We walked on, talking about this and that till we came to the Gurdwara on the left and stopped by to eat some of the yummy prashad. The jostling crowds, the sights and sounds of the walled city, were all so vibrant. This part of the world seemed to be caught in a time warp. There were people getting their ears cleaned on the pavement, oblivious of the crowd. The cleaners seemed to be doing their job with the concentration of a surgeon. There were photographers with cameras that must be at least fifty years old. Suddenly, the sharp crack of an air gun set hundreds of pigeons off in flight. They automatically sought shelter in the Bird Hospital nearby. The call of the muezzin from the Jama Masjid summoned the faithful to join the afternoon prayers. All this was so familiar and yet so strange. I had not realized, until then, how much this city meant to me. We kept walking and ignored the vendors on the pavement, who were selling everything from imported condoms to cigarettes. I stopped to buy one single cigarette. Kapil packed a few meetha paans for the family.

We walked on until the smell of parathas indicated we were home. We climbed the steep ladder-like stairs and reached Kapil's room. He had a poster of Amitabh Bachchan near his study table. Then, he opened his cupboard and pointed out a poster of Rekha that was camouflaged behind a pile of shirts. I discovered more about Kapil in the thirty-minute conversation before lunch than I had known in the last three years. I learnt for the first time that Kapil had lost his father in a train accident and had moved with his widowed mother into this house that belonged to his Mamaji. His uncle had since then been the father figure that Kapil looked up to. Nobody seemed to be more aware of this than Mamaji himself.

'Chun Mun! Lunch is ready.' Kapil's mother announced, before he could jump up and silence her physically.

The damage was done.

'Chun Mun? You are called Chun Mun at home. CHUN MUN? I don't believe this.' I said, almost whooping with laughter.

Kapil just turned a fiery red.

At the lunch table, I was finally introduced to the honourable Mamaji himself. He wore a spotless white kurta pyjama, and chewed paan continuously. The man had the air of someone who is used to ordering the rest of humanity around to do his bidding. He looked at me as if he was sizing me up, before deciding to shake my hand, and seemed to know a lot about MIJ. The fact that I had gotten into MIJ seemed to make me worthy of his attention, at least.

'You must try and make friends with the senior managers. When the time comes automatically you will be getting offers to join the Steel & Iron Company. I have told Chun Mun that he must do the IAS. His personality is more suited to that,' he opined, while I focussed on the gajar ka halwa.

After having gorged on the endless stream of parathas appearing out of the kitchen, I sprawled on a chair in Kapil's room. It was the right time to ask him about Priya. Kapil told me that he had met her just before she went off to sing in a hotel in Simla and that she had talked to him a couple of times.

'I once met Priya Bhabhi walking only with one another boy, Neelu. She is still having the Teddy Beer that you gave her as gift. I purposely then told Neel-ji that Priya Bhabhi is already due for marrij with my friend. Priya Bhabhi just started getting upset so I stopped,' said Kapil, describing his brave attempts at warding off evil from Priya's life.

After that, he said, he had no news of her at all.

I was disappointed, but I then had to be polite and listen to Kapil tell me about his own life and his plans.

Kapil Aggarwal's dream had been to set up his own little branch of the family 'bijness' but Mamaji had insisted that he write the Civil Services exam. Kapil was surprised by the sudden pressure on him not to do what he had always believed was his destiny—joining the family bijness. But being the obedient nephew, he had given in and was beginning to believe it was what he was cut out for.

'Mamaji feels that bijness can give you money. But I think being IAS gives you power. Closest to being a raja. Everyone has to please you.'

I couldn't imagine Kapil as the district magistrate, lording over the life of the lesser mortals. That was not logical. But then life doesn't always follow a logical path. My own life was a case in point ...

Before I knew it, the year was at an end. It was time for the annual New Year's Eve Party at the SP Marg Railway Colony Club. It was all so predictable, so routine. But we would have it no other way. The club always had a make-shift dance floor. This year, some wise guy had put up disco lights in the form of the railway guard's signals. Looked pretty weird. The club had six long playing records. Each reflected the musical tastes of the six club secretaries over the past six years. There was one album of M. S. Subbalakshmi's bhajans, a Ravi Shankar album, an album of Punjabi folk songs, one soundtrack of Dev Anand's *Guide* and an LP each of Abba's hits and Boney M. The last two had probably been chosen by the club secretary's kids. We all knew the last two albums by heart. But the club couldn't buy new ones because the governing body had not been able to come to a consensus over the past three years as to what kind of music should be bought with public money.

Hence, every year the New Year's Eve party meant hearing '*Daddy Cool*' or '*Fernando*' at the stroke of midnight. Every now and then, some adventurous youngster would bring in his own LP—like the time one fellow brought some Pink Floyd and got booed out. So we all went back to Boney M. There is a certain warmth and comfort that comes with predictability. Between dances, we'd go to the meal counter of our club and ask Ramaswamy to make dosas. Swamy, his wife and five sons were permanent fixtures. They used to run the club canteen. Swamy dished up hot crispy and paper-thin dosas. After that, it was time to go for a midnight stroll in a big group. I had never missed that ritual.

Only this year, I went out alone. I removed my jacket and walked out in the freezing winter night clad in a half-sleeved shirt and my jeans.

The temperature was at 8 degrees Celsius. The fog hung around the streetlight like a giant firefly. I enjoyed feeling the cold winter air chill me to the bones and shivered as I lit a cigarette and blew out the smoke. Long after you had finished smoking, you could still blow smoke rings into the night, in this weather.

I thought of the many evenings I had spent in the Railway Colony, growing up with a group of kids, sharing games, books, comics, dreams, fights... Every few months a new face would replace the ones that had left the colony when the parents had been transferred. These were strange friendships. We never wrote to each other once the person moved away despite the passionate and well-meaning promises we made. They were like friendships that develop during a train journey only to finish off at the destination.

It would probably be my last New Year's Eve at the Club—the thought was not pleasant at all.

Recently, the college crowd, hanging around together, laughing hysterically at some inane remark, had begun to irk me. I had to worry about finding a job and earning a living while these irresponsible kids were wasting their lives away.

'Were you not the same until the other day when you went to DU?'

'Let's not get into that. I got into MIJ...'

'You know that was serendipity at its best.'

I was to return the next night to MIJ. That afternoon, while we were sitting at the dining table, my father said, 'So you will have to apply for jobs now, I believe? Have you decided which companies to apply to? Public sector companies are better—they pay good salaries, and there is job security. Plus all benefits you get...'

Asmita seemed to have become less opinionated, 'What do you want to do, Bhai? You could still write the Civil Services exam if you want to. An MBA cannot hurt.'

I promised my father I would bear his advice in mind before I gave my acceptance.

Typically, he hastened to add, 'No, no this was only a suggestion—after all you young fellows know better—it is your choice, your life…'

On the train, I had enough time to think, brood, sort myself out. To the backdrop of the rhythmic clatter of the train, I spread my life out before me.

Three women—Priya, Ayesha and Keya. What did they all mean to me? I thought that chat with Fundu had cleared my doubts about where Ayesha and I stood vis-a-vis each other. But I wasn't so sure any more. Keya changed the way I had looked at women. Meeting her was another act of serendipity. So was losing her? Nah. Much as I tried, I couldn't deny the fact that I loved her. A heck lot, at that. But what happened to her? She claimed to have cared for me. So what if I was a little self absorbed for a while, did that mean she should leave me? If she genuinely loved me, what had happened, suddenly? Why had I not bothered to find out what went wrong? Why had I not tried hard enough to salvage the relationship? She was such a wonderful person and so full of life. Maybe I knew it was too good to be true and was expecting it to end anytime, anyway. Maybe I didn't want a relationship and was just living up to Kapil's advice, 'Have a good time and no falling in love and all that, baba.' I felt so hollow. I needed a real relationship.

Like in the case of most first loves, things had not worked out with Keya, but she would always remain very special. Would she? I felt confused. Maybe Keya was not my first love.

Maybe Priya was actually my first love. I wanted to kick myself for even harbouring that blasphemous thought. She was proof that a girl could unconditionally love an ass like me. Wonder how she was...

Did she need me? Was she happy? Was she singing cheap cabaret songs in a hotel under a crazy pseudonym?

I could visualize the posters in the lobby. 'Miss Chandaa?' Or 'The Hot Sensation—Goldie?' Naah. That sounded much too crass.

Why could she not write to me? At least call? Or send me her phone number so that I could call! Maybe I should call her mother. Would that get her more worried? Would that reassure her? Fuck knows! Then the practical MBA in me resurfaced and I said to myself that I would think about her after placement.

I put Priya down on a lower rack mentally and resumed my inner dialogue.

'I have never seen a more selfish human being than you.'

'Listen, I have my future to worry about. I need a job. I HAVE to concentrate on getting one. My CQPI is not exactly the envy of my generation. So I need to work extra hard.'

'You KNOW you will get a job. Everyone gets it. After all, the stamp of MIJ is in itself a passport to the corporate sector. More than half of the personnel managers of the country are part of the alumni network. They can't let MIJ become yet another institute, that would bring down their market value. They will always be there for you—even if it is out of self interest.'

'You sound so much like Rusty. He is the one you spend the most time with. You have become his sidekick. His little puppy. Wagging your tail every time your master throws a nugget of deviousness your way. You hang on to that like a puppy guards a bone. Isn't that proof that you will be hired.'

'What about Priya?'

'I don't know and I don't care. Why complicate life at this stage?'

My head was spinning. I just had to stop this self examination. At the next station, I got off, smoked a cigarette and felt better. I would not have believed it three weeks ago if someone had said it to me, but now I was actually looking forward to getting back to the MIJ Boys' Hostel.

Chapter 20

I was back in MIJ. Placement season was on. You could feel the strong undercurrent of tension in the air. All conversations began to turn to applications, questionnaires, jobs, work life, corporate lifestyles and other such areas which had seemed like distant concerns just two months ago. The same MIJ that had been so relaxed and laidback seemed to be picking up speed scarily, like the athlete in the last lap of the marathon. Everyone wanted to breast the tape before others—only winning mattered. And the prize at the end of the race was a career. So the stakes were high. Anything and everything could be sacrificed and would be.

The summer project appeared to have injected a sense of impending doom in all of us. I felt a perceptible tightening of my stomach muscles every time the word 'placement' was mentioned. Posh had told me that a good CQPI was the ultimate insurance policy. Looking over my academic track record, I knew it was going to be tough. I was already having sleepless nights.

In the silence of the night, I could hear the conversation in Joy's room.

'Do you think I'll get a job?'

'Of course, you will. I probably won't.'

'No I mean, will I get a *decent* job? My CQPI is pretty fucked, you know. Not like yours.'

'Depends what you define as a decent job.'

'Cock up Chumma, answer the question, yaar.'

'No, da. Just CQPI alone doesn't matter. You've got a pretty impressive extra-curricular record on your CV. You've won prizes for theatre and cricket, da.'

'Ya, but I am not going to apply for a job as a cricketer. And I am told some interviewers don't like people who can act. They aren't genuine, they say. Shit. I'll probably remain unemployed.'

'What are the companies that are coming to campus this year?'

'The usual stuff—some MNCs and some pub sector buggers. This year Balwan Paper and D-DOC (Dehra Doon Oil Company) are coming to our campus for final placement. That's the company to go for if you want to go live in Dehradun. Great place. I believe booze is cheap and plentiful out there. D-DOC does not make you slog either. They pay well. You know our Super Senior Naidu is there. Fellow comes drunk to office.

Of course, nobody would know the difference if he came in sober.'

'We should start reading a newspaper regularly. I am sharing a copy of *The Telegraph* with my roomie. Buying newspapers is such a drain on resources. I have better uses for the limited funds I have.'

'I want to read that too. They have a hazaar cartoons. I'll come to your room and take it at night after you've read it.'

'Then why don't we split the cost of the paper.'

'Cool. Rusty is buying *The Economic Times*. I find that boring. But I am told it helps you a lot in the interviews. Maybe we should subscribe to *Competition Success Review*.'

'Don't be an ass. That's only for the IAS types.'

'What companies are you applying for?'

'All of them. Whoever gives me a job first will have me. But, man, suppose I don't get a job…'

'If I get past the group discussion I'll con them in the interview. All companies should just go by CQPI.'

'Yeah, then you'd be the only one to get a job.'

It was 2 a.m. This was so depressing. I had to mail the rather elaborate questionnaire that Hindustan Soaps Ltd. wanted all applicants to fill out. Selection of candidates for interviews would be based on this, and I was stumped as usual. In desperation, I knocked on the Zen Master's door for help, as always.

'Wondering what to write for the strengths and weaknesses questions, eh Abbey?'

Was Rusty a mindreader? I just stared at him.

'Tell me, what have you written?'

'Er ... nothing so far. It's a very unfair question, Rusty. If I told them what my weaknesses are, why would they hire me? They would think I am mediocre. Huh? If I wrote equally candidly about my strengths, they'd call me arrogant. Either way you lose, man!'

'That's the idea, boss. They want to see if you fall for the trick. When you write about your strengths, always mention teamwork as your first strength. Nobody wants an ape who will sulk in the corner of the cage. Then whatever else you write as strength is inconsequential. For the weaknesses, write stuff that will again be counted as a strength of yours. For example, if you say that your greatest weakness is that you drive yourself and your team too hard when it comes to completing any task, it will make any employer salivate.'

'Maybe I should say, I am too much of a perfectionist. That sounds cute... Good, I get the drift. Thanks, pal.'

I was about to leave the room when it struck me that Rusty was remarkably calm. I couldn't stop myself from asking, 'Enna da Rusty, how come you aren't all worked up about applications and questionnaires? What are you planning to do?'

'Well, remember that Sheikh you saw me with in Bombay? He has offered me a job. Only I cannot talk about it now. Someday, I will tell you...'

I just shrugged, and strolled back to my room, feeling quite relaxed now that I had the power to control my destiny. Going for an MBA is the second major national pastime among college-goers, some survey had proved. Was this why so many of us wanted to join B-Schools every year? To be prepared to give up a little bit of ourselves in exchange for the good life? To learn the rules of the game of the corporate world? A world whose existence I was unaware of, whose rules I did not know. I joined this set up with the eyes of a curious tourist in the rainforests of Amazon. There was little that was familiar. There were no maps available; the undergrowth was dense and tangled. The path you trod on was littered with the corpses of the gullible, unwary of the lurking danger, and there were only a few experienced guides who shared the folklore that evoked feelings of awe, pity and disgust all at the same time.

Hell! DU and SRCC had been a cakewalk compared to this. From the star debater shining brightly on the horizon, I had now become one of those million faceless bodies that dotted the night sky. And I wasn't liking it at all.

Chapter 21

In addition to preparing our resumes—Rusty had drilled it into me to call it a resume—Bastard, knew it all!—this time we needed photographs as well. So there was a lot to do. We all made a beeline for Flunkey's Studio in Bistupur. Mr Flunkey (maybe it was his employee) made me sit on a strange three-legged stool and placed four scorching floodlights on my face. Then he placed what looked like a white umbrella somewhere on the side. Did he expect rain, I politely enquired. He ignored the wisecrack.

He asked me to aim my right shoulder towards the camera and then hold up my chin while he tilted my face around like a Rubik's Cube. I felt like Rajesh Khanna. But the picture looked vaguely like me, only with a rather pained expression. All our classmates went through this drill and were equally unhappy with the results.

When we complained to Mr Flunkey, he dismissed us with a rude wave and said, 'Well that's what *you* look like. So that's what you will see. The kemra never lies,' all the while staring at Alps' 'healthy lungs' and scratching his crotch.

Every day, we would look at all the companies that had put up their one page write ups, the number of vacancies they had and the most important point—how much money were they willing to dish out—and then apply to them all.

Rusty offered advice in one-to-one coaching sessions. I needed that more than most since I wanted a job in Delhi, preferably.

Placement began with the first set of companies coming in around the 15th of January and petered off around March. Those companies that came in the beginning got the largest number of applications. Everyone applied to them. And then, with each job offer that was accepted the subsequent companies had less garbage to sift through to find their 'future CEOs.'

When it came to career choices there were three kinds of MIJ-ites. The first category believed in the 'Son of the Soil' policy. They would apply to a company depending solely on which city the job would take them to. The job in itself did not matter. Among the Delhi companies, one would naturally have to search for the one which paid more; living in Delhi was not cheap. And you couldn't be doing a shitty job either, living in the capital.

If you managed to shortlist the equivalent of Ms Right (or Mr Right), it was not necessary that Ms Right would select you. So, life could get very complicated.

The second group in MIJ made their career choices using the 'Auction' approach. Very simply, you sold your fundamental rights to the highest bidder. Rusty advised me to go for this approach. Someone who paid you more than the market price would be more than willing to fuss over you and keep you happy.

'Look at it from the recruitment manager's point of view,' said Rusty. 'That bugger wouldn't want to see a rapid turnover after paying someone an obscene salary. How would he explain to his boss why a bright management trainee quit even when their company paid more than their competitors? The recruitment manager can be blackmailed into submission right through your stay.'

I was not convinced. 'What if they treated you like a piece of shit because they knew you wouldn't get this kind of money anywhere else?'

Rusty laughed.

'Forgotten our class on negotiation skills already? Remember, your bargaining power comes from your own perception, of whether you see yourself in a position of strength or not. Like in judo, you use the opponents' weight and strength against him.'

'I don't know of a single recruitment manager who knows judo. My career is well and truly buggered. I need to get a drink.'

'How can you, Abbey…' Rusty began, then stopped, disgusted by my frivolity.

The third kind of MIJ-ite was the kind that went in for job satisfaction and quality of possible learning on the job before they applied to a company. Predictably, they were a mere handful.

Rusty was contemptuous of such idealists.

'They'll be the first ones to switch jobs. Because after a concentrated phase of pure learning like we've had in MIJ, any job would seem like an apology for education. And learning on the job is another oxymoron, man!'

'Besides, what are these types going to learn in Delhi, given how little learning Delhi has to offer as a city,' I added, in mock seriousness.

There was more to this recruitment process than application forms and photographs. There was a standard dress code to be followed. Very few guys had their own blazers or suits. As a result all the blazers in the Men's Hostel had been booked more than a month before the D-day. The paranoid kind like Gopher had 'booked' two different blazers for each day. Along with two ties, 'One for the prelim round of the interview and the other for the final interview, da.'

I had a problem. Rusty's was the only blazer that no one had reserved. But it was too tight for me.

'Carry it in your hands and walk in with panache,' said Alps helpfully.

'Starve yourself Abbey, you might lose some weight,' suggested Joy. 'You never know, it might work. Otherwise the job may not...'

I kicked myself mentally for not having planned this better.

'Just then I saw Ganauri walking down the hallway and I let out a whoop of delight.

'Ganauri, I need a suit. Or at least a blazer.'

Ganauri pretended to be really surprised at my request, 'Why are you asking me...?'

After a round of swift negotiations, Ganauri organized a blazer that fitted me perfectly. The charge was a bit steep—fifteen bucks if I got the job offer from an interview, a ridiculous price to pay but hinging on my success. I would attend with the blazer on.

'You could further hire it out to someone else. Three bucks for each interview. If you get selected for the final round, then the charge would be ten bucks. You could make enough money to buy your own blazer.' Said Rusty, the shrewd business consultant!

I smiled smugly. I had already loaned out my blazer to Joy for the D. DOC interview.

Chapter 22

It was Day 1 of placements on the MIJ campus. I don't think any of us slept the previous night. There was tension in the air. The Mess was quiet. Everyone finished dinner and then walked back to their rooms briskly to be able to make some last minute changes in their resume. Although the placement season went on officially for a few weeks, most of the companies were landing up at the same time. And the placement committee was going nuts trying to draw up elaborate timetables and logistics charts. It was tough since the reputed and sought after fellows generally threw their weight around and got away.

Two 'good' companies would almost certainly schedule one prized candidate for an interview at the same time. The placement committee would try and keep one of the two busy with repeated rounds of tea and coffee and engage them in small talk, praying all the while that the fellow in the other room would get the interview over with fast enough to attend the second interview. In the process, some feathers got ruffled. Some egos got massaged. Many were bruised.

I saw my name in the 'shortlists' of two Delhi companies.

'Imagine, yaar, Chumma, if this is what just acquiring a blazer does, imagine what wearing it would do.'

'Bloody idiot, you are! Don't get so excited. It only means they have agreed to let you run the obstacle race. You haven't been chosen as yet.'

The insomniac Chumma had shaved, showered and dressed in a suit by 6 a.m., in a sharp contrast to his usual norm—shaving once a week. Only he had not been shortlisted by any of the companies that day. I could see him turning green at the edges.

'Abbey! You moron, what are you doing out here? They are looking for you in the Balwanpur Paper Group Discussion Room. Run and join them before they strike your name off their list!' Alps was screaming hysterically.

I adjusted my tie and ran. Not a sprint but a brisk, executive-like stride. Understated elegance, was the name of the game. As I entered the group discussion room, I saw twelve of my batchmates sitting around giving me filthy looks. The four girls were all dressed in saris, but were obviously not used to wearing them. It made them look distractingly pretty, if a trifle uncomfortable. Only then did I realize that I had not worn the blazer I had paid fifteen rupees to Ganauri for. SHIT!

'It's okay, Abbey. Think positive. Relax. Cool it. Maybe that's what will make you stand out in the crowd.'

The guys, all wearing ties, looked like dogs on a leash waiting to be taken for a walk. The leader of the interviewing panel got up and cleared his throat.

'The topic for this discussion will be decided by the group itself. In the next twenty minutes, you will identify a common topic and then debate the pros and cons of the topic. Your time starts now. Please give everyone a chance to speak. During these twenty minutes, please ignore the presence of the panel. We will, however, be making notes as you speak.'

Ignore our presence! Hah! Here we are, all thirteen of us trying to impress the daylights out of the panel and they ask us to ignore them.

There was a moment of silence. Each one was trying to figure out what strategy to adopt to best impress the panel. So much for their advice! I was weighing the options—should I start off first and be seen as a guy with initiative (at least that's what *Competition Success Review* would advise) or would I be viewed as an impatient jerk diving face down into the muck.

But the decision had been made for me. Gopher had started off the discussion. And realizing the golden chance was slipping away, the rest of us jumped in simultaneously. What, until then, was just Sumo wrestling, now turned into verbal rugby! The ball was nowhere in sight. For a long time there was verbal mayhem, and it showed little sign of ending.

'Can we have some norms here please?' That was Chumma, trying to bring sanity to the group.

'That's what we were deciding,' said Joy.

'Let's discuss the merits or demerits of having a dictatorship in India,' proposed Curly Venky.

'No!' A unanimous, collective groan.

End of the road for Curly Venky, I guess. I could visualize the panel writing 'Unable to influence peer group—rejected' against Curly Venky's name.

'Two minutes more,' said Mr Panel.

We were all getting desperate. I tried to propose something that everyone wanted desperately—more time.

'Let everybody get a chance to say why we need more time,' I bleated.

Surprisingly, no one heard me. Each one was using the air time to make his or her voice heard.

'If the entire purpose of their exercise was to see how we work as a group then we have all failed miserably.' Wise words from Madam Ayesha.

'That will be all,' announced one grim looking panel member, dismissing us summarily. Later, when the list was put up for Stage II, which was the interviews, only Ayesha's name figured on it. Sethu and I were waitlisted.

Most people had had at least one offer. Even that dickhead Gopher had been placed. He had an offer from Clearwill Chemicals, Pune. Only Sethu and I had no 'final offers' in hand to boast of. I could only console myself thinking that if I felt bad, Sethu must be feeling infinitely worse. He was the topper of the class after all.

My inner voice piped up again.

'Accept it, Abbey. You are mediocre. But arrogant.'

'But I am an MBA.'

'So what? What extra rights does that confer on you? What did these two years teach you? Some jargon? Some table manners? Just because you have a stamp from MIJ, should the world stop to kiss your feet?'

Perhaps that was true. I was mediocre. Mediocre is what being shortlisted means. I was good only as an after-thought. Second best. I hated the thought. I disliked consolation prizes.

Envy, disappointment, anxiety led to all kinds of meanness. Loose talk was one of them. 'Ayesha is the first in our batch to be called for an interview. Naturally da, with her assets, she's sure to get it.'

'Ya, when all rational criteria are absent, looks will help. After all, who doesn't like to see a pretty face in the office first thing in the morning?'

These and other equally rude and crude remarks floated around. Sour grapes, obviously, though no one would admit it.

A consoling thought struck me. Technically, I did not owe Ganauri any money because I had not been wearing the blazer at the time of the interview. And I had witnesses to prove my case.

Chapter 23

Placement season was not going well for me at all. Despite my bravado, in my heart I knew things were looking bleak. I was on the shortlists of *exactly* two companies, one of which was the Dumduma Gardens Ltd, Assam.

Rusty called me aside and said, 'Don't take it. Avoid going there if you have the slightest doubts. If you don't like the job, you won't be able to look for another one. The whole town will know when you are going for an interview. Stick to the metros. It's easier to change jobs there, da.'

'But I need a *job offer* first, Rusty, before I can change jobs,' I almost wailed. Anyway, I took his sage advice and requested the placement office to strike my name off the DGL shortlist. Only Gur stayed on— and was promptly rewarded with a job as Assistant Manager of Personnel.

'I will be getting a three bedroom bungalow for myself. You guys are all welcome to plan your honeymoon there, yaar. Even the petrol for my jeep will be paid for by the company. I will drive you guys all over the beautiful tea gardens.' Gurpreet was ecstatic.

He had grown up in Guwahati and could go on and on about the beauty of Assam. He had a million stories about facing rhinos and elephants when he had accompanied his dad, who was an IPS officer there.

'The three bedroom bungalow must be the guest house,' said Arunesh, sarcastically.

'Recruitment criteria for this job must be height and weight. I had a higher CQPI than Gur.' Gopher couldn't help himself. He was just that kind of bastard.

Gur's smile vanished. Here he was feeling good about a job offer that no one else wanted and all we jealous jerks were drinking rum that he was paying for and openly displaying our resentment of his success.

'What's wrong with height and weight as criteria, Gopher? DGL was in the news recently when their personnel manager was killed by union leaders. Gur has the perfect qualifications for the job. He is the one who will be celebrating his honeymoon there first. Right, Gur?'

'Which newspaper was this?' Gopher, asked suspiciously.

'BBC World News,' said Rusty and shut everyone up.

That was a typical Rusty ploy. When he wanted to say something and make it look authentic, he'd attribute it to the BBC.

Later that night, as we drank ourselves silly, Gur kept worrying whether drinking rum in the tea garden was illegal under the Industrial Disputes Act. Arunesh got out his guitar and sang '*Hai apna dil to awara*'.

I was happy Gur had got what he wanted. But it was hard to be really thrilled when my own job offer was yet to happen. I was terrified that I would be the only one to not get a job offer on campus. Only Joy knew what I was thinking about.

'Stop worrying, Abbey. No one has ever left MIJ without an offer.'

'Yeah and I don't want to start a tradition. I need this job, Joy. I wish I had studied a bit harder. I can never go back home like this.'

'I am sure Haathi will have enough influence with the Bawas to find us something.'

'I would rather get something on my own.'

'Relax, Abbey, two more companies coming in tomorrow. Maybe, I will be paying for the booze tomorrow. Maybe you will... Who knows?'

I tottered back to Room 209 and opened the door gently so as to not wake up Fundu. He had got a job as

Personnel Officer for Bombay Vidyut Ltd in Bombay, and he was contented. His life was set.

A few days into the placement season and the unspoken hierarchy and labels that had stuck to us for two years had changed. Many rank holders, including Sethu, had been attending innumerable interviews with no success, whereas some of the laggards in academics had got really good offers. It caused much heartburn and misery among the less fortunate ones.

All of us had our own speculations as to why there was little or no correlation between academic brilliance, employment opportunities and employability! Everybody was at Dadu's Dhaba celebrating yet another day of job offers. But I felt like a pariah, going for these celebrations. Even the prospect of free rum was not enough to entice me. My self-esteem had hit a new low. And I did not want any theories or sympathy. I pretended to buy cigarettes and tried to tune in to the conversation.

'The job scene is different, yaar. There's no place for theories, only practical stuff,' said Gurpreet. Now that he was Asst Manager Personnel, DGL, he could no longer be addressed as Gur. At least for a short while. He also had the right to offer insights about getting jobs.

'O bhayncho, if grades were anything to go by, Sethu would have got a job on the first day of placement. He is still unemployed—like Abbey. Bhayncho aaj tak job nahi mili usko,' said Funny.

Joy defended Sethu's honour by mimicking Funny's accent, 'By the same yardstick Funny oye, you'd have been the last one to get the offer "latter"'.

'Abbey, here, have a drink, yaar. This one is on me.'

'This may have to continue for the rest of your life, bugger. I am still without a job. What do you say Sethu?' I had been driven to weak jokes.

Sethu must have been dying a hundred deaths too, like me. It was not easy celebrating somebody else's success when it poked a million holes in your ego. Sethu silently gulped down a large peg of vodka and went off to Dadu to buy cigarettes.

I knew failure drove people to drink. But being driven to smoke? Sethu was not a regular smoker. Before I could remark on it, somebody shouted, 'Don't be such a loser, Abbey. Sethu and you are the only blokes holding back the GRAND BOOZEOUT. Jaldi karo yaar.'

'Bhayncho, jaldi is for the companies. They need to send an offer letter. Oye Arunesh ... let's sing a Dylan da gana shaana, yaar.'

Arunesh strummed the opening chords of Dylan's '*Shelter from the Storm*':

Come in she said I'll give you shelter from the storm... '

Neetika held up her glass of gin and said, 'Cheers! Here's to Gur's new career.'

With this, she gave an unprepared Gur a very wet kiss. Gurpreet looked considerably embarrassed and shut up for the rest of the evening.

Chumma must have smelt the booze flowing.

He ran in our direction, waving his coffee mug, 'Bastards, how can you have a party without inviting me?'

'No one was invited, saale. Neats is hosting the first tea party of the Placement Season. Bhayncho, ek toh free booze and you want an invitation letter mailed to you, is it?' Funny could not conceal his sarcasm.

It is true that no one was 'invited' to these booze parties. Everyone was just there. One checked out the successful-at-job-interviews list on the placement notice board and followed the trail of rum or whatever else was being served in gestures of forced magnanimity. Most people would buy a few bottles of Old Monk rum and pour it into a bucket, then each one just dipped his or her mug into it and carried on drinking ad nauseam (pun intended). Occasionally, someone felt generous enough to contribute a bottle of vodka, like Neetika had done, even though it was Gurpreet who had gotten placed.

Vishy was showing off to Neetika. 'I got my final offer on the phone today. Pharmaceutical companies are the ultimate in style, enna? Calling up gives it a personal touch. And Neetika, when will you get your "Ultimate Placement" da? Now that Gur has a job, it makes the next step very simple.'

'Gur has written to his dad. We will let you know the shaadi ka dates. All of you have to come over. OK? No excuses. We will host that Batch of '84 reunion.' Neats flashed her dimples. Amazing how many sardarnis have dimples when they smile!

Joy stood up on a broken chair and cleared his throat to announce: 'CEOs, Managers and Vice Presidents. Lend me your ears. Gur and Neats have just announced that they are getting married. Cheers to the first wedding of our batch.'

'So Gur where is the shaadi?'

'Depends on Neats's folks. Her dad is the Navy types, yaar ... Slightly unpredictable. But now that his son-in-law is not unemployed anymore he should feel happy. Neats, no more excuses left ,yaar.'

'Okay, yaar, Dad was just trying to see how serious you are. He always told me these campus relationships never work out. Wait for the day he gets a job and then see if he proposes to you, he told me.' Neats giggled.

'Neats, I told you on the first day you are the girl I will marry. You never believed me only.'

'Will someone please pour some more rum into the bucket? I am dying of dehydration.'

'Cheers! Here's to Gur and Neats!'

'Idiot! I paid for these two bottles of rum. At least wish me luck before you get drunk.'

'Next year in February, we'll be meeting during our convocation. Hope all you buggers will make it. We must come in a day early and lagao a hike up to Dalma Hills and stay in the Steel & Iron Company Guest House.'

It felt like the last page of an Asterix comic, when all the adventure was over and the villagers had gathered for a feast and tied up Cacophonix.

So we were all probably a little too drunk to react immediately when we saw smoke coming out of the Boys' Hostel. Until someone shouted, 'Shit! 108. Sethu's room!'

Chapter 24

Fortunately for Sethu, the watchman on duty 'Pocket Bahadur' (called so because of his 4'10' frame) had noticed smoke coming out of the window and had broken into the room.

The room was full of smoke. Sethu was sitting on the floor with a pile of burnt paper in front of him. He still had the half-lit cigarette we had all seen him buying from Dadu's half an hour earlier. What could've happened? Sethu was still in a state of, what is politely called, inebriation. There was a dazed expression on his face and he was muttering incoherently. We tried asking him what had happened but he would not respond. Suddenly, Gur figured it out.

'Shit! He's burnt all his certificates!' he gasped, horrified.

'These bloody certificates have no meaning... don't get a job. So what if you come first in class... doesn't mean you get a job first, right? Don't need them... gone, all the evidence... burnt...'

All of us were stunned, like idiots we kept repeating, 'You *burnt* all your marksheets?'

'Bhayncho pagal ho gaya hai kya?'

'Are you crazy?'

He had destroyed all his certificates from school and college which showed he had been way ahead of the class. Until placement season came along.

Then his face crumpled and he began to sob like a child. None of us knew what to do. Fundu and Rusty sent us all away and spent a long time talking to Sethu.

The fire had been put out thanks to Pocket Bahadur's alertness. We would have been of little help, considering how our collective level of alertness was lower than his, thanks to the celebrations that evening. Fortunately, Sethu had escaped serious injury to his person. Except for a blister, courtesy the cigarette he had tried to stub out. The next day, Sethu went around apologizing to all and sundry and thanking them. But in MIJ, anything done under the influence of liquor was always pardoned. Everyone carried on as if nothing had happened.

Sethu came to no bodily harm but his ego and his world were shattered along with his confidence. He got into, what in management jargon is called, a 'downward spiral.' Since his confidence was so low, he did not perform well in any of the subsequent interviews. He was rejected each time. That lowered his self esteem even more, if that were possible. It was a vicious cycle. Soon, Sethu became a shadow of himself. He started praying for longer hours. He had lost a lot of weight because he was fasting on most days. He smeared himself with ash, and wore beads and stayed cooped up in his room. We were all genuinely sorry for him.

As the placement season drew to a close, it became harder for him to understand why he was one of the few who was without a job. Most MIJ-ites had one job in hand and were trying to improve the deal in the next couple of interviews—trying for more money or trying to get a location of choice.

That afternoon, we were sitting around after lunch under the Bodhi tree waiting for letters and money orders from home. The extended postal strike had wreaked havoc with my finances. Then, the stillness of the afternoon was broken by an incoherent shriek.

It was Nikhilesh, our placement coordinator, charging out of the Mail Room like Archimedes had done. He was fully clothed of course, and he did not scream 'Eureka,' but his excitement was no less. He was waving two envelopes . The first one was from United Metals & Minerals with their famous golden eagle logo on them. In spite of being completely out of breath, Nikhilesh insisted on reading out the letter.

Dear Mr S Madhavan,

With reference to the interview you had with the undersigned on 22nd January 1984, we are pleased to offer you the position of Personal Executive on a starting salary...

The rest of the letter was lost in the crowd's cheering. Everyone rushed in to Sethu's room and kicked open the door.

'Sethu! You stupid dick. You were the first one to get a job after all. They had given the wrong address and Pin Code for MIJ. No wonder the letter got delayed.'

Sethu was reading, mugging, more likely, PL Malik's *Industrial Law.* He was so overwhelmed that he started to laugh and cry at the same time. In sheer relief and happiness, Joy tore up PL Malik and threw the pieces up in the air. Collective insanity slash euphoria prevailed.

'Sethu, you bum! When you come back for Convo next Feb, don't forget to get personalized stationery for all of us,' yelled Gur who was carrying Sethu around the hostel in a kind of victory lap.

'Provided Jakes get cigarettes for all of us, ITC.'

'And Neetika gets us shampoo ...'

'No, she'll be hoarding it for Gur!'

'Why did Ponds cream?'

'Because Max Factor.'

The lowest form of humour was back in evidence. A sign that all was well in the men's hostel of MIJ in the spring of '83.

The second envelope held my own appointment letter from Balwanpur.

Funny hugged me and said, 'Thank god, your letter came through. Bhayncho how much more could we have waited for the Grand Boozeout?'

I was numb. Could this have happened or was I just making it up? I could see general screaming and bonhomie all around. But all I could hear was Ma's voice saying how proud I had made her. I could imagine Baba's response. He would say, 'Even though you were the last to get placed let that not deter you from giving your best to this company for having placed their trust in you.'

Placement season was effectively over.

If Sethu's appointment letter had created a stir, Pappu's getting a job was equally unusual. I have to tell you about that one.

Known for his inability to wake up by 8 a.m. to get ready for interviews, he missed every single interview where he was scheduled. And none of us had the time or inclination to make sure he was there. Under the circumstances, that was too much to expect.

The Seekers said in one of their songs, '*There's always someone for each of us they say...*'

By that, the songwriter surely meant jobs not girls. And Pappu eventually did manage to wake up in time for an interview at 6 p.m. The panel from Krishnamurthy Enterprises had missed their connecting flight and landed up at 5 p. m. instead of 8 a.m. The interviews were rescheduled for late evening. So while all the other applicants who had been waiting since the morning were looking like wilted flowers, Pappu was there, fresh as a daisy and ready to answer every question in the interview. They were very impressed with how alert and bright he was, even at that time of the day.

Joy came into my room to tell me about Pappu's coup, and to congratulate me on my own.

'So Abbey, you got a job and that too in Delhi. Better late than never.'

'Make that "Better laid than never." This is too much, yaar. I still cannot believe it. I am Personnel Officer for Northern Region in Balwanpur Paper, that too in Delhi...'

'So what are you contributing to this evening's do?'

'Shit man, my money order still hasn't come! I forgot all about it in the excitement.'

'Now that you have a job offer, your credit will be

good—anyone will give you a loan!' he said, thumping me on my back as we walked towards Dadu's.

That afternoon's mail included my money order—and another letter. The handwriting was familiar, so I knew it was from Priya. I decided it could wait. I put it in my shirt pocket with a mental note that I would read it later that night, in the solitude of my room.

That evening we had the Grand Boozeout. We drank until we were incapable of holding even the glasses, let alone ourselves, straight. Arunesh sang the Diana song, even though all the girls were sitting there gasping at the profanity of the lyrics.

I somehow managed to sway back to my room and all I could think of was sleep, sweet sleep, perchance to dream...

When I woke up the next afternoon, I noticed the blue envelope lying on the table. Shit! The letter from Priya! I tore it open and read through it quickly. Was I still drunk? What was this girl saying? I sat down on my bed and read through it again.

The hotel did not renew my contract because Neel fought with the Manager. So we are both back in Delhi. My album contract in Bombay may still happen if Neel manages to contact RD. Neel said that he tried calling RD once but I believe RD was on a concert tour.

We will have a small ceremony at the temple next Tuesday i.e. 14th February 1984. I do hope that there will be a miracle and I will see you at our wedding. I know you hate Neel. But he is going to be my husband. I would really like you to be there on this special day. You must be a successful corporate executive by now or may well be on your way. I am so proud of you. Hope you have not forgotten me.

My best wishes always,
Priya
P.S.: Are you an MBA, yet?

Chapter 25

With placement season having come to an end, life in MIJ lost its lustre. There was an air of deflated balloons about all of us. We seemed to have lost our raison d'etre. The cut-throat competition of the group discussion, the elbowing each other out of the way, was all over. We were friends again. What an anticlimax after those adrenaline filled days!

The same placement interviews which had been the source of so much stress were now the subject of conversations during lazy afternoon adda sessions.

'Did you hear what Funny did at the D-DOC interview?'

'Yeah, that one where he had mentioned his hobby was following current events in newspapers and magazines. They asked him which news item had recently intrigued him the most.'

'And pat came Funny's reply, news about Diana having had twins.'

The interviewer was surprised he had never heard this mentioned on BBC or something. Until Funny clarified that he was referring to Phantom's wife Diana, who had had Kit and Heliose that weekend in *The Illustrated Weekly* comic strip!

With a job in hand, we lost the last dregs of motivation to attend the remaining few weeks of classes. The only way to get us out of this ennui was to rekindle the competitive spirit that had driven us. Even the fear of poor grades not getting us jobs had gone, now that that myth too was broken.

Whenever we met our profs in the campus, we felt a little embarrassed about bunking classes, and not taking assignments seriously. But I suppose it had happened every year and they expected it of us. Most of them would congratulate us on our jobs. Some would even compare our salaries with their own and remark (not without a tinge of envy and regret) how most of us were starting off on salaries higher than what MIJ was paying them.

It was damned unfair, now that I think of it. Here was a professor who taught us about marketing and graded our strategic plans as a B+ or C. And now armed with the same knowledge base (and heaven knows how pathetic that base was) some arrogant MBA lands a job that has better perks and salaries than the prof. Life was a bitch after all.

To add insult to injury some of us would actually get to invite the same profs to our organizations to consult. And if they didn't do a good job of it, we would actually suggest to them how they could have done it differently. This was the concept of poetic justice.

I made plans to invite Chatto some day to the place where I would be working and get him to do some consulting work for us. And I would give him a 1.17 out of 100 and then tell him to work harder the next time. Or do the project report all over again. What a thrill that would give me! But there was one little hitch. I couldn't figure out what consulting project he could possibly do, one which involved drawing up the Mean, Median and Mode of a table of figures. But one could work on that!

'Hey Abbey, I am bunking class tomorrow.'

'Why? Date in the library?'

'Don't be an ass, yaar. I'm going to Dalma on a trek. This is the right season to see elephants in the wild. Want to come?' That was Matchis alias Asif Matchiswala, my new sidey from the Junior batch. He was the resident wildlife lover and conservationist of MIJ. The guy did know a thing or two about wild animals. Since none of us knew any better, his views and opinions always went unchallenged.

'Who else is going, Matchis? Any girls coming?' I enquired.

Matchis gave his verdict, 'No girls and no mushy couples. This is serious elephant business.'

'Arunesh can bring his guitar and you can join in. Ask Pappu. We are getting Junior Venky along. Don't invite Chumma. He is a dead bore. Maybe Rusty could join in—though I am not sure he will. He never does anyway. I will bring the booze along. And carry a jacket or something. It gets damn cold at night out there.' Joy had assumed he was invited.

'Steel & Iron Company has a guesthouse on top of the hill. Can't we try and stay there? Camping out in the open can be dicey. I didn't mention wild elephants on the rampage...'

'Why don't you ask Keya's dad to book it for you? Aiyyo! I forgot da... you have broken off!'

Was Gopher really forgetful? Was he doing it on purpose? I could never be sure with that slimeball. But he achieved his objective. It hurt. Was not just below the belt—between the legs to be precise. But I maintained a brave exterior and laughed off the remark. I sent him to eternal hell and damnation in my heart though.

'So is it a yes or no, Abbey?'

'Yes, I'd love to go. But tomorrow Professor Parihar is teaching us SWOT analysis. What do we tell him?' Unbelievable but true. I actually *wanted* to learn about all this stuff.

'Ask him to bugger off. We are all big boys now. You are Personnel Executive of Balwanpur Paper. And you can't take your own decision to go on a trek?' Joy was insistent.

'I told you I am going. I have to borrow a jacket from Reddy.' I had resigned myself to giving in to group pressure.

'I tell you, Matchis, the whole Junior batch is so much better equipped to deal with life in all senses of the term. Did you notice that while we all were borrowing blazers for the final interviews, the Juniors all had suits even for the summer interviews? Seriously, you guys are all spoilt,' said Joy.

'He's got a good one. Hey guys, but how are we going to climb with all this gear, food, booze, jackets, guitar? We'll need a Sherpa or something.' I had traumatic memories of hauling myself up when I had last gone there with Keya.

'That's why we are taking you, bastard,' laughed the irreverent Matchis.

I wanted no more of this conversation. The nerve. That too coming from a Junior!

We did not see any elephants—only the vast amounts of elephant shit that marked the trail. How did I know that the shit belonged to elephants? Matchis said so.

The next day was Holi. Then one more week to go, and MIJ was all over. Finished.

I felt a strange mixture of emotions as I sat in Dadu's Dhaba sipping tea, for once in solitude. This was the phase when you start ticking off everything as the very last time you did this, went there...

The uppermost emotion at that moment was guilt. I'd felt it when I sat in the last class and wrote my last exam. I felt guilty at not having studied hard enough, with all the opportunities I had had. I thought of the countless times I had made presentations to profs without having read even a page of the case study courtesy Rusty's coaching.

Felt a twinge of regret for the pain I must have caused Keya. To this day I don't know why she walked away.

Anger. At some of the profs—especially Kamini Mishra. I had paid Banerjee Babu vast sums of money to type out her term papers. But she only gave me a B or B+. I could have drunk better brands or at least more litres of Old Monk with that money.

Felt happy at settling Dadu's bill with the caution money that was returned to me by MIJ. The old man managed to take most of it away!

Thought of all my batchmates—especially Ayesha. Both of us had been posted to Delhi. I did a rain dance at the thought. But the next moment, I felt a dip of depression. Besides, Ayesha had other preoccupations in Delhi. That asshole Khosla of the motorbike-fame had got a job in Delhi too. This diminished my chances to single digits.

Ayesha had a new look. She had grown her hair.

'Bhayncho, Ayesha looks like a Playboy Bunny now with that new hairstyle, yaar,' said Funny.

'Bunnies don't study for a living. Others study them,' said Rusty, spot on as usual!

Holi that year was special. It was the last festival we were to celebrate before leaving the cosy world of MIJ behind, to start another chapter of our lives. At 8:30 a.m., I was woken up by a knock on the door. I was still groggy, struggling to make contact with the earthlings, and I opened the door unawares to paint-smeared faces grinning at the sight of their latest victim. Someone grabbed my hands and dragged me straight into the vortex of chaos. A million hands simultaneously rubbed colour powder, paint and poured water on me, screaming 'Holi Hai,' as if I would have never guessed from their behaviour.

Just the previous evening I had told Fundu that I was going to feign sickness to avoid playing Holi. When I saw him standing in the corner grinning away, I decided to go after him with vengeance. Over the next few minutes, we were all transformed—much like the two years at MIJ had transformed me. After everyone had their fill of dunking people in the little pool of coloured water and getting everyone coated with a million colours, we settled down to the next phase of celebrating Holi: singing songs and drinking bhang. Arunesh Nanda brought out his Yamaha guitar and sang '*Rang barse*' from the film *Silsila* five or six times before we ran out of steam. This was followed by some drunken dancing, after which Arunesh abruptly got up and announced that he was going to his room. Everyone was too sloshed to protest.

Besides the Old Monk bottles that were de rigeur at MIJ, we had gotten a huge container of thandai and sweets laced with bhang. Bhang is a very potent substance—is the universal verdict of anyone who has dealt with this intoxicant's effects. I saw a couple of MIJ-ites have a glass of thandai, eat the solitary laddu and feel proud of their immunity to the effects of bhang.

'This is nothing. I can easily have a couple more of each,' when suddenly BOOM! The bhang worked its black magic and hit all of us between the eyes, the solar plexus, the shoulder blades. It made us go into a loop. We kept on repeating whatever we were doing when the BOOM happened. So Joy and Chumma were laughing hysterically for five minutes when realization struck us that we might be doing something like that soon. Ratina and Alps withdrew into their hostel to sleep it off.

The effect of bhang was showing on Rusty too. I felt my legs slowly becoming heavy as lead. Seeing Rusty stagger, I thought I should escort him back to the safety net of his room. As soon as we reached his room, Rusty sat on the floor.

'I should not have had all this. I am not used to it and there was no point taking chances.'

Blame it on the bhang, but I was feeling a little sentimental. 'Rusty, you have been a great friend. Keep in touch. I know you will make it big someday... you will roll in the big bucks. Don't forget the struggling proletariat.'

'You knew? I didn't. I've had to struggle every day of my life to get all the things that you take for granted... I know you guys think I sponge on others. I DO NOT! I earn my fee to bail them out. Why should they resent that?'

'That sounds very reasonable. Why should people grudge you your dues?'

'Abbey, I know you thought I was really cheap when I asked you to pay for a month's subscription for the newspaper after I'd bailed you out of that first term paper... Do you want to know why I offer my services for a fee? I have no rich daddy who will send me money at the end of the month. I have to maintain myself.'

I was embarrassed by Rusty's revelations. But I was also curious.

'Where are your parents, da?' I asked innocently.

'Well, my father used to work in a small factory in a town called Kodungallur about thirty-five kilometres from Trichur. Since I had done very well in the Higher Secondary exam, the local bishop suggested to my father that he send me to Loyola College in Madras for my graduation. To make some spending money, I started doing odd jobs. The local bookstore helped me by letting me sell magazine subscriptions. That's when I got interested in business magazines and started taking detailed notes on each company.'

He paused to drink some water. I sat and stared at him, lost for words. How different people's lives can be, I thought.

Rusty continued, 'After some time, I had a good enough database about two companies to carry on an intelligent conversation with anyone who had worked there. I would open my sale to the executives by talking to them about stuff happening in other companies, especially their competitors. Once they realized they knew nothing about it, selling them the subscription was easy. Some of them became friends. They enjoyed my company. Others felt like helping me. I was fine with that, as long as they were up front about it. That's how I went to all those fancy clubs and bars, and met the who's who of the industry.'

'So you were not lying when you talked about Nusli Uncle and Jeh?'

Rusty nodded.

I was still a bit skeptical. 'But MIJ? How did that happen?'

'I met Haathi at an MIJ alumni meeting where I had taken a stall to sell subscriptions. I told him about my dreams. He took a chance on me. He gave me admission and waived my tuition fees. He gave me a small stipend to manage my expenses initially. After the first month, I did not have to take that money either. There were enough people who needed my advice. In exchange, I would get them to pay for my expenses. I owe everything to Father Hathaway. He gave me what my parents couldn't.'

'And how did you get this job with this Sheikh in Dubai?'

'You must have heard of Sheikh Rashid, the ruler of Dubai? His cousin had come to Bombay to identify investment opportunities. I met him at a hotel near Churchgate station. We got talking. I told him if he took my advice and invested in three companies, he could make a 40% profit in a week. He got curious and asked me how much I would charge.'

'You asked him to pay for a month's stay in Bombay, right?'

'No. I told him it was a gesture of friendship. He acted on my tips and made his money. Before he left Bombay, he made me a deal—to go and manage his portfolio for him in Dubai. So technically, I am the first student of MIJ to get a final placement offer—abroad, in a company I have not even worked for!'

No wonder Rascal Rusty had not appeared for any interview during the placement season. The guy was amazing.

The effect of the bhang was wearing off. I sleepwalked back to my room and slept till the sun shone on my face the next morning.

The following day all of us lined up on the lawns of the men's hostel to pose for a Class of '84 photograph. This was a formal affair, a photograph that would hang in the offices and homes of all of us years later as a reminder of this moment, forever frozen in time, and symbolic of two very special years in our lives. The guys were all dressed in formal suits or blazers and ties, the girls in saris. Haathi was in his usual crisp white starched cassock.

Fundu taught me that word, 'That's not a frock, Abbey. It's a cassock.'

'Just a habit, Fundu.' I couldn't help myself.

Father Hathaway was glowing with pride. Maybe it was pure joy at the thought of finally getting rid of us? The same Mr Flunkey came from Bistupur with a huge camera with a massive lens that could well have been the muzzle of a gun. We stood with frozen smiles and waited while he focussed, on more than the Alps, I hoped. When he was satisfied, he ducked under the black cloth covered camera again.

'Pleej stand *absolutely* still. Otherwise you will istand in sun until I am satisfied. You there, please keep your chin up...'

'Please specify which chin for Hairy!'

'Shut up, Chumma.'

'OK, everyone, let's put on our best smile and say cheese,' said Haathi.

'We don't get any in the mess, Father.'

At last, after much buffoonery and re-takes, Mr Itchy Groin decided to let us go. The professors were all talking to the students in ones and twos. Haathi gave us all a small envelope each.

'Read it only after you have left MIJ.'

I was overcome with admiration for this man, a man who had spent his entire life building an institution of higher learning. Surely he must have had his moments of doubt? What did he get out of it? Did it ever bother him that every year a fresh batch would come in and he would have to start from scratch again? Did he ever get tired of doing this?

On the last day, we began to bid farewell to each other, promising to write and call up (only on company account). Joy donated five music albums to our music room. He had been paid airfare to attend three job interviews in Delhi. But I had to hand it to him; whatever he had saved, he spent on these five long playing records of dance music and wrote on each one of them 'I wish to thank Haridwara Industries for three interviews they called me for without which this gift would not have been possible.' Typical!

There was no more time to waste. Joy had organized a bus to take us to Tatanagar railway station. We had to board the good old Tatanagar Express that would take us back to Delhi. The Delhi gang—Joy, Pappu, Funny, Arunesh, Gur and Neetika were all going back home to Delhi. Then there was Gopher, who had gotten a job in Delhi and did not want to lose out on 'seniority' by taking time off to go home. He was joining immediately, unlike the rest of us. Sethu had left for Bangalore to visit his cousin, who was getting married. Then he would spend a week in Kerala, before joining up. Ayesha was to meet us at the station itself. She had too much luggage, she said. Sunaina and Tina were going trekking in Sikkim. Vishy and Alps were also going home. They were scheduled to take the Bokaro Steel City Express to Madras on their way to Munnar. Alps was planning to take a course in film appreciation in Pune for three weeks. Rusty was off to Bombay with David and Fundu. He was flying to

Dubai and had promised to supply all of us with duty free scotch and cigarettes each time he came to India.

The bus drove out of the campus and through Bistupur Market on its way to the station. A pensive silence reigned right through the ride. We waved out at Chatto and his wife, who were shopping for vegetables in the market. I must have dozed off for a while, but I woke to hear Gopher shouting hysterically.

'We have to catch the train, bhaiyya. Please sir, please...'

A large truck had its axle broken and had blocked the traffic on the single lane road to the station. We were stuck behind a long line of vehicles, crawling along in single file.

'What can he do, Gopher? He is driving us as fast as he can.'

'Why don't you get out of the bus and direct the traffic.'

'I don't know how we will catch the train today.'

After a brief period of excitement, we somehow made it to the station and wove our way through auto-rickshaw drivers, cab drivers, porters, vendors and on to the platform. Ayesha, dressed in her tight jeans and a tighter light green T-shirt that said 'Only a Rat wins the Rat-Race', was already there and had identified our berths on the train. Her father ordered Thums Up for all of us.

'Hurry up, guys, we have just a few minutes left,' warned Ayesha, as we gulped down the drink.

Gopher, who insisted on sucking the life blood out of his bottle, handed the bottle back with a satisfied burp.

The engine was blowing its whistle and people were saying their last goodbyes. I was watching people who had tears in their eyes, waving to their loved ones; others obviously delighted to be making the journey, when I heard my name being called. Pushing through the crowd was Keya. I rushed to the door.

'Don't lean out like that, Abbey, you will hurt yourself.' She said. 'I... I... came to say... I... have lots to explain, Abbey. I am coming to Delhi in August... Don't go away, Abbey...' and started to cry.

There was no time to console her. The guard was waving the green flag. Stop! Stop for just a moment, I wished. But the train started to move. Taking me away from Jamshedpur and Keya.

'*Why did she come at the last minute? Couldn't she have come over yesterday?*'

'*You were stuck in that traffic jam. So was she. She could have come over yesterday. That's true. You could have gone over too, to say bye. Did that even cross your mind?*'

'*I swear I thought of doing that. But I was busy packing all my stuff and saying goodbye. Then in the evening I was in no shape to do anything. I know I should have... Is she coming to Delhi to meet me? Has she got a job in Delhi? Is she getting married to someone out there? Is she on her way to someplace?'*

Seeing Keya at the station left me with a wave of emotions and questions. My head reeled. Ayesha knew what I was going through. She came and sat next to me. For a change she did not say anything. She just looked at me, quietly squeezed my hand and then left me alone.

The train was moving past the overbridge. I could see the familiar outline of the steel factory, the Dalma range of mountains. I was leaving behind a slew of memories of two years in MIJ that had changed my life. I thought of Haathi and remembered I had his letter in my shirt pocket. What could he have written? I opened the letter and read it. It was a short note, was written in Haathi's neat, unmistakable handwriting, each word carefully formed.

Dear Abbey,

As you step into the world of work, you are bringing to it the freshness of ideas and the power to change things. And yet, there is the danger that all too soon you will forget why you came to a place like MIJ. No, you were not here to understand the corporate sector or the intricate theories of management. You came here to understand yourself and your strengths. To believe how easy it is for you to make a difference. That is the purpose of higher education. To instil in you the belief that you can make the world a better place.

Whenever you feel unhappy about something around you, remember, you have the capability within to improve it. So whether you choose to change it or choose to walk away and just complain — you have made a choice. As a professional manager, you will have opportunities to make things happen. You have had the education that will tell you what to do and how to do it. But it is only your heart that will tell you <u>why</u> you ought to.

There are no limits to how we can grow as human beings. Every morning we get up and make a choice about how much we will do to make a difference. Every day we choose how much we will touch the lives of the less fortunate. Too many people give up the opportunity because they do not believe they can change things. I do hope this education has given you that belief within.

Never underestimate your ability to make a difference.

Nihil Ultra – Nothing is Beyond.

Truly,

Ed Hathaway

The Tatanagar Express was on its way to Delhi. Was it the crimson smoke from the chimneys of the steel plant that blurred my vision of the city skyline? Or was it the gathering tear...